DONE With CRAZY

DONE with CRAZY

Welcome to BonHaven

BOOK I

For Ashley and Alyssa, my Southern Girls at heart;

Thank you for always standing by me as I chased my dreams. I always told you, as my Momma told me, you can accomplish any dreams you have, you just need to get going on it.

With all my love "To the Moon and Back",

Momma

(Aka: Mo, Merva, Mert or whatever nicknames your Dad has for me this month)

ACKNOWLEDGEMENTS

Writing a novel is everything it is described to be, exciting, rewarding, difficult, stressful, nerve wracking, soul searching, narcissistic, and ultimately fulfilling. It also alienates you from your family for days at a stretch and can drive you to drink. During this process, I came to understand why many writers become alcoholics. Luckily, my drink of choice is usually Diet Pepsi. Writing is also extremely hard on your ego and self esteem, due to rejection letters that begin with "While your story is extremely well written and your characters are very unique, I am not sure where your novel would fit....or "I love your distinct Southern voice and the blending of genres in your storyline but I'm not sure where your novel would fit…" See, tough on the old self esteem. Again, luckily I am a pretty tough cookie.

So, here we are.

If you are reading this right now, it means either you have been courageous enough to risk your hard earned money and take a chance on my first book, or someone has passed along their copy with their recommendation that it's a good way to spend a couple hours. I thank you for whatever route you have taken, you are here. I love nothing more than to lose myself in a great story of any kind. As long as I get transported into that world, I'm good. Especially if at the end of the book, your first question is "What's next" and frantically hit the internet to see if the author's next book is in the works. Hopefully that is how you will feel when you get to the end of what is in your hands or on your device. Thank you for taking this journey with me and I hope you tag along for more.

Since the moment I woke up in the middle of the night with these characters creating their world in my head and the storyline a runaway freight train, I knew I had to get this series written. I liberally borrowed names from my eccentric southern family and off we went. The characters constantly talk amongst themselves in my head making for some interesting conversation at our family dinner table. As long as they are talking you will hear about it; the characters, not my family.

I would like to take this time to thank several people.

(I)

When I first decided to actually write this book, I discussed it over lunch with my best friend since high school. I was a little nervous thinking she would say I finally lost it. I have had a lot of crazy ideas over our friendship timeline. Singing in a rock band, running a business, wacky inventions and a short stint in politics, I was afraid this might be the idea that finally makes her say "Just stop. Please, for the Love of God, just stop."

Nope. Her response? She picked up her wine glass, gave a brief salute and said "Why Not?" Although, I must confess, that line has gotten us into more than one or two sticky situations over the years.

But, with that, I was off. So, thank you, Lori Balog.

I also would like to thank those who were my Beta Readers extraordinariarre.

Gloria Blanco, who gave me that first and very difficult to hear but life changing helpful critique, and yes, Damn it, you were right. Natacha Costa, Jeana Nishihara and of course my Mom, Mom in Law and my daughters who all had to endure a million emails with one or two word revisions and the inevitable question; better one or better two, or maybe…..

My sister Jennifer Kirby who never once insinuated I might need professional help when I discussed my characters dialogue as if they are real and my sister in law Jennifer Bell; thank you for all of your wonderful advice!

Mom and Dad, I can't thank you enough for always encouraging me to pursue my dreams, whatever they might be. I hope I can pass on the enthusiasm you have for life and compassion for everyone around you. You touch lives and make the world a better place.

My daughters, Ashley and Alyssa; I cannot express how proud I am of the young women you have become and the impact you are making in the world. Levi and Marcos, my daughters have chosen well.

And last but never least, my husband of forever, Paul. Thank you for being understanding of all my pursuits, however silly and insane you thought they were, especially all the time spent in my office and having my "me time".

I love you and THANK YOU all for indulging my crazy.

(II)

1

Welcome to BonHaven

I am so done with crazy.

Good Lord, I'm actually speaking out loud to MYSELF. That's a first; although with what happens to me on a daily basis, nothing should surprise me, least of all talking to myself. I suppose I should give a little background to that statement. If I'm gonna do this, I should go whole hog, right? My best friend Ashton, who is usually called Sugar, which is short for Sugar Plum, and yes – he is gay (but more on that later), suggested that I keep a journal to keep track of the crazy things that go on around BonHaven. Who knows, maybe someday NASA will come knocking on our door; or at the very least, the X-Files writers trying to get material to resurrect the series? Momma always says begin at the beginning, so let's just start with the basics:

My name is Alma Sue Babineaux. Now wait! Before you go raising your eyebrow or having a good snicker, ya'll need to know a few things.

I am from the Deep South where double first names are not only perfectly acceptable but expected – it means I BELONG and I find that comforting. And believe you me; I need all the comforting I can get. I think you will understand later on. Keep reading.

1. It's a family name that is passed down through the generations of Babineaux's every seventy-five years and YAAA!! I win the draw. Ha.

2. I have a wicked right hook, wrestling moves that won me a full ride scholarship through college and I am much tougher than I look; being called Barbie growing up gave me a huge chip on my shoulder. It comes in handy and has served me well. Again, read on.

Our family home is in Blakely, Alabama, just south of Mobile, on Bon Secours Bay. It's actually a rather large house – okay, it's really a plantation –there's just nothing else you could call it. It even has a name, BonHaven, listed on the National Historic register. Not in its previous splendor, to be sure, but still impressive to come upon according to the new folks who are visiting for the first time. Very cliché, but its home and all I know. A Babineaux has lived on this land for three hundred years. Longer if you believe some of the Uglies stories, but as they are notorious liars, I don't. Ooh, I am getting ahead of myself – Ya'll don't know about the Uglies. I'll explain in a few pages.

Explain? Explain how?

I stop writing and put the pen in my mouth. In a completely subconscious move, I decide to break my old college record and personal best of chewing on every pen I touch to the point of ruination. Sugar gleefully likes to call out this act as one of my nastiest flaws. Personally, I'm kind of proud of the sheer number of writing instruments I've gone through!

Momma even tried to break me of the habit by purchasing beautifully made, very expensive, writing pens and using a heavy dose of guilt. Didn't work. Turns out the more expensive and higher quality the pens are increases their susceptibility to teeth marks! Scientifically proven.

From this subject my thoughts scatter as they race through my head, hitting every other formed and half formed thought floating around in there and bouncing off into the empty spaces with frightening force and a touch of echo. How in hell do I even begin to describe life at BonHaven? I can't be too detailed or I would freak out anyone who even flipped through the first few pages. I find myself daydreaming and my mind wandering even further from the subject I'm supposed to be writing about.

I have always enjoyed reading a good book, usually several a week actually. Ever since learning speed reading in a high school English class, I have to force myself to slow down to really enjoy what I am reading. Damn you Ms. Sheehy! My respect for writers just increased tenfold. "How do they do it?" I asked out loud. My voice echoed off the wood slat floors and high ceilings of my bedroom. The rest of the house quiet as it was pretty late. I probably should have been on the alert with the quiet as Thurman was around somewhere, but I was determined to get this journal started. Journal. Back to the subject. But really, how do writers stay focused. I like to think I am an intelligent person with a fairly active imagination. Good Lord! I wouldn't survive three days around here without it! So how do they get a whole book with fully formed thoughts and words on paper before they escape their imagination or get distracted? Seriously, what's their secret?

"I can't even get through a page on a stupid journal!" I think as I lay my head on my pillows and burrow in to get comfortable, tossing the journal on the bed. That's the last coherent thought I had before I drifted off.

Al was rudely awoken by her nose scraping against the ceiling; the fifteen foot high with beautifully ornate crown molding from the late 1800's, ceiling. They were quite detailed, especially this close up. I've never really noticed before she thought; then comprehension dawned in her sleepy brain and she realized her face was on the ceiling and she was getting claustrophobic fast. Wallace had to be behind this.

"Damn it Wallace! Put me down!"

Looking down over the side of the bed, she idly noted the floor far below, really, really far below, and heard giggling.

Thurman.

I should have guessed. A prank at three AM would involve them both. Good Lord! How did I end up being head Chair on the entertainment committee for BonHaven's cantankerous ghost and a precocious creature from Aunt Merle's nightly reality displacements? I had to be at the police station for my shift in less than two hours, identify the victim carved with voodoo symbols tied to a tree on my property and figure out how to handle Jimmy-Don's latest screw up. Come on Alma Sue, think.

Luckily, my sister Lyci was walking down the hall and heard the commotion.

"Wallace, put her down!" and he immediately obeyed; the bed slowly lowering back to the floor with Thurman gleefully dangling his legs from the edge.

As usual, she read my thoughts. "Don't worry Al; you know if leather were brains, Jimmy-Don wouldn't have enough to saddle a June bug." With a slow shake of her head and a small smile, she continued walking down the hall. I suppose the thought of why was my sixteen year old sister was walking down the hall at four am should probably have crossed my mind, but around here it takes more than that to set off alarm bells in my head.

Just as the bed settles gently back on the floor with a small whoosh like a contented sigh, my cell phone on the side table begins to vibrate violently startling Thurman. He jumps into the air like a surprised cat and skitters through the doorway, pinballing off the walls as he scrambled down the hall. I vaguely hear thumps and bumps as he must have taken the turn to the stairs too quickly. I could tell when he landed at the bottom as he let out oomph with the breath he had been holding on his way down. I couldn't help but smile. Wallace looked up from where he was slouched against the wall by the doorway and made eye contact as he vanished through the wall; but not before I caught the ghost of a smile on his face that mirrored my own. Ha. That's funny; a ghost of a smile on the face of a ghost.

I roll off the bed and place my feet firmly on the floor. Just checking. Reaching over, I grab the phone off the side table and scroll down the message. It's from Bobby, my partner and best friend from high school. Looks like we may have caught a big break on one of our cases and according to him, the Captain said to "get my ass to the station."

"Thanks for the wakeup call Wallace" I said out loud knowing Wallace was still lurking around somewhere. The rapid fire two knocks on the wall was acknowledgement I was right. Since I had to head into the work early anyway, it really was nice to get a jump on heading in to the station. I truly meant the compliment even though, me, giving Wallace a compliment was a foreign thing. It felt more than a little uncomfortable coming out of my mouth; like trying to pull a single cotton ball away from the clump out of a just opened bag.

As I grabbed out my uniform from the closet and untangled the shirt from the sticky plastic covering, I mused on Wallace, one of the two Uglies that have been in the house the longest and my least favorite. I much prefer dealing with John.

Uglies are basically ghosts; more like poltergeists really. If you can classify ghosts, I guess that would be their genus, species ghost. The main difference between ghosts and Uglies are basically their attitude. They are always in a bad mood. If they are ever in a good mood, then you are really in trouble. That's when they will play their meanest pranks.

This is where the southern term "Don't be Ugly" or "Stop acting Ugly" comes from. Although, if you were in Chicago, I doubt you would hear this being yelled by parents to their children. It pretty much covers all bad behavior from tantrums, being mean, not sharing, brattiness, or in adults (especially teenagers) to being bitchy or pissy.

Our Uglies have been around since shortly after the house was built. On one hand it's been great. We always had the best book reports at school because they were like our own personal encyclopedias – long before the web was invented – we had access to all kinds of information.

A perk to having been around for the advent of all sorts of inventions and knowing firsthand of past governments and politicians. And they love telling you of their knowledge. Actually they just like to rub it in your face that they know something you don't.

The drawback is they come and go as they feel. Where they go I have no idea. I am still working on that discussion and to be honest I am a little afraid of learning the answer. They also are always being obnoxious. John is not so bad, but Wallace is just a pain in the ass. For example, when you are getting dressed and just when you have your outfit laid out and you're feeling pretty pleased with yourself and getting excited about your day or god forbid , your date, one of them – usually always Wallace – will follow you down the hall spouting his nasty opinion.

"Are you sure that is the most appropriate attire? You really don't look your best in that color. It makes you look a bit pasty; and, your hair? Really? It is most severe looking worn that way, not flattering to you at all, though to be honest, not much is."

To be fair, it is usually just me that is treated this way. Or at least is bothered by it. I know Momma is never spoken to this way. I'm not sure if it is because she is always perfectly dressed or if Wallace is afraid she knows how to or has the power to banish him from the house. And Lyci could care less. Plus, everyone loves her, even Wallace. He doesn't bother Aunt Merle either, but I know for a fact – he is definitely afraid of her. He won't even be in the same room with her if he can avoid it. He is afraid she will sneeze and he will disappear

I look in the mirror as I button up the last button on my uniform. After a quick sweep of my hair with a brush, I pull my long hair into a ponytail and make a bun. Done. It's funny really how a police uniform makes such a transformation. Without it, I am usually mistaken for a co-ed on break from U of A just visiting the folks. Once dressed, there is no mistaking who or what I am. I still have to fight to earn respect, but in one way or another, doesn't every one?

One last glance and I puff out my chest; with a SUTU said out loud, I'm off.

When Sugar and I were in junior high school, we were always into something. Momma lost count of how many times we were invited to Mr. Carmichael's office, our assistant Principal, by eighth grade. The first time it happened, we were scared shitless. So to make me laugh, when we were escorted into his office, Sugar puffed out his chest, whispered "Uh-oh gotta face the music" straightened up and pretended to adjust boobs in a bra. Then even more quietly "Shit's up – Tit's up" and marched to his fate with me stumbling behind him trying not to laugh out loud. You can imagine this did not help our punishment. But from that day we made a pact, no matter what, we would not rat each other out. So every time our names were called over the intercom, which was audaciously frequent, we would look at each other, puff out our chests and give each other our signal; SUTU; Shits up, Tits up. For some reason, we thought this was hilarious. It was our way of giving the middle finger to everyone without being openly obnoxious. We thought we were being so clever and in the minds of two smartass thirteen year olds, I'm sure we were. But for whatever reason, the saying stuck. It's actually much more appropriate in adulthood. The added benefit is you feel more confident before walking into any situation. It is more of a mental exercise, kind of like a breathing mantra. It also works as a warning. This has saved my butt many times. If Sugar walks into a room and say SUTU, I am ready for anything. With my family any kind of advance warning is helpful. It actually prepared me for wrestling against guys in high school and college. While all of my friends were trying out for the cheer team as was expected, I went out for the wrestling team and made it. All through high school I was known for my wrestling moves. Went all the way to state and placed second in my weight division. It was good enough for a full ride to U of A, our family almamator. All of us were expected to go to school there, which we did, at least until my brother Bug went to Auburn and almost killed my parents. It still causes stress to Momma if it is brought up in mixed company.

For years, people have asked me how I did it; wrestling guys twice as big as me, going through the academy when I was constantly berated and belittled for being female. The wrestling thing seems like an unusual thing for a girl to do, but I cannot tell you how many times those wrestling moves have come in handy, both in my police work and everyday life! Most of the time I look more like the cheerleader role. I'm tall for a girl at 5'8 with long dirty blonde hair that I usually wear in a ponytail for work. You can imagine how much grief I get at the station. They call me Barbie cop behind my back, but it's all in good fun as I have proved myself over the years as much tougher than I look. There is no one on the force that won't have me as a partner.

The truth is I had an edge. SUTU gave me an attitude I could carry with me anywhere, making me feel ten feet tall and bulletproof. The fact that I carry a gun helps, although, remember, down here of course, everyone usually carries a gun. Its best to always assume even the polite little grannies shopping at the local Piggly Wiggly are packing a .22 in those big purses they always seem to carry. Although most academics will advise against it, I have found that a little assumption goes a long way.

I enjoy being part of the force here in town. I originally wanted to join the force in Mobile where I went through the Academy, thinking that there would be more action than in our sleepy little town of Blakely – or so you would think. But lately, BonHaven seems to be a magnet for all kinds of adventures; case in point, the four-thirty "get your ass to the station" call. Sugar frequently likes to point out how important it is that I keep a journal to accurately retell what goes on around here. He likes to think it may keep someone out of jail one day.

He may be right. He likes to spend his free time hanging out here because and I quote "BonHaven reminds me of a real life Disneyworld Haunted Mansion; the crazy Eddie Murphy version, but without the singing."

I made my way downstairs as quietly as I could; and considering the creaking of my leather service belt, that's no small feat. I was fixin to head to the kitchen to grab something to eat real quick when I decided to just stop on my way in to the station. A coffee and a cream filled donut warm off the conveyer belt at Krispy Kreme sounded like an awesome idea. It's always an awesome idea, but at 4:30 in the morning it takes on a life of its own and as an officer sworn to uphold the law, who am I to snuff out that life? As I sneak out the front door, I give a silent Thank You to Hollis, our caretaker, for keeping the door hinges oiled. I close and relock the door with hardly a sound making sure to not to wake anyone still asleep. Creeping across the front porch, all I can think about for some reason is Sugar's idea of BonHaven being like a Disney attraction. It's all I can do to get the image of floating heads following me to the station serenading me with barbershop quartet versions of popular songs and I have to hold my breath to keep from laughing until I get in the car. My truck purrs to life with the push of a button and I let out the laugh I was holding in. I was feeling pretty darn proud of myself for getting out of the house quietly and without incident when a big, red clay-filled dirt clod splattered on my driver's window with a thump - splat sound. Thump because this dirt clod had a goodly amount of clay mixed with the Alabama dirt. Splat because it was still wet and squishy with the morning dew so blew apart when it hit the glass surface.

Thurman.

Maybe this would be a good time to explain how I feel about Thurman.

Thurman showed up about six months ago and Thurman is a Trow. Trows are close cousins of Trolls: members of the Fae genus. That's a fairy to the lay person. But whatever you do – Do NOT say that to Thurman. It makes him a little crazy. And trust me, Thurman has enough crazy. Trows are mentioned throughout history, but usually they get it wrong and refer to them as Trolls. There is a BIG difference. At least to those who can actually tell the difference and I think there are more of us than people really know or at least admit to.

Trows are smaller – much smaller than Trolls. Trolls are actually exactly like they are depicted in storybooks. Giant, usually ugly, and like to hang out under bridges and underpasses. Likes to give humans a hard time. Have you ever noticed how Troll and Toll sound alike? Think about it. Most sayings in our time are derived from truths from another time. Most folks who hang around BonHaven for any piece of time will confirm this. Anyway, Trows are much smaller, usually about three feet or so tall and funny looking. Not ugly, just......funny looking. Each one is very different from another. Some have arms and legs, some no legs (these have an interesting way of travel, either scooting or kind of bouncing on their butt. Strange, but highly entertaining to watch.) They are known for being mischievous. They steal things, move things and hide things. Historically in the past, they would kidnap people. Especially babies and musicians. I guess they like music – or Not.

Anyway, their most interesting trait is they can only move around at night. It must be after dusk, full dark, or they cannot travel. They have to be underground by sunrise. If they are above ground after sunrise, they freeze, exactly where they are, until dusk falls. Still as a statue, just like stone, it's pretty cool to see. And with Thurman being who he is, it happens at least a few times a week. It's kind of the family joke these days. Having Thurman around is a lot like having a really nasty toddler that never sleeps. Sometimes, I actually think Momma has fallen in love with him. She thinks he is adorable. Although, since he got into trouble by "playing" with Cooper, Momma's beloved dog, and Momma had to lay down some ground rules about playing to rough with poor Coop (torturing would be a better description), those feeling may have cooled off a bit.

Thurman and I have a special relationship. I say that with sarcasm dripping like nectar from a honeysuckle bud in full bloom, from every word. Thurman doesn't like me. At all. His favorite pastime is hiding things from me. This is surpassed only by his love of throwing things at me. His newest entertainment is throwing large clumps of dirt at me when I leave for a shift. Ladies and Gentlemen of the jury, see driver's window as exhibit number one. Luckily, his throwing arm is wild. He usually misses by a mile. Usually. Again, see exhibit number one. This is a good thing, as evidenced by the thump splat effect, Alabama dirt is red with a goodly amount of clay mixed in. This means not only does the clay make the dirt hold together so that it hurts when I am hit, but the red stains whatever I am wearing. But, when he gets lucky, I usually end up at the precinct with a big red stain on my back. It's a running joke with the other officers. Hey Al, you got that last quick roll in the hay in before you came in? You can imagine where this goes. On and on and on…..

"Hell of a way to wake up." I state to no one backing out of the circular drive. I have an interesting habit of talking out loud. Actually, most times, even if I'm alone, I half expected an answer; half of the time I get one. In my experience, that's just how it is. I don't turn on the headlights until I have the truck headed down the driveway so my lights don't reflect off the windows of the house. I keep the speed to under 5mph so I don't kick up too much of the crushed shell drive; it sounds like mini gunshots if you go too fast. Not nice before five in the morning. By the time I come out on the main road, the sun is just starting to pink the horizon. I pause for a second to take it in. I'm usually on swing or graveyard, so I don't get to see the sunrise very often. It's very majestic. And very quiet. It's a little unnerving actually; I usually have some sort of back ground noise in my life. I put the truck in park and stay that way for a moment, soaking in the tranquility. BonHaven is very secluded and most of the time, we feel very secure in knowing the antics that go on around here will go unnoticed by anyone.

2

Our closest neighbors to BonHaven are the Giles, James & Bettina who have a few acres to the east of us. From where I'm stopped at the end of our private drive, I can see the beginning of their property line across the road. We hardly ever see them anymore, even in town, but according to family records, they are very distant cousins. But unfortunately, I can't say the same about one of their offspring.

They have two adult children, Ellen & James Jr. who goes by Jimmy-Don. Momma frequently points out Ellen married a Yankee and moved to Chicago a few years ago. She usually leaves out the Yankee part and just focuses on the married part. I heard she recently had twin girls and loves to hold court at the neighborhood cocktail parties as Southern Royalty. As if! Whatever makes her happy. Maybe her twins are like the little girls in the Shining. One can only hope. I definitely have too weird an imagination. At least I come by it honestly! I know. Deep breath. Focus!

Jimmy-Don is the proverbial prodigal son and a pain in my ass. He returned home two years ago after trying college, vocational school, and working on a cruise ship. None of these were a "proper suit" according to his momma. He has no intention of leaving home. His parents just won't admit it yet.

Jimmy-Don's latest hair brained idea, and there have been many, is to be a ghost hunter. He has watched every episode of the TV show and fancies himself to be the next ghost hunter on the show. He is convinced if he can make a name for himself; they will come knocking on his door begging him to be on their show. So with the notion he could convince his drinking buddies to be on his "team", he got a loan from his Daddy and went on a buying spree at Best Buy.

The salesman at Best Buy thought he was dreaming. It was a slow Tuesday, all he had sold was a USB drive to a twelve year old boy for his science PowerPoint, when Jimmy-Don walked in and started looking at digital recorders. After finding out why Jimmy-Don was there (he actually said to buy ghost hunting equipment, for Christ's sake!), he knew he had a live one! So after convincing him he needed no less than ten digital recorders (for different rooms for full coverage), EMF detectors in different sensitivities, video cameras with ultra sensitive recording capabilities, tripods, Polaroid cameras, and multiple other equipment and items he couldn't possibly work a case without, the salesperson went for the kill. He was gonna make that bonus! He was finally going to be employee of the month! He had his shirt and tie picked out over six months ago waiting to be chosen for that photo that hadn't yet been taken. So he showed Jimmy-Don the ultimate thing he HAD to have – a very expensive high resolution digital camera with infra red sensors, slow motion, stop action and frame by frame reply in High definition.

After Jimmy-Don purchased his equipment, he then had to hire a "crew". Naturally his first thought was to recruit his drinking buddies and his best friends since second grade, Buster & Jason, (better known to all as Bubba) and Pink, the kid with the reddest hair anyone had ever seen, to join him in this new "business adventure". Jimmy-Don convinced them that they would become famous and get their own T.V. series. "Guaranteed chick magnets" he promised. Idiots.

His first case was Miss Jane from Spanish Fort. She was positive she was experiencing paranormal activity in her house. She had called the police many times to report disturbances. I had been on one call out there myself. Each time the officers that responded concluded the "disturbance" was usually caused by her cats, which, of course, was promptly dismissed by Miss Jane as just another example of a cover-up. Miss Jane's latest concern is that things are disappearing and reappearing around her home. And of course, Jimmy-Don and his crew are only too happy to charge her to "solve" the disturbance.

Miss Jane's neighbors were curious too say the least when Jimmy-Don pulled up in front of her house in his neon orange and black Chevy truck with the Chaser's logo on both door panels. This is my favorite part. Jimmy-Don was extremely proud of his logo. He felt he was being witty with his double entendre of a cartoon ghost holding a shot glass of Jack Daniels in one hand and a beer in the other with "Chaser's" underneath. Only in the South would a couple of rednecks think this was the epitome of advertising. But wait for it, there's more. When he pulled up to the curb, he has a speaker on the outside that has the nee-neer-nee-neer horn from the Ghostbusters's hearse. He is then joined by the two other morons in their monster trucks. I have heard it's quite a site.

So of course they "investigated". After dark of course – as if paranormal activity only happens at night. God forbid they step foot inside

BonHaven at lunchtime! So they took EMF readings, and had Q & A sessions with their digital recorders. But it was a bust. No activity. If they would have only listened to the neighbors who all tried to be helpful and relate Miss Jane has had Alheizimers since 1998.

So needless to say, Miss Jane's is "an ongoing open investigation".

Unfortunately, Jimmy Don is always pestering me about something. He thinks if I will agree with him on any of his harebrained ideas, me being a cop will lend some sort of credence to his theories. Even though he seems to be on to something, no way will I ever let him and his merry band of idiots. Even though Lyci assured me he won't cause trouble, I have an uneasy feeling as I look across to the road to where our property lines join marked by a huge ancient Spanish Oak tree dropping with moss and shudder with a premonition of dread.

I put the truck back into drive and goose the engine to shoot out onto the road spraying crushed shells everywhere. Krispy Kreme, Here I come!

Pulling up in from of the donut shop, Jerry the manager is just flipping on the lights in front. I walk into the sound of the bulbs still buzzing as they wake to life.

"Morning Jerry" I say with a wave.

"Hey Al" He drawls as he slides the last tray of donuts into the old fashioned display case. "Surprised to see you here this early. We usually never see you in the daylight. Had a running bet you were a vampire that sleeps during the day buried in some dark basement out there at Bon-

Haven." He chuckled at his humor.

"Well damn Jerry, now that you've found me out, I'll have to come back tonight when I transform and bite you on that wrinkly old neck of yours." I drawl back as I rest my hand on my belt making the leather creak.

Jerry swallowed hard and placed an empty cup for my coffee to go and two crème filled glazed donuts in a bag and handed them to me over the counter. He wiped his hands down his apron, tickled that I was playing the game, but also a little nervous. Not many folks were brave enough to actually make a comment about BonHaven. The rumors had persisted for so long, no one was quite sure.

I decided to put the old guy at ease. "Vampires? Really Jerry? Now that's a good one. But can you picture me sleeping in dirt? That hurts. You really know how to wound a girl's self esteem." I grin as I take my cup over to the coffee station by the enormous plate glass window that looks into the kitchen area with the conveyer belt that carries the donuts from the ovens.

"Now Miss Al, you all know you're a looker. Just have to look into that glass you're standin in front of to see that." He said with a smile. "And I'm not buying that pitiful line about hurtin' your self esteem. You're a tough'n, you can take it. Your Daddy brought you up better than that." He looked at me with sadness in his eyes and walked to the back. I saw him through the glass as he went back to kneading dough.

I sometimes forgot that Daddy spent a lot of time hanging out here the last few years. When Daddy went missing a few years back, Jerry took it pretty hard.

As I looked through the glass at the donuts rolling down the conveyer belt and sliding onto a large metal shelf waiting to be filled with crème, a memory popped into my head. Me, Daddy, and my brother Bug standing right here in this same spot. I couldn't have been more than five or six, my brother Bug maybe nine or ten at the oldest. Daddy was trying to convince us there were little elves under the metal table that filled the donuts with crème or jelly filling. They wrestled around underneath fighting over whether they would use jelly or crème for each donut; the winner got to fill the donut then toss it up over the side so quick no one saw. Daddy swore if we were quiet enough and really paid attention and stared really hard we would see a tiny hand come up and snatch a donut off the end of the conveyer belt. Bug, being the fussbudget personality he is, was adamant that was not true.

"No. That's just not true Daddy." He adamantly exclaimed and promptly went on to explain the process in detail. Me, on the other hand, stood there in a fit of giggles, almost believing it. After all, I saw things at BonHaven that opened my eyes to other things, even the young age I was.

Daddy knew that and fed into it. Maybe it was all part of his preparation for me. It definitely helped form me into who I am today.

Bug. I missed my brother. . Bug's given name is Lewis, but when he was born, supposedly, every time someone met him for the first time, they all said "Well, isn't he just as cute as a bug!" and the name stuck.

Southerners and their nicknames; makes life more interesting if you ask me. Anyway, he has spent the last few years of his life since passing the bar trying to convince everyone to stop calling him that. "It's not proper to call a lawyer that!" He is so straight laced, he still has not figured out we all only do it to make him crazy. If he didn't react each time, we would have dropped it a long time ago! He now has a law practice up in Birmingham and vague aspirations to politics. We shall see...... I should call him today and check in; it's been too long.

While I was deep in thought, stirring my coffee, I didn't hear the ruckus at the counter. A few more cops had walked in and were joking with Jerry. I almost jumped through the plate glass window in front of me when a hand was laid on my shoulder. Looking up into the reflection I saw it was Bobby and relaxed.

"What the hell Bobby Glen!" I said giving him an irritated look in the glass reflection. "Now I gotta start over" I muttered with hostility as I moped up the coffee that had spilled everywhere.

"Jeeze Al, Sorry" Bobby said with a giggle and sly smile, not sorry. He was pleased as a tick on a coon hound. He never got the better of me. I was always on guard so he never was able to sneak up on me. I wasn't gonna live this down anytime soon.

"I'll see you at the station." I huffed and slid out the door.

3

Driving into the station parking lot, I rolled down my window and inserted my key card. As the gates rolled open and I drove through, I spotted an open slot and pulled in and threw the truck into park. I hurriedly went inside. I wanted to be at my desk before Bobby got back. If I was engrossed in something, maybe he would leave me alone. Not likely, but maybe.

A full ten minutes later, Bobby and several other officers sauntered in.

"Hey Al, heard you were a little shaken up this morning. Maybe morning shifts aren't such a good idea for you huh?" A sleazy officer named Norris said with a leer. Ugh, I really didn't like that guy. And I really, really didn't like that he saw what happened with Bobby. I didn't think anyone saw, but I should of known. If he was there, then he was watching.

"She just didn't have her coffee yet dude. One cup and she would have kicked my ass before I even got with a foot" Bobby said coming to my recue.

"Good info to know" Norris said with a leer.

"Good Lord. " I said putting my head down on my desk.

Before the conversation could get any weirder, Captain Sampson popper his head out of his office and bellowed like only he can "Babineaux, Taylor, LaRue, get your asses in here now. Where have you been?"

We all scrambled into his office and stood against the back wall to his office. Bobby sat in a chair in front of his desk and placed his hands in his lap like an obedient school boy ready for the day's lesson. Kiss ass. I kicked the leg of his chair.

"We caught a break on the robbery case from last week; well maybe caught a break. That's why I wanted ya'll here early. A teenager may have seen the thief climbing out of the back of the house from one of the victim's house."

"Which vic?" I asked pulling my notebook out of my back pocket.

"White Victorian over on South Eighth." He said checking the report on his desk.

"That's the one with the old tapestry rug right?" Bobby pointed out. "Didn't the victim say the time of theft was around three am in that case? That would explain the teenage witness. Who else is up at that time?"

"Me, for one." I said sarcastically. "Where does the witness live?" I asked the Captain

"On South Ninth. Kid was coming home past curfew and was trying to sneak in his bedroom window in the rear of his house. He happened to hear noise in the yard behind him and looked over to see someone crawling out of a window of that house.

"And how are we hearing about it?" LaRue questioned.

"Kid is grounded and called and left an anonymous tip on our hotline asking if he had information to exchange, could he get a reduced sentence from his Mom." Captain said with a chuckle. "Gotta give it to the kid for trying."

"So, how are we supposed to handle it? Good cop, bad cop? What are we offering?" I said

"Just routine questioning. We aren't offering anything. I know his Mom and she won't budge on his grounding." He said with a laugh. "Just see if he knows anything. It's the first break we have had on these robberies and I'll take what I can get. These thefts aren't normal, especially for around here. Who takes old things but leaves the TV's and computers? It's starting to unnerve the residents. So go do something!" He said shoving the contact info into my hands while shooing us out of his office.

Back at my desk, I look down at the name of the possible witness. "Oh Good Lord" I said to Bobby. "I think I might know this kid. I think he's my friend Jenny Katherine's nephew. He's a real piece of work. Making her sister crazy. From what I know about him, he won't be easy to find and even harder to make him cooperate. He's known to take off for weeks. Last I heard he was grounded for life." I sighed and handed the paper to Bobby.

LaRue had already disappeared, probably to the lounge. He slept whenever he could and fell asleep within seconds. War World III could be going on and he would be in a corner sleeping on a pallet of water bottles snoring like a bear.

"All right" he said shrugging his shoulders. "Let's go."

With a sigh, I got up and headed towards the door.

Three hours later and still no kid; his mom said she hadn't seen him since last night when they argued after he was caught sneaking in his window at three am. She gave us the names of his friends and hangouts, but nada.

After a big lunch at Maude's Café, I was nodding off at my desk. I was ready for a nap.

"Bobby, I gotta go take a nap. I'm usually sleeping right now and can't handle this day time stuff."

"I know, me too. Let's call it a day. We can try again tomorrow, maybe he'll show somewhere." He said with a yawn.

I looked at my phone. It was 2:30. "Hey, if you want to swing by for dinner before shift, I think Sadie is making gumbo."

"Magic words. I'll be there."

"K. See ya." I said heading for the front door. As I got in my car, I hoped I heard Sadie right. I'm pretty sure she said she was gonna look for the bag pan in the attic to make gumbo tonight. Man I hope so, she makes a mean gumbo. She says it's an old family recipe, but she always says it with a wink. I really wonder what that wink actually means, but honestly I'm afraid of the answer.

Sadie. Where do I even start?

To this day, I honestly am not sure who Sadie really is to my family. I guess you could say she came with the house. Literally. All family accounts mention Sadie dating back to my great great Granddaddy's household ledgers. We don't dwell much on thinking this through. We just accept that she is here and takes care of us. On the surface, she appears to be the quintessential stereotype of an old world southern cook/maid. But that is not who or what she is at all. Her skin is an exotic blend of colors that back in the old South days would be referred to as mulatto. Her pale green eyes that could be faded from age offer no clue either. Even though she appears to be old, her hair is still black as the darkest night. No gray in sight.

The only thing I know as an absolute is she is as old as the house.

Actually, she came first.

I did not believe this at first, even after several family members recalled what they knew. It was Daddy who had me believing it first. But the clincher was Wallace. In a momentary lapse of his usual protocol of provoking me, he accidently slipped and retold a portion of the story that matched Daddy's, but with more details. Things Daddy didn't know. The fact that Wallace immediately back peddled, recanted and said the whole thing was hogwash then walked through the closest wall was what convinced me.

The story goes that Sadie was actually a Banshee. Not really the truly evil type, as technically a Banshee is one bad evil spirit, capable of making one's life miserable. Supposedly, Banshees remain in the material world as they are afraid to cross into the void as they will have to answer (Insert my obvious question of "To Who??" here) for their evil deeds and receive eternal punishment. Sadie's story is she grew to prefer remaining here and be with humans. She gave up all of her power to remain on this side, but evidently she still has quite a few connections, if you know what I mean!

Our family loves her as if she were from our lineage. Who knows, in this crazy family that might actually be true! Everything about my family and BonHaven all seem connected somehow.

This story might help explain my Aunt Mae. Well, not really, but it may be a start.

As I pull into the drive and head around back to where the family garages are, I take notice of several cars parked in front of the house. Hmmm. Lyci must have friends over. Great, that means they'll be staying for dinner probably. As I get out of the truck, I hear splashing and laughing from the rear yard by the pool. That verifies where Lyci and her gang are. Good, I can't hear the racket from my room, so I can still sneak in a nap. As I enter the rear porch, I catch a whiff of something good wafting on the humid air. Gumbo! At least I heard Sadie correctly last night. Bobby won't be disappointed in the dinner choice; although with Sadie's cooking no one is ever disappointed.

I headed up the back stairs yawning loudly.

"Oh really Miss Al, must you make such repugnant noises?" Wallace said drolly thrusting his upper body through the wall to throw his hands up in the air then disappearing just as abruptly.

If I wasn't so tired, I might have thought of a witty comeback, but then again maybe I was just kidding myself.

I shuffled to my room and flipped on the ceiling fan before throwing myself facedown onto my bed sinking into the duvet. Ahh, my bed. I was sound asleep within thirty seconds of kicking off my shoes.

4

I awoke refreshed from my nap, but after taking a glance in my mirror was wondering if I slept too hard. Mascara smudged and hair sticking up like Medusa.

"A quick shower will hopefully help with that" I said aloud.

The message written on the steamed glass was meant to quickly dissuade me of that notion. After turning off the water, I wrapped my wet hair in as towel and stepped over to wipe the steam off the mirror. As I lifted my hand, I looked up.

Written in perfect script was Wallace's message; "*Did NOT Help*!"

Good Lord, he was hateful!

I had an hour before dinner, so decided I should use my time wisely. I grabbed my pen and pulled the journal out from under the bed where it had landed after my morning magic carpet ride curtsey of Wallace and Thurman. I sat on the floor and leaned against the bed pulling the cap off my pen to contemplate where to pick up. I'm still not sure what to explain, or even if there even is an explanation. I guess I should tackle it like I do when I am writing up a police incident report. "Just the facts, Maam."

So, I don't live alone; I think I mentioned BonHaven is REALLY big, so I am glad it's not empty. Well mostly glad. There are a few residents living (and I use that term VERY loosely) here that I would not miss if they were to disappear. And I mean that literally and figuratively.

First, there is Uncle Howard. He has rooms at the north end of the house. But we try not to hold that against him. When he first moved in, he convinced his brother (that would be my daddy –Fraser) to let him build a private entrance and small porch off the new kitchen veranda. The new kitchen was added in 1927, which isn't so new today, but compared to when the house was first built in 1794 – it's new. Anyway, I side tracked. Man, I'm easily distracted. Wait, what was I talking about? Ooh – Uncle Howard.

So, Daddy has always felt a little guilty as he is in charge of BonHaven even though he is the youngest of six children. I guess my grandparents thought it made more sense to have the youngest son take over the property as there is such a large age difference from the first son, Uncle Howard, who is now 68. Daddy would have been 56 this summer. Anyway – Uncle Howard built his own entrance and comes and goes as he pleases. Sometimes I don't see him for days. The only sign of him is the sound of his old manual typewriter drifting down the front hall. Once, we did not see him for over two weeks. It took us that long to figure out he was actually missing. But that is another story for later.

My Aunt Merle also lives at BonHaven. Aunt Merle is a really interesting person to live with. Mostly because of her habit of bringing unusual creatures, objects or animals back home with her when she accidently time travels in her sleep (and occasionally when she sneezes.) I must say in her defense that she does not purposefully set out to create havoc in the universe. It just happens.

Then there is Aunt Leila Mae. She lives with us part time. And believe you me, part time is plenty! You can only take Leila Mae in small doses. She is blindingly beautiful, even at her age of 63. She seems to radiate energy. Who knows, maybe she actually does; wouldn't surprise me. Anyway, while she radiates energy, conversely, all the energy seems to be sucked from the room when she is in it. Talking with her for any extended period of time is exhausting. I may need to look into this at some point. Leila Mae has a small home across the bay in St. Elmo's. I have only been there twice and that was under most unfortunate circumstances, so maybe it's unfair of me to judge, but wow, talk about being in another reality. And trust me, later we will.

Of course, Granddaddy, is always home. He has the other master suite in the house. The original master suite, which was his and Mamaw's retreat from the usual craziness, Momma and Daddy had the other master suite in the opposite wing. Mamaw died right after daddy disappeared. He was always her unspoken favorite child and everyone pretty much agree she died of a broken heart. I was really close with her, as my grandmother on Momma's side is always so stuffy and formal. It has been hard to maintain any kind of relationship with her. The most unusual thing about Granddaddy, and again that term is applied relatively, is he thinks he is a necromancer. Maybe he is and maybe he isn't. It isn't really debated much. Weird things happen around here all the time, and everyone fights to take credit for it. Who knows? I have learned not to ask too many questions around here; at least when I'm off duty. It helps with my sanity. Since Bug moved to Birmingham a few years back and with Daddy gone, I have fallen into the role of being in charge. Everyone looks to me when it is decision time. This is partly because I am a cop and carry a gun, but here in the South, everyone carries a gun. Either way since I'm in charge, my sanity is important.

Of course my little sister lives at home with me and Momma. Lyci Leigh is sixteen and lovely. That should cover everything…. But it doesn't. Lyci is one of those people who are instantly loved and adored by everyone she meets. That includes the "things" that follow Aunt Merle back. This makes things even more difficult most of the time; interesting and mostly entertaining, but difficult. Lyci is a junior at Fairhope High School and all the normal things that usually entails. But Lyci is not exactly normal. She has inherited our family gift of being not only a medium, but extremely psychic. We all learned long ago, if Lyci has a hunch, we all go with it. I cannot iterate how many speeding tickets she saved me from when I first started driving! Speak of the devil; I can hear Lyci and company creating a ruckus downstairs. It must be getting close to dinner time. I reach up and grab my phone off the bed to check the time; 6:45. Wow, I didn't realize it was that late. I have to keep blackout shade on my windows because of my sleep schedule, but it really screws up my daylight hours. Tossing the journal back under the bed, I head for the door. As soon as I open the door I am assaulted by the mouthwatering smell of Sadie's Gumbo and walk quickly towards the landing. I briefly consider sliding down the banister like when I was a kid, but just as quickly discard the idea. Can you imagine the flack I would get from Wallace? The squeeze just isn't worth the juice.

Just as I hit the last stair, Lyci came flying into the foyer to stand by the door with her hand on the knob. She looked at me for a count of three, grinned, and then flung open the door. "Hey Bobby!" she laughed, and took off back into the front parlor with her friends.

"I still think that's weird. I hate when she does that" Bobby said with a slow shake of his head.

"Hey" I said. "You should be used to it by now. She's been doing that to you since she was three years old. You should be flattered. It means she's connected to you like a member of the family. Think of it as an insurance policy against ever being kidnapped. An internal GPS."

Bobby cocked his head and stared at me really hard with an indecipherable look. He then dropped his head to his chin, sighed heavily, and turned and walked away. I followed him into the front parlor with a smile on my face. One point for me; almost even for this morning, not quiet, but it made a dent.

Walking into the front room was like entering another world. The large arched windows with its stained glass beveled panels cast brilliant starbursts of color over the entire room. The lowering sun was hitting the glass just right to create a jeweled and bedazzling world just in the room. Combined with the company assembled in the cavernous space was enough to take your breath away. But that may be attributed to Aunt Mae who was seated in the corner chase with a Cheshire grin on her face. Momma was in a seemingly exasperating conversation with Uncle Howard and Aunt Merle on the sofa.

The boisterous noise coming from the sitting area on the left side of the room drew my eyes over. Lyci and her friends were telling jokes.

"No way!" screeched Ashleigh and Jackson. Lyci's wannabe boyfriend, Crockett (what the hell kind of name was Crocket anyway? did his parents watch too many Miami Vice episodes?), was bending over pantomiming something coming out of his nose. Whatever the joke was, it was pretty hilarious watching him act it out.

Bobby was just standing just inside the room taking it all in, probably on sensory overload. I came up behind him and pushed him further into the room towards the open love seat. He shuffled over and sat down.

"Hello Bobby" Momma said graciously.

"Hey Maam. Thank you for having me over for dinner. When I heard Sadie was making her Gumbo, I begged Al for an invite."

"You know you are always welcome here. Look at this group." She gestured with a flick of her wrist. "With all this racket, who even knows when there is one or two more." She smiled warmly.

Uncle Howard stood up and crossed the room to shake hands with Bobby who met him half way.

"Nice to see you young man. Always good to up the testosterone in this house." Uncle Howard was serious. Bobby squirmed uncomfortably. I decided not to save him, it was too fun.

Wallace chose that moment to be offended. He appeared on the far end of the coach where the kids could not see him and whispered "I do declare Howard. I believe you must be mistaken in thinking just because I am not fully present in the flesh does not mean I am not a man." He crossed his legs and proceeded to pick at an imaginary piece of lint at the crease of his pants. Then glowed vibrantly for a brief moment then faded slowly.

"I do believe he made his point Howard." Aunt Merle said wringing her hands together. Aunt Merle was the sweetest woman. Any type of disharmony greatly disturbed her.

"Poppycock!" Uncle Howard said and picked up his cocktail and took a long swig.

I caught Lyci looking over to where Wallace was just sitting with a big grin on her face. She always thought Wallace was a great source of entertainment. If she were on my end of his "entertainment" she might think differently.

The large sliding pocket doors separating the dining room from the parlor rumbled open. "Dinner's ready, Come and get it." Sadie announced stepping into the room from the open doors

The teenagers bounded as one into the dining room and Lyci assigned them seats. The table was a huge piece of oak darkened from age and polished to a shine that could blind. Legend has it the oak came from a Spanish Oak tree on the original piece of property BonHaven was eventually built on. That would make the table over three hundred years old. It was huge and could seat twenty comfortably. As everyone else took their seats, Momma noticed Granddaddy was missing.

"Alma Sue, would you please go find Granddaddy and inform him dinner is ready please?"

Great, now I had to go search the house for him. Who knows where he could be? With my luck he was wandering the grounds somewhere and I was hungry. I almost whined out loud, but caught myself at the last minute and whirled around to head out through the kitchen.

As I passed through the butler's pantry, there was a thump inside the pantry door. I made a mental note to put an entry into the journal. There's something that lives in the pantry. No one is exactly sure what it is. The fact that none of us has really looked into it should be extremely telling. Our family usually has more important fish to fry. It pretends to be a ghost, but it's not as Wallace has vehemently assured us. Maybe it doesn't even know what it really is. All I know is it's always pissed off and constantly has tantrums. Lyci says it's a bogey. Again, still not sure what that is, but since it stays in the pantry, it doesn't really bother anyone. Much.

I change direction and head to the library. Better check inside the house first just in case. As I approach the library, I hear voices. Found him. But who else is here? As I barge into the room, I stop short. Granddaddy is deep in conversation; complete with wildly animated hand gestures, with an old Indian man dressed in what appeared to be a loincloth and full ritual headdress. I could see straight through him. Important fact, Granddaddy is half Cherokee Indian. Both of them stared at me as if I had interrupted some extremely important discussion. Granddaddy raised one eyebrow at me in warning. So I bowed my head, backed out of the room and closed the door.

On my way back to the dining room, I was deciding on my story. The truth or nothing. As I entered the dining room, Lyci caught my eye and shook her head. OK, nothing.

"Well?" Momma asked.

"He'll be along shortly." I said with a smile. Lyci smiled back and I knew I made the right choice. I sat down next to Bobby and reached for my wine glass that someone had conveniently filled for me. The chattering of the teens across the table was a pleasant distraction. Bobby leaned over and bumped my shoulder. He knew something had happened while I was gone and was just acknowledging it. We have been friends for a long time and he could sense when something was up. By this time the sun had started its descent and full dark was almost upon us. Sadie had come in to turn up the lights in the dining room and light the candles in the hurricane globes scattered around the table. With the candles lit and the fragrance of the floral arrangements in the center of the table, it created a very elegant but casual atmosphere. For us, it was a nightly ritual, but for Lyci's friends it was something new.

"Wow Lyci, this is awesome" Jackson said in awe as Ashleigh elbowed him. "What? I was just sayin it's awesome."

"Don't be embarrassing." Ashleigh said turning red. "I'm sorry Mrs. Babineaux; he was raised by wolves and has no manners." Jackson was Ashleigh's boyfriend so she obviously felt responsible for his actions. It was sorta cute.

"Don't be silly. Thank You Jackson." Momma said. "So" she continued. "What will you all be doing this summer?" she asked of the group in general.

All of them started chattering at once.

Lyci reminded everyone she will be a fully certified lifeguard at the beach this summer. She was proud she had worked her way up from junior lifeguard.

"I will be attending a three week classroom at sea. I leave on a tall ship out of Mobile. It's supposed to be awesome!" from Crockett.

"That sounds lovely Crockett." Momma said with a smile

"Crockett? What the hell kind of name is Crockett?" Uncle Howard questioned, genuinely confused. He looked around the table for an answer. I just raised my wineglass to him glad it wasn't just me. Everyone else ignored him accept for Aunt Merle who shot him a dirty look. Aunt Mae just chuckled, thoroughly enjoying his confusion. She's like that.

"I'll be working for Mo and Blo's all summer." Jackson said obviously resigned to his fate.

"Mo and Blo's?" Bobby asked. "They're still around? I worked for Mo for three summers. Hot a hell, but I got a lot of free lemonade and sympathy from the neighborhood moms and it gave me enough to buy my first car. Nothing wrong with that." Bobby said to Jackson with a point of his finger.

All of a sudden I smelled smoke. Just then I noticed the curtains shaking very lightly. I thought maybe the breeze was coming in through the open windows, but I realized they were closed. The AC was on. I looked around. No one else was reacting to smelling anything unusual so it was just in my head. Then I noticed Mae and Merle lean towards the floral arrangements and sniff. Oh Crap! In our family, the coming of an event is accompanied by a premonitory smell, usually flowers for most, but has always been smoke for me.

Lyci reached across the table for the bowl of Sadie's special dirty rice and beans that she always serves with her Gumbo. "Yep, it's coming" she stated matter of fact.

"What's coming Lyci?" Ashleigh asked.

Lyci looked around at all of us then shook her head. "Oh, I just meant Sadie is bringing out the Gumbo soon."

Great! Now I have this to add to my list of "Things to Worry about". Sadie brought in the Gumbo just then right on cue and the kids started jabbering at once again. While Sadie ladled out the soupy mixture into everyone's bowl, I again noticed the drapes moving. As I looked closer, I notice a pair of small wrinkly feet sticking out of the bottom edges. Just as it dawned on me what I was seeing, Thurman stuck his head out from behind the thick draperies to peer at the loud teenagers. His eyes were huge and glistened with tears. It was almost as if….he were AFRAID of them! Wait a minute, Thurman afraid of teenagers? This was too good to be true. Maybe I found his kryptonite! Good to know, I can work with this. I smiled to myself as dinner carried on in its usual raucous fashion. There were no arguments, major ones that is and no food was thrown.

It was a good night.

5

The next morning I awoke to clear skies and cicadas already at maximum decibel levels. The humidity was making the sheet mold to my body so that it took a few seconds to unpeel like a cocoon skin. It was gonna be a scorcher today. I started to dress for my shift, but since it was so hot already, I just threw on an old uniform shirt over a tiny tank top and daisy duke shorts. If I left early enough I could change at the station so I would have a better than average chance of at least starting with a crisp shirt. The outfit was pretty ridiculous, but better that than arriving at the station in full uniform, but a sweaty mess.

Actually, all I could think about at the moment was stopping by Lum's and grabbing a few banana Moon Pies for my break. Yeah, Yeah, Yeah, I know; Cops and their donuts. Granted you will find several cop cars at Krispy Kreme at any given time day or night; that's a given. But a Moon Pie is not a donut, not even close. Ever! It's an all gooey, banana flavored piece of southern heaven! Southerners love their Moon Pies! Plus, I love shopping in Lum's. Lum's is an old fashioned corner store that carries the old fashioned candies and treats. It has been there since 1908 and hasn't changed much since the day it opened. With its wide wooden slat floors and original barrels for pickles and iced drinks, it evokes everyone's childhood. The minute you pull up to the front door and park under the tin roof stretched out over the old filling station pumps, you are transported back in time. It even has the original pumps with the glass globes on top with the Pegasus logo. But the best part is walking under the faded red and white stripped awning over the front door on a really hot, humid day, and stepping into the cool darkness. Inside, the shades are always drawn from the heat, and two huge ceiling fans spin drunkenly around and make a wonderful swooshing noise each time the blades cut through the swollen humid air. They are the original fans and rock on their extension poles making you wonder if you will be underneath them when they finally come crashing down. And you know it's only a matter of time, but you don't care.

You just want to spend as much time there as you can! Then there's the smell you're assaulted with the minute the door is cracked. Man, there's nothing like it anywhere! Candy, cinnamon, even a slightly acrid smell of full ripe pickles in their barrel, pipe tobacco, a slight dusty smell, and the cool , still damp smell of long ago children, old men and secrets. You relax just walking through the door. It is impossible not to. It's magic. If only it could be bottled and sold, Lum would be a rich man! Then there are the Moon Pies! You can hardly find them anywhere, but Lum always has a great stock of all the flavors. Again, it's almost magic!

Oooh, Moon Pies. It always comes back to the Moon Pies!

I was still in my Moon pie trance, and just reaching for the door, when Momma caught me in the front hall.

"Alma Sue, please tell me you are not going anywhere other than to your gym dressed like that. That's not appropriate for even the Piggly Wiggly. Who knows who you may run into?" Momma said from the top of the landing.

I closed the door and turned around (so slowly I could have been in the Matrix – still didn't help). I took in Momma.

Marianne Elizabeth Hanlon Babineaux.

Five foot seven, wearing an immaculate pale pink channel skirt with matching shell pink silk tank, she could pass for a twenty eight year old coed. Definitely not the 51 year old mother of three who deals with assorted craziness all day – every day. Her Dark Blonde hair was styled in a perfect chignon. Southern humidity would not dare frizz Momma's hair. Her light blue eyes are legendary – even outside our family. Like lasers when she chose, I am surprised NASA up in Huntsville hasn't registered them as a Weapon of Mass Destruction. These days they usually just twinkle with secretive mischief.

When we were little, we seriously thought she had the power to hypnotize us. Maybe she did. Does. She's doing it now! Look away! Look away!

"Momma, stop doing that!!"

"Al, stop being so dramatic. Have you seen your sister? I want her to try on her dress with the latest shoes I picked up in Mobile. I need to see them together." Momma said losing patience.

The junior prom. Good Lord, I had forgotten about it, at least for the moment! More likely repressed the idea of it. Since Lyci announced the date of the prom two months ago, that has been the topic of every conversation with Momma. Well that and the Huntington Gala. One or the other. Styles, colors, textures, designers, jeweled or not jeweled, short or long. The worst part is everyone in town is talking about the Gala. I can't get away from it!

Good Lord, I hate fashion and hate discussing fashion even more! Poor Lyci! Oh Well, better her than me, she can handle Momma!

I served my time in fashion hell in high school, then in college with my sorority Kappa Delta. Ugh, talk about fashion purgatory; I had to attend sixteen different formal events in the first semester alone! That meant sixteen different visits to fashion hell with Momma. But to be fair, when she was finished, with her shopping and dressing me like a Barbie Doll, I did always look awesome. My sorority sisters to this day, think I am some kind of fashionista. Ha! More like the Idiot savant of the fashion world!

Lordy, the memories this prom is bring up might just kill me!

"Momma, it's just the junior prom, not her cotillion." I said with a classic eye roll.

"Why Cher', I know that! But prom is very special for a young woman. Every detail is important. Even you gave in and let me help you dress for your prom and you were beautiful!"

"O.K, O.K." I said throwing up my hands in defeat. "I get it, but No, I don't know where Lyci is. I think she's over at Ashleigh's house." I said trying to be helpful. Ashleigh is Lyci's BFF. They are usually inseparable. Find one and you'll most likely find the other.

"Well, that's a change." Momma said "Ashleigh is usually here."

Just then the front doorbell chimed.

"I have it Momma."

As I open the door to see a nattily dressed older gentleman, his expression was one of surprise. It took me a few seconds to realize the state of the uniform, well, it really couldn't be called a uniform, not really, but the size too small shirt I had on currently was still unbuttoned. I probably looked like I was auditioning for the lead role in Busty Cops III.

After he closed his mouth and gathered his composure, he spoke as he handed me his card. It said Mr. Desmond DeCompanse. DeCompanse Antiquities.

"Hello young Miss. My name is Desmond DeCompanse, proprietor of DeCompanse Antiquities and I have an appointment with Mrs. Babineaux." He said. His voice was gravelly. It did not fit his appearance at all. It made me feel a little off balance, but that could have been the air conditioning and my open shirt.

Before I could answer, momma finished her royal descending of the staircase, pausing on the first landing, quite aware of the impression she was making.

"Of course, Hello Mr. DeCompanse, it is very nice to see you again. I believe last saw one another at the Huntington's Spring Gala, yes? It is very gracious of you to come here to BonHaven to view the lamps. It would be very cumbersome to bring them in to be valued." Momma said.

"Of course, it is not a problem a 'tall Mrs. Babineaux." He actually bowed a little as he spoke.

"Please, call me Marianne." Momma said as she extended her hand. "I must say I was surprised you knew we had the Radio lamps, much less to have a buyer that would go to such lengths to obtain them."

As Mr. DeCompanse stepped into the foyer, he keep glancing my way – almost as if my presence made him nervous, but of course that was because I was still partially dressed, I'm sure.

"It is actually a common occurrence in this business, I assure you. The way information is spread in this day and age is quite amazing." He sniffed. "And my understanding is you have a matched pair with the Green crackle glaze, that is the most difficult color to find as they only made a few. The blue was more popular at the time."

I saw my chance for escape here before they started in on the whole "young people these days" speech and looked for me to confirm or deny.

"It was a pleasure meeting you Mr. DeCompanse." "Momma, I will see you later." As I turned to leave, I saw a look come over Mr. DeCompanse's face. He had turned to follow my progress out of the entry hall and stopped to stare at something down the hall. The only thing there was the antique sideboard. I figured Mr. DeCompanse thought it was valuable and Momma was about to have to discourage him on the sale of another family heirloom.

As Momma was ushering him into the front parlor, I grinned as I heard her asking "So you said on the telephone your buyer wishes to remain anonymous. I just find that a little sordid, don't you agree?"

I was still laughing to myself as I snuck out the back door in the kitchen. That poor antiques dealer was in for it and didn't even know it yet.

6

There is always something interesting going on here at BonHaven. Take today for example. My shift didn't start until three, so I had time to putter around. I slept later than I usually do probably because it was awfully quite upstairs. That should have set off alarm bells, but I was determined to relax this morning, so was not on my toes. I usually have really good spidey senses – You have to have them in this family! So I threw on some sweats – the kind from my academy days that drive Momma crazy-and headed downstairs, drawn to the smell of Sadie's biscuits.

As I reached the second floor landing the din of voices rose, but like a family argument in church. You know the kind you see every Sunday where the mom is trying to stop the arguing of the kids and keep Dad out of it. All while remaining aware of where you are. There was the same reverence to the tone of voices. O.K. now my spidey senses were on full alert. I hurried down the second set of stairs and ran to the source of the noise. I was moving so quick that I actually did a Risky Business slide on the hardwood floor in my socks as I slid into the rug under the breakfast room table.

Now I knew why it was so quite upstairs and probably everywhere else in the house. Everyone was in the breakfast room. I mean everyone, even Uncle Howard. Aunt Leila Mae, Momma, Granddaddy, John and even Wallace were gathered in the large dining room. Wallace never sits with the family, ever. The person sitting at the head of the table had a plate full of fresh biscuits and sausage gravy, eggs perfectly over-easy, grits and red-eye ham. All the while, Sadie hovered over him to refill his plate. Our guest, who was telling stories in between shoveling forkfuls of Sadie's best, had just finished chewing and was about to speak.

Now you could hear a pin drop.

"Sadie, these are the best biscuits - best since Momma's o'course. It's the lard isn't it? Boy, I sure miss lard."

"I'll be in my grave many times over before I cook with that low fat olive oil that's in the Piggly Wiggly these days!" As she realized who her outburst was in front of, she shuffled off to the kitchen to hide her embarrassment.

It was amazing! He actually had a visible energy radiating from him. I have to admit, it was pretty cool. But, I am the voice of reason around here, so I put on my best stern cop face and glared over the room.

Ever the southern gentleman, as he realized I had come into the room, our guest, Elvis, THE Elvis, stood.

"Hi Darlin'." He gave me his famous lopsided grin. "I hope you don't mind. Sorry 'bout this (as he spreads his hands over the table). I sure miss the food more than anything —even the young cuties".

As I stare, I am stunned. It's not just the fact that Elvis is sitting at my family table, it's the effect he is having on everyone. Even Wallace is sitting quietly- enwrapped. I am so freaked out that I am starting to get the whole Wallace being quite thing.

I finally manage to blurt out "How did you get here?"

I watch in awe as he delicately dabs his mouth with one of our heirloom linen napkins thoughtfully provided by Sadie. He then carefully places the monogram face up on the table and walks toward me.

I gotta tell you, the Elvis walking towards me (circa 1950's-in his prime Elvis), took my breath away. So much so, that out of habit, I find myself putting my hand down to my hip where my gun would normally be whenever I felt a threat. As he approached, he closed in and put his arm around my shoulder and gestured to walk with him. As we walked away towards the French doors leading to the gardens, he turned his head and gave Sadie a final compliment.

"Maam, those were the best grits I ever had…and (he actually giggles) those biscuits were to die for". And with his famous crooked grin, we were gone.

"So, Elvis, again, why are you here? HOW are you here?"

Elvis pulled away and looked at Al like a little boy who knows he's in trouble and is ready to try to charm his way out.

"Now don't go blamin' Merle-it wasn't her fault –exactly."

I slapped my forehead and sat down on the stone bench between the hedges.

"Why didn't I guess that right away? I must be slipping! Okaaay, out with it."

"Well Darlin', like I said it's not really her fault. I was sittin' around, just being bored, there's not as much to do on the other side as you would think, at least for someone like me." The grin was back. I saw a bright light flash -sorta like those bulbs on cameras that got real hot after they flash, then you throw 'em out- remember those?"

I did remember actually. Uncle Howard had one of those cameras. He was very proud of it. It was cutting edge technology at the time. I remember playing with the strip of bulbs and thinking how alien they were. He was constantly taking pictures when he first got it. We were blinded most of that year.

"So, what IS going on? Why are you here? We'll get to the how later." I said. I must have had a dazed look on my face because he just stared at me for the longest time. I thought I was going to have to ask him the question again. Maybe he wasn't even with me anymore. Who knows how these things work.

"Well, the light was what first got my attention. So I came closer to see what was what, and that's when I saw the gauzy curtain kind of things bellowing out in the middle like it was being blown gently by a light breeze". He gestured with his hands and said "You know how those fortune tellers at a county fair always say things like "let me look behind the veil to see your future"? "That's exactly how it is! Reality is really just a thin layer of, well, I can't rightly say exactly. It's like a sheer stretchy fabric that tears slightly when you pass through; more like spider webs, silky but sticky at the same time. And there's this sighing noise when you pass through. It's almost as if the reality is resigned to being passed through. Then it repairs the tear immediately when you pass through".

"Okay" I say. "But how did YOU get here?"

Elvis looked serious, then leaned forward. "It's like looking through a window with sheer curtains. Some windows are more brightly lit than others. Your windows were like beacons - a lighthouse on a dark ocean! I couldn't resist checking it out to see what was causing the light, so I walked towards it and ended up here, in your garden." He spread his hands, palms up, indicating the expanse of the gardens.

"Alright. I've heard more farfetched stories. Actually, for this family, that makes perfect sense." I said.

I got up and then threw myself down on a plush wicker chair a few feet away and leaned forward with my head in my hands.

"WHY are you here?" The words came out muffled as I was talking through my hands.

But evidently he understood because he answered.

"Well Darlin', it's like this. Have you ever heard of Palisphor?"

"Vaguely." I said squinting, trying to recall what I knew. "I'm pretty sure I heard Aunt Mae talk about it once or twice. It's supposed to be another reality parallel to ours right?"

Elvis had moved to the wicker loveseat opposite and nodded, leaning in towards me. Then he reached over and pulled my chair closer to him, while scooting to the edge of the loveseat. We were so close our noses almost touched. Man, his eyes are sooo blue, almost violet. Oh Good Lord Alma Sue, get a grip! How often will I get another chance like this, to talk to the King?? Unless I'm actually having a stroke right now and I'm imagining all this. Jeeze, pay attention. I need to look into getting Ritalin or something. I definitely have adult ADHD. I blinked several times to refocus.

"Right" Elvis said. "But it's pure. Untouched by human or mortal influence. It's a refuge for all mystical creatures, except Demons o'course."

"Of course." I said solemnly.

"Well, there's been some strange things happening there, and seeing as my schedule was clear, I volunteered to poke around and see what I could find out."

I was nodding my head as if I understood what he was talking about and said "O.K., but why are you HERE, in my house? I'm afraid to ask, (and even more afraid of the answer), but what does any of that have to do with this reality? Or with my family? I asked, still floating in those flower like eyes of his, or maybe it was more like floating in a turquoise colored pool.

"Baby Doll" he drawled. "I'm not exactly sure, but I was drawn to the bright light on the other side, so I thought I'd check it out. Then o'course I ran into Miss Sadie who invited me to breakfast. Then I met your family and was really just enjoying myself." He grinned like a schoolboy caught being naughty – again. I got the feeling he was naughty a lot, so has had lots of practice with that grin.

"I've met John, and I ran into Thurman , literally ran into Thurman early this morning – knocked the funny little guy right on his butt, and of course I already know Wallace. So basically, I'm just passing through. And I like to slip between realities. It's pretty cool." The grin was back. "I like that feeling you get when you pass through, like you just misplaced something important. It makes you feel a little sad, but hopeful to find it. There's also the sound, that soft sighing noise as reality slips back into place. You should try it sometime." He nods his head towards me.

"Umm, thanks, maybe I will." I say with a matching grin.

"Well, I better be going, lots to do still." He says standing.

Just as I was starting to stand, Lyci came skidding across the patio, knocking both her and me to the ground. She popped back up, bringing me with her in a tangle of arms and legs.

"Wow, I had a feeling you were here!" She said out of breath. "I just can't believe it would really be you. It's so awesome! I felt something was here, but just figured Aunt Merle brought back something. But I didn't figure it would be you! This is the coolest thing she's ever done and ..." I put my hand over her mouth mid-sentence to shut her up while shrugging at Elvis.

"Sorry, this is my baby sister, Lyci" I said while still trying to corral my struggling sister. See, my wrestling moves still come in handy. "She has a thing for you. She has all your music and even the DVD "Live from Las Vegas".

"Hey little Darlin'. Come on over here and give me a big hug!" He said while ogling and holding out his arms towards the suddenly limp body of my sister puddling to the ground.

"Um, remember King, she is only sixteen!" I teased.

"Can I take a picture?" Lyci asked as she took the picture.

"Umm, I'm not sure that's such a good idea." I said reaching for her phone.

"Don't fret over it. Anyone that sees it will just think it's an impersonator." Elvis said with a laugh. "I'm always on the cover of that magazine, can't think of the name of it right now, shoot, tip of my tongue." He snapped his fingers and had a look or real concentration on his face.

"National Inquirer?" I offered as I made a face.

"That's it!" He pointed at me. "Don't you notice there is always a story about me, even after thirty years? Well, me or an alien. MOST of them aren't true" he coughed on the word MOST.

"Wow." Was all I could think of to say. I think my brain short circuited. Again.

"I really gotta go lots of stops to make. Maybe I'll see you around." He turned to leave, and then turned back. "Wallace knows where to reach me if you need anything."

"Wallace??" I said with my unhinged jaw on the floor. I didn't see that coming.

"Sure. Wallace knows everybody!" he said with a grin and a wave.

And before I could recover, he was gone.

7

Later that day, after supper, we had one of those mellow family nights that I have read about in books, but never really experienced. Or at least one that remained mellow. They usually start off that way, but never stay quiet. It's expected in our family and a kind of tradition we are actually proud of in a weird sort of way.

Anyway, we were all on the back veranda enjoying a spectacular sunset, drinking a last glass of Merlot before settling in for the night. The conversation was easy, with Merle, Howard and Momma telling stories of their childhoods. I always enjoy hearing how they amused themselves as kids; especially the tales of Momma behaving extremely un-Momma like. I sometimes think they say things just to see if I will be shocked or grossed out. Lyci is at her BFF's, Ashleigh's tonight, but if she were here, she just shrugs her shoulders like she has seen it all before. And what with her abilities, she probably has. Literally and figuratively. My favorite tale tonight is the Flying of the June Bug. In a very specific time frame in early summer, a special kind of insect comes around. They are a beautiful shade of iridescent green with disproportionately giant wings and delicate long legs that feel both sticky and prickly at the same time when they crawl along your skin. They are awesome to see, once you get over the shock of them arriving. When they were little, they would catch June Bugs and tie kite string to their legs. Then when they took off to fly they would fly the June Bugs like a kite. This sounds cruel, but I am assured they untied them and let them go unharmed. This is marginally better than the stories of making jewelry out of lightening bugs tail. Uggh. Have you ever accidently squashed a lightening bug?

They stink to high heaven! Why would you want to put that on your skin? It takes a week to get the stink washed off. Nasty

As I am trying to decide whether or not to believe this latest tale, I see Aunt Merle holding up her glass, looking at the wine she was swirling in her glass. "Marianne, this Merlot is really quite good. Have we had it before?"

"No. It was recommended by the young man in the wine shop today. Something about it being a very good year in the Siena region when this was bottled."

"Oh, I visited there when I was in my twenties - went on the European tour you know. I so enjoyed it. The food, the hospitality, and of course the wine! Those Italians really know how to cook! Oh and the young men…." Aunt Merle looked as if she might actually swoon.

"Poppycock!" Uncle Howard grumbled. "I-talian shmalian. Nobody cooks like a Southerner!" And with that he was off to his room. Soon after, the sounds of his typewriter drifted on the sultry breeze to compete with the increasing volume of the cicadas as the dusk turned to evening. Classic Uncle Howard.

Aunt Merle was awfully quiet after that. She was so lost in her memories a spaceship could have landed in front of her and she wouldn't have noticed. I use that example because it HAS happened before. I decided to get another glass of this exceptional wine and pay attention this time when I swallowed it. I am constantly trying to become a connoisseur, but I can never remember what I learned the next time I go to buy wine. Momma's glass was still half full, and Aunt Merle was still lost in thought as I wandered down the hall towards the kitchen. I could hear Sadie banging pots and pans as she cleaned and was singing to herself. I recognized the tune, but couldn't place exactly what it was, so I was not really paying attention to where I was walking.

So you can imagine my surprise when I bumped into the large man dressed as a Sea-Captain pointing his saber at me.

"Damn the Torpedoes, four bells! Go ahead, Jouett, Full speed!"

"Damn it David! You scared the BeJezus out of me!" Meet First Rear Admiral David Farragut. The Union Officer most famously known for the aforementioned saying. He likes to pop in every now and then just to yell his infamous Bon Mot. Since Bon Secuers Bay is located so close to where the battle was, he is sort of a local legend. He has been here since his death in 1870. Why here you may ask? Who knows? Probably for the same reason the others all stay around. Maybe it's the party house of the other world. Although frankly, I'm surprised Thurman doesn't run most of them off. David never stays very long, as someone usually yells for "the damn Yankee to leave!" What everyone has conveniently forgotten is that David was born in Tennessee, but since he fought for the Union (otherwise known as "the WRONG side"), he is forever a Yankee.

It's not that he is scary in any way, it's just he shows up when you least expect it. But that is the way of all of our non-living guests. The other interesting fact is when David appears to Momma or Lyci, he usually bows, excuses himself, and says things like "Pardon me ladies", or "Excuse me, Maam." Really??!

Sadie comes barreling through the swinging kitchen door, which has passed through David of course, but hits me in the forehead. As I stagger back, Sadie is bending over laughing.

"I can't believe that ole' fool still scares you. I would 'a thought by now ya'll be used to 'em."

"He doesn't scare me – I'm just surprised. When he just shows up right in front of me, poking a sword in my face, it's kind of…surprising."

"Lordy, Lordy, Lordy, I declare." She clucks, shaking her head slowly back and forth with a slight grin. Looking down at my empty wine glass she stated; "Im'a guessing you need another one of those" and disappears back into the kitchen.

Good Lord.

8

The house is unusually quite again this morning. As I walked down the stairs there was only the normal volume of voices coming from the breakfast room. Thank God for small favors…maybe today will turn out to be a normal day. Although, now that I think about it, I wouldn't recognize a normal day if it threw itself in my face and rasp berried me with a huge tongue. One can always hope! For the normal day, not the raspberry.

Only Uncle Howard was still seated at the table. The light coming in from the three huge arched windows was very bright with the morning sun. The way the light refracted through the ancient beveled glass created thousands of miniature rainbows splashed across the large room. It took my breath away every single time I noticed. "Good morning." Howard said looking up from his paper.

"Good morning. Where is everyone? I thought I heard you talking to someone?" I said as I looked around.

"Nope, just me. Oh, John just left, he was looking for Wallace. Had something important to discuss with him. He actually seemed flustered, the way he was wringing his hands in that way he does when he is agitated. He obviously had something on his mind and I tried to get it out of him, but he just said he need to discuss it with Wallace first."

"Hummm." I frowned as I sat down and poured myself coffee from the silver decanter Sadie had left on the table. "That's strange; usually John is headed the opposite way from Wallace, not looking for him."

From behind his paper Howard said "I thought so too. But I have learned from the past. Stay out of their business and they will tend to stay out of mine. I recommend you do the same and I did try to offer my help."

I was quiet for awhile as I sipped my coffee and thought through different scenarios of what Wallace and John could possibly have to discuss on this quiet morning. It must be something pretty important for John to be in such a god-awful hurry to stir up something with Wallace. Nothing exciting had happened yesterday and the excitement from Elvis's visit the other day had finally calmed down. Oh well, it would eventually be brought up, I'm sure.

"Good morning everyone!" Aunt Merle said brightly as she sashayed into the room. "Notice anything different?"

"Oh, Good Lord! I don't want to play this game. It's too early." I groaned slipping down in my chair.

"I'll play" Howard said. "Well Merle, Let's see…I see a new gray hair. And is that a new mole on your left cheek?" Uncle Howard loves to tease his younger sister.

"Oh stop it. I'm not falling for your goading this morning. I'm in too good of a mood." She said as she walked to a chair opposite me and sat down in a big production. "Now, Alma Sue, Do you notice anything?" she said as she pulled her hair away from her neck to reveal a beautiful necklace and matching drop earrings, well one earring. One was missing.

My eyes bugged out of my head and my mouth must have dropped onto the table because I actually heard a thud. I gaped at the necklace. It was made of intricately woven filaments of delicate gold that wrapped each jewel in a frothy bed that showcased each jewel independently. The jewels were each the size of a large jelly bean with smaller diamonds between each piece. The rainbows I noticed earlier from the windows danced off the jewels, making them appear as if they were exploding with color. The effect was amazing. At least I think it was the lighting, I hoped it was the lighting, Oh Jeeze, I prayed it was the lighting! But the crowning jewel, pun definitely intended, was the huge oval emerald that appeared to float at the apex due to how the filaments were around the jewel. The earring was a miniature version of the sides of the necklace.

"Alma Sue, Dear, please close your mouth, it's not a look becoming to a young lady." Merle sniffed with pretend indignation. "Your mother would have a conniption." She could barely hold back her giggle. She was having waaay too much fun with this.

"Holy Crap. Where did you get that? Please say you didn't steal it. Please say you didn't steal it." I was having a little trouble breathing at this point. "You do remember I am a cop, right"

"Seriously Al, calm down" Merle was looking a little alarmed now at the color my face was turning. "I woke up wearing it, if you must know. You know how these things are dear."

By this time, Uncle Howard had put his paper down and was seriously interested in the conversation. He stared at Merle, then at the necklace, then at me, then back to the necklace.

Oh No. It's not the lighting. They came from somewhere where light exploding from jewelry may be normal.

"O.K. I am ... calm now." I said between taking deep relaxing breaths. "So start at the beginning. How did you get the necklace?"

"Well, remember our conversation last night on the veranda, after dinner?" She said as her hand fluttered to her chest, then to the necklace, then back to her chest. "When ya'll were discussing the Merlot we were drinking, it brought back memories of when I was young and traveled to Europe. I had so much fun. Especially in Italy. We traveled to this village somewhere in the Tuscany region, and visited with a family whose ancestors had been there for centuries. They gave us a tour of their family stronghold – a castle by most standards. In their gallery, there was a picture of this beautiful young woman. A girl really. She had the most pitifully sad eyes. She was wearing this necklace in the portrait. There was some sort of story involved with her and the necklace, but I can't remember the details now."

"Oh, but I do recall the name of the village now, and isn't it funny, it's the same name as the wine we were drinking yesterday! Oh my! I do remember (at this point she is gesturing wildly with her hands); the drawing of the castle and the vineyard on the bottle is the very same one we visited! Good gracious, I remember everything now! The young girl in the portrait wearing the necklace, her name was Sienna. Sienna

D'Arbia. The story was she was the only daughter of the castle Lord. Something about her getting sick and turning a funny shade of blue. It happened just after the commissioned portrait was completed. There was more to the story, but I just can't remember anymore." She said as her hands fluttered to her neck and came to rest on the necklace.

I must have been staring at her with my "get to the point" look because she said "Anyway, I was musing on the past when I went to bed and when I woke up this morning, I was wearing the jewelry." She made a washing her hands motion with the end of the story. And to Aunt Merle, this really was the end to her. No big deal. Happens all the time. What's the problem?

Uncle Howard was laughing at this point. "Well Merle, this is a new one." He said. "Maybe we can actually profit off your "activities". That would be a nice change. Usually these antics end up costing us one way or the other." He chuckled.

It was at this moment that Wallace chose to walk by the dining room. He looked straight at me and burst out laughing. So much for a normal day. As I got up and walked out of the dining room, I could swear I heard the sound of Wallace making a raspberry noise. I swear to God. One day I'm gonna ask Aunt Mae how to get rid of ghosts.

Good Lord!

9

There was something about Aunt Merle's story that kept pulling at me; something tickling a memory. Oh well, first things first. The Jewels. Maybe if I can just go sit and veg awhile, it will come to me. Well that and more coffee. And why the hell was there only one earring? Probably the least of my worries, but still weird.

Just as I had gone out the rear French doors onto the veranda to finish my coffee and figure out what to do about the priceless jewels we were now harboring under our roof, unbeknownst to me, Aunt Leila Mae was breezing through the front door. Again, where the hell are my spidey senses when I need them?

"Hellooooo. Anyone home?" Mae called out as she walked through the door. Leila Mae, better known to the world at large as Mae, breezed in as though she still lived at BonHaven. As she had grown up here, she still thought of it as home. Mae glimmered in her beauty; impeccably dressed as always, today she wore a designer sheath dress in pale blue, the exact same shade of her eyes. With her hair down, she looked much younger than her actual age of 63. "Not bad for an old gal" she said out loud as she checked her reflection in the hall mirror. She tossed her purse and sunglasses on the sideboard as she unwound a Hermes scarf from her neck and backtracked to toss that on the sideboard as well. "Helloooo. Anybody home?" She called out again as she headed towards the parlor.

"In here Mae." Howard called out from the dining room.

"Oh. Thank goodness. I was afraid ya'll were out for the day already!" she exclaimed as she walked into the dining room. She stopped short when she saw Merle at the table with her head down fanning herself with her hands. "What happened?" she asked as she sat down and proceeded to pour herself a cup of coffee from the almost empty silver decanter.

"Just the usual." Howard said as he got up from the table. "This is my cue for ya'll ladies to work out the kinks." He said walking swiftly from the room. He was obviously waiting for any excuse to leave Merle alone rather than deal with her distress now that she realized the situation could present a problem. "Nice to see you Mae – Good Luck" he threw out as a parting shot.

Mae carried her cup over to a chair next to Merle and sat down. "My goodness Merle, what's happened?"

Merle was wringing her hands as she repeated the story she had just told to Al. "I really didn't see any problem. I just woke up with the jewels. You know how these things happen to me. Al seemed pretty upset when she left. Oh dear. I've really done it this time haven't I?" She pleaded to Mae.

"I'm sure you're overreacting. Al is just a little high strung. Is Marianne here? We can discuss the situation calmly with her. I am sure she will have a few suggestions." Mae said soothingly while checking out the necklace. She had a look on her face that if Al were present would recognize it for exactly what it was; cold calculation. "It is quite beautiful." Mae was reaching for the necklace. "Do you mind if I try it on?" She purred. Mae had already unclasped the necklace and was putting it on before Merle knew what was going on. "I have been looking for the right jewelry to wear with my dress for the Huntington's Annual Benefit Gala next week.

This would be absolutely perfect! It is the exact shade of green! I was beginning to despair I wouldn't be able to wear the outfit as everyone knows the accessories are the crowning jewel, so to speak. It's a shame you only have the one earring, the complete set would look magnificent!"

"I know!" Mae exclaimed. "I will keep it for you. That way it will be out of Al's view for awhile so she'll have time to cool off. Bless her little heart; she has too much on her mind as it is."

"I guess that would be O.K." Merle said cautiously as took out the single earring. Merle walked through the doorway into the hall and placed the single earring in the dish on the entryway antique sideboard.

"That's it. It's all settled!" Mae said as she breezed out of the room. Mae always had perfect timing and she knew when to make her exit. "Oh, I almost forgot why I came. I will be out of town for the next week, so I won't see ya'll till next week at the Gala. Can you let everyone know?" And with that she was gone as quickly as she had come.

10

On Sunday morning, when Sugar walked in with his head down and his hand over his forehead and whisper shouted SUTU with Momma fast on his heels, I took a deep breath and attacked first.

"Good Morning, Momma".

"Don't good morning Momma me young lady. I just heard from Uncle Howard that you said you were not going to buy any more new clothes – ever - and that included shopping for another cocktail dress for this year's Gala, did he hear you correctly?" Momma said with one eyebrow arched and that voice that was an octave lower than normal.

Uh-Oh. Of all the things on the list that ran through my head, I wasn't expecting that. Jeeze, this is worse than I thought. I can talk my way around most any subject, but not the fashion thing. And the worst part is, it's true. I did say that at breakfast last week when the Aunts were asking what I was wearing to The Gala. I didn't expect Uncle Howard to be the one to turn me in to the fashion police. Mae maybe, but not Howard. OK, get a grip.

"No Momma, he must have misunderstood. I was just saying I have so many dresses that would work, it was a shame they couldn't be used again. Sugar and I plan on heading to Spanish Fort next week and Dillard's is at the top of my list." Spanish Fort was to the closest shopping area that was acceptable to Momma's standards and Dillard's carried her favorite brands.

"Sugar," She looked at him for confirmation. "You WILL be helping with the selection process?" Momma cocked her head to the side waiting on his answer and demanding he do just that at the same time. "I actually have several evening gowns on hold for you there already. Evelyn was just waiting to hear from you for the fitting."

"Absolutely Miss Marianne, we have an appointment with Miss Evelyn in Designer wear for Monday morning. Al just wanted to surprise you when we came home with the perfect dress!" Sugar lied while smiling his cat that ate the canary smile. Wait, he was enjoying this waaay too much. Something's up. And I'm beginning to think I have just been outsmarted by them both.

"Well, bless your little heart" Momma said while grabbing Sugars arms. "I knew I could count on you". And with that, she breezed out of the room.

I turned on Sugar as quick as a cat sneeze. "What do you mean, about the appointment on Monday?"

"I know your aren't working on Monday, and I know you have to get an outfit for the Gala. Nothing else. I figured we can get an appointment, especially since she is expecting you, so technically, it's not a lie," He shrugged.

I was fixin to get mad when it hit me hard that he was right. I had to do it anyway, so there was no reason to get mad. He was always accusing me of being able to start an argument in an empty house, so I decided I wasn't gonna prove him right. At least not today.

Sugar knew he won this round and followed Momma out to the Veranda to talk fashion.

I still couldn't believe Uncle Howard threw me to the wolves, or wolf so to speak. As I was sinking into the realization that I was actually going to have to put in time trying on dresses, a plan to get even with Uncle Howard came to me.

Uncle Howard had an obsession with his favorite food. Potted meat. Even those who love it don't really question what it is made up of. Like I always say, there are some things you just don't question. Not everyone understood this Southern staple, but to those who did, it was constantly on hand and our pantry was no exception. He constantly was eating it; either as a sandwich or spread on crackers. Preferably Ritz, although Saltines worked in a pinch.

I sauntered back into the dining room pretending to pick up a section of the Sunday newspaper lying on the table paying particular interest in the advertisements. I waited long enough for him to have forgotten what he just discussed. That way he would never even know I could possibly be upset and therefore not be suspicious of the next thing out of my mouth. Knowing Uncle Howard would be eating a sandwich for lunch and there were at least a dozen cans of his beloved staple stacked where they should be, I threw out "Oh, I noticed you were out of potted meat. I can pick some up tonight on my way home. I hope your weren't planning on it for lunch." The look on his face as he threw his chair back to go check took some of the sting out of the dress shopping thing. I didn't feel even the least bit guilty; well maybe some, but I still would do it again.

I wasn't usually so vindictive and plotting, but dress shopping? That was the one thing guaranteed to push me to my dark side. I was still smiling when I reached into my back pocket to answer my buzzing cell phone. That smile quickly faded when the desk sergeant on the other end asked if I could come in tonight to cover the graveyard shift for a sick co worker. Maybe it was Karma.

I was unbuttoning my uniform shirt as I walked out the door of the station, another shift safely done, ready for the afternoon off. It was getting pretty warm, but you could tell it was going to be a great night. The twilight was sultry, but there was enough of an ocean breeze blowing in off the water to make it really nice. You could smell and even slightly taste the tangy salty water with every humid breath. I was looking forward to a big glass of sweet tea on the back veranda. I was almost dozing on my drive home as I imagined the soft, caressing breeze of the ceiling fans, their blades performing their lazy dance, and the soothing hum they made as they whirred around.

"Jeez, I need to pay attention to the road" I said aloud shaking my head to clear the cobwebs trying to make a beautiful glistening palace in my head. I made the unfortunate head shake at the exact moment as I looked to my right just as I was passing The Jureaux sheep farm. Ugh! I grimaced and made a face of disgust. I hate those damn sheep!

They really creep me out! Lamar Jureaux raises Heritage Jacob breed sheep. These poor sheep have the most unfortunate luck having two or even three sets of horns. It makes them look diabolical. Like something straight from a Stephen King novel. Why Lamar raises these demon sheep beats the hell out of me. Evidently they are prized and can sell for big bucks. I want to know who BUYS these scary looking sheep, and for what purpose; to give small children nightmares?

I shudder as I pass two of the sheep looking out through the slats of the wooden fence, slowly and deliberately chewing their cud. Both of them stare intently at me as they follow my progress as I slowly pass, probably filing the information for some sinister purpose only they know! Yikes! I goosed the accelerator and the car shot forward. Sometimes it was nice to have a hemi engine when you needed the power, especially if I wasn't footing the bill for the gas guzzler.

As I was pulling up the drive in the cruiser, I noticed Jimmy-Don and his crew nosing around Bastian, the ancient Spanish Oak tree that sits straddling or property lines. As if it's not bad enough that I had to pick up the ten to five AM shift yesterday for Joey B who ate some bad crawfish, now I have to deal with Jimmy-Don and his idiots. I had heard talk that Bastian was his latest fixation, but I was hoping it would just go away.

Evidently not.

I can understand the fascination though. Everyone around the greater Blakely area thinks the tree is haunted and has special powers. It's not really because of its appearance. It's more of a feeling associated with Bastian and that inexplicable things have been attributed to the tree over the years. It's a good thing in general that people don't know how right they are, and I'm certainly not talking!

There have been a number of incidents in the past, both recent and very long ago, that have contributed to Bastian's lore - the most recent being little Jenny Saunders going missing for five days and found incoherent in Bastian's upper limbs. All everyone knows for sure is that there is NO way she climbed up there on her own. Again – I'm not talking. There have been many times over the years that the massive tree was almost cut down by an out of control superstitious mob, only to be backed down by a member of my family. Since the tree is on our property line, we have the final say.

But it seems Jimmy-Don does indeed have his sights set and I better put a stop to it if I can. He'll only make a mess.

He has tripods with cameras set up to record and all kinds of other equipment that I have no idea what it's used for.

"Hey Jimmy-Don, What're ya'll up to this early?" I yell across the car through my open passenger window as I pull the cruiser over to the group.

"Oh, hey Al." he says as he trips over a tripod leg as he walks towards the car. "We are doing an experiment. The Ghost Hunters producers said to send them a tape of us in a r..r..real investigation. Kind of as an aud..aud..audition." Jimmy-Don finally got out. Did I mention Jimmy-Don stutters when he's excited or nervous? And he is definitely both right now. He knows from my voice that I am acting on official business.

"Well, that sounds great and all, but this tree is on private property, and I know for a fact that you don't have permission." I say.

"But, it is on both our properties according to my momma and daddy." Jimmy-Don smiles in what he thinks is his most charming, don't be silly woman, kind of way. But I see him swallow hard when he is finished talking. If it weren't six AM, I bet I could see him sweat, but I'm tired and not that into details.

"You're not exactly correct Jimmy-Don, but either way you would need my permission, and I'm not sure I want my part of the tree pestered with. I'd bet you Bastian would say the very same thing if he could talk, so ya'll go on." I say hoping that the tired in my voice is mistaken for anger. "So why don't you and your boys pack on up and go have breakfast."

"Okay; and maybe that there tree *can* talk." Jimmy-Don says with a secret grin. "No problem. Come on boys, it's a wrap"

I probably should have been more worried about that grin, but like I said I was tired.

Buster, Jimmy-Don's lifelong best friend and partner in crime was holding the new Best Buy video camera, filming Jimmy-Don, flipped the camera cover down and headed for his truck. He was like an obedient little puppy. Another rough around the edges guy I didn't recognize was holding down the button of a specialized pocket digital recorder and filming away pointed towards what appeared to be the direction of BonHaven, which didn't make sense to me, but whatever. He had a baseball cap with the Chasers logo on the front pulled down low so most of his face was hidden; the rest was shadowed by the small camera. BonHaven was far enough away so I wasn't worried about anything being seen. The Spanish Oaks lining the edge of the property made a good screen anyway. I decided to stay around for a bit watching to make sure they are packing up for real, which it looks like they really are which makes me even more suspicious. For Jimmy-Don to give in so quickly means he probably really is finished. Since when is he intimidated by me? Especially enough to shut down production of his life-long dream? But I figured he won't cause any real harm, and really, he is an idiot, what could have happened? He was just filming the tree.

But I figured wrong.

11

When most everyone, normal, everyday regular humans at least, look upon Bastian, what they see is this; imagine the most beautiful Southern Spanish Oak tree you have ever seen. Its massive trunk reaching out through the ground, claiming all space around it as if it's claiming the land as it's due for being on the earth for so long. The branches caressed possessively by fluffy Spanish moss that gracefully flutters like gauze dreamily in the warm humid breeze. The image evokes thoughts of drifting off into a delightfully restful nap while leaning against its steady trunk, reassured by the fact that you would be protected under its canopied branches, as it has weathered so many seasons under the relentless Southern suns. Bastian makes you feel secure, protected, even loved.

NOT.

What lies underneath that warm and fuzzy exterior Bastian projects, is the stuff nightmares are made of. If you really stare at the tree and really focus, another image comes to mind. Not what you see, not, with your eyes, it's more of an image that superimposes itself over the "pretty" image. And believe you me, the real Bastian is one scary dude, and yes, I mean dude, as in a person.

If you close your eyes and imagined what a haunted tree looks like, Bastian would be it. Classic menacing gnarly limbs and roots growing up from the ground like an open wound. Like it knows what scares you and is only too happy to oblige. Near the base is a large gaping opening, exactly where a mouth would be if a tree had a mouth. Actually, now that I really think about it, it probably is Bastian's mouth.

See, Bastian was once a human. Many, many centuries ago, Bastian was actually a very beloved member of the Chamonix of France family. He was a third son, and therefore not much was expected of him as his father had his heir in his oldest brother Cedric. Then his next brother, Cecil, was expected to fulfill the familial duties if anything happened to the eldest. So Bastian spent most of his time being mischievous and playing pranks on everyone in his village. One day he was so bored, that he concocted his most outlandish prank, just to see what would happen. Unfortunately, the prank extended to most of the countryside. His big idea was to put the dye used to color clothes in the village well. Really not that big of a deal, but what happened was no one really noticed.

That is until some people started turning blue. The drinking water was turning the skin of some folks blue. Not everyone, just some of the fair skinned ones whose skin was evidently more susceptible. One of these people was a young girl who was the daughter of a wealthy land baron. When his daughter became ill, he sent for the village healer, a kindly old woman named Marceline. She was a typical healer of the day, and generally thought to be a witch, but was left alone because of her healing powers.

Anyway, the concoction she gave the young woman was just an herb mixture to flush the toxins, including the blue dye, from the body, nothing harmful. Unfortunately, the young woman had an unknown allergy to one of the herbs and had a severe allergic reaction that caused her face and ears to swell, which caused her husband to blame Marceline and throw her off his land, which is where her cottage was located. She was forced from the village and no one ever saw her again.

But she put a spell on the one responsible for the incident, which as we know, was our Bastian. The spell was;

"To the One with Mischief in his heart, with his body will soon part. After Death will join with Nature far across the lands, and will do mischief only where he stands. Just to be sure, to keep all away and safe, he will be looked upon with the fright of face."

So....Here he is. And no one's the wiser. Well, usually no one. Only those with an additional sense can see him.

And evidently high resolution digital cameras with infra-red sensors, slow motion, stop action, and frame by frame reply.

12

Unfortunately, I did not realize, or more likely, never really cared, that time lapse digital photography and videography has come so far technically. Things that were undetectable to the human eye are now being discovered, or re-discovered in some cases. This new technology has given so much to the scientific community, from new species, to a new color being added to the color spectrum.

What the world needs to know are that some things are Supernatural and should remain so – and this is coming from a police officer! Not everything needs an explanation. Many secrets of other realms around us have been secret for many millennia for a reason. Whether it is just to be able to look at Nature around us with a sense of wonder and awe, to bask in the golden rays of warm sunshine on a beautiful Autumn day afire, or watching the full Harvest moon crown over the lapping waves of the ocean to watching a hummingbird drink thirstily from a flower blossom in replete bloom, not everything must be explained, just enjoyed.

Maybe this attitude is just a survival mechanism for being in my family, but hey, a girls gotta do what a girls gotta do, right?

I first heard of "The Tape" as it is being referred to all around town, in line at the Piggly Wiggly. I was just on my way home from the station and stopped in to grab a jar of pasta sauce as requested by Sadie for dinner. As I was standing in the checkout line I heard the first "Well, I declare!"

As I turned to see who was so excited, low and behold it was none other than Miss Ethyl and Mrs. Pender. Miss Ethyl, AKA Biddie to her closest frenemies, has the dubious distinction as the biggest gossip this side of the Mississippi. If she didn't have the latest gossip to spread, then she made something up and spread that around like fresh manure in a spring garden, very liberally. Mrs. Pender seemed to be listening intently rather than with just a half hearted effort, like most people do when talking with Miss Ethyl, normal people that is. But as I mentally hit myself upside my forehead, I reminded myself that normal is a very relative term.

Regardless, since I was captive in line anyway, I eavesdropped.

"So, I heard it is actual proof that "That" Tree is haunted." Miss Ethyl repeated to Mrs. Pender.

"Well, I Declare, that's just nonsense Biddie." Mrs. Pender sniffed, trying to look indignant.

"Well, I have seen that videotape and it is most definitely true!" Biddie stamped her foot for emphasis.

Uh-Oh. Bastian. Dammit! What did that idiot Jimmy-Don do?

I leaned over to the other check out isle. "Excuse me, Maam" I said to Miss Ethyl.

"What did you say about that tree?"

Both women looked at me and stood up a little straighter. My uniform has that effect sometimes.

"I was just explaining to Mrs. Pender that I saw a videotape of that dreadful old Spanish oak tree off route 48. You know the one, it sits…" Ha. She just recognized me. "on your property".

"Yes Maam. I know the one. What about it?" I asked politely.

"Well, I just came from Jenny Katherine's house and she had a copy and was showing it to everyone. She just bought a really nice big screen TV. She made her husband Wiley hang it over the fireplace to show it off real well. But it turned into a God Almighty fight as Jenny Katherine made Wiley move that ugly painting he insists is Art. You know the one; it was in the paper last year when they were running a series on folk art and Lore. Jenny Katherine has hated that painting since the day it…. "

"Maam, could you tell me what you saw?" I interrupted her.

"Why, yes, I was telling you." She looked genuinely confused. "I was going to say there was a really nice shot of BonHaven with that tree off to the side, then all of a sudden the video goes all out of focus, but then a different image comes on the screen. It's still the tree, but not. This tree looks really scary. And mean. It looks real. I mean like a real person, not a tree."

I must have been giving her my patented "Now tell the truth" look, because Miss Ethyl said "No, really. I know how that sounds, but I saw it with my own eyes!"

"So then what?" I asked trying to sound bored and disbelieving when actually I was freaking out trying to think of the best way to handle damage control.

"Well, nothing. The video went back to normal." She said as if that was that and explained everything.

This was my big chance. If I could convince Biddie, the biggest gossip in town that the video was a prank, she would spread it around and that would be the end of it. Cut the head off the snake so to speak.....

"Why Miss Ethyl," I said with a wave of my hand, "That tape is just a prank that Jimmy Don came up with. He was going to send it as a joke to that TV show "Ghost Hunters". "He worked on that editing a really long time to make it look convincing. I heard he was doing it, but I didn't think he could pull it off. You know that boy's brain rattles around like a BB in a boxcar. Evidently he is better than I thought!" I said laughing. "I don't think I would tell anyone else about it, or you'll just end up looking silly." And then I went for the final blow. "You don't want to lose your credibility now. Then no one will believe a single thing you say....."

The look on her face said it all. Mission accomplished.

"Well I for one did not believe a word of it. Not a single word!" Mrs. Pender said as she placed her items on the counter to be rung up.

Miss Ethyl was unusually quiet as she waited in line.

I said my goodbyes and stepped back over to my checkout lane and put my pasta sauce on the counter. As I gave the clerk my cash, I did a mental fist pump. By tomorrow Miss Ethyl will have burned out all the towns' phone lines killing any hopes of anyone believing anything they see on that tape. God Bless little old ladies with a mission!

13

The Huntington Gala was an event attended by anyone who was anybody-meaning Momma and Aunt Mae had to be there and I was dragged along. Granted it is a benefit and raises badly needed money for multiple children's programs in the tri-parish area. But I hated to dress up and play the part of social butterfly. I would much rather be hanging with the guys having pizza and beer after our shift. But noooo, Momma has me in this ridiculous evening gown. Although, I must admit, I do clean up well. I also have spotted a really cute guy at the buffet table who has glanced my way more than once. Maybe this won't be a bad way to spend a Saturday night after all!

Just as I am making my way over to Mr. Hottie, I hear a hush fall over the room. As I pull my attention away from my intended target, I see what all the commotion is about. Figures. Aunt Mae has made her entrance and as usual, she is stunning. Oh Crap. She is wearing the necklace Merle brought back. Oh well, nothing I can do about it now. There is no way anyone would know what it is anyway. Our family has money, but not THAT much money. They'll just assume it's a really great piece of costume jewelry that she found at that specialty shop in Atlanta everyone talks about. I hope.

While every person in the entire ballroom's breathing has been suspending staring at my Aunt, my intended goal for the evening had snuck up behind me.

— 91 —

"She doesn't hold a candle to you, you are the only one with the beauty of echrassa." was whispered into my ear.

I whipped around so fast; I think I caused the earth to tilt off its axis by a degree or so. I whirled so quickly my heels got caught in the hem of my dress and I started to keel over. Hottie reached down, grabbed my waist and steadied me. I reached for my gun, forgetting I was in an evening gown, not a police uniform. Initially disappointed, but after finding my gaze on Mr. Hottie as I looked up, surprised, then thrilled. He looked even better up close!

"Reaching for your weapon Officer? Wow, I must have lost my touch." The blond Adonis said. I really need to find out what his name is so I can stop with the clichés in my head. "Usually women don't feel the need to shoot me when I try to introduce myself" He said with a hangdog expression on his face. And I'll be damned if he didn't mean it!

"I'm sorry" I said. "It's just my training. Wait, how did you know I'm a cop?"

"It's kind of obvious if you know what to look for." He said with a grin.

I was getting nervous now. I didn't want to be obnoxious in front of him as I still was interested, but now curiosity won out. As I scrunched my eyebrow I said "And you would know what to look for because......."

"Sorry. I'm Carlyle Baveras, but everyone but my mother calls me Lyle. I just transferred from down from Birmingham – started today." He said extending his hand. His hand was huge, warm and rough. I liked the feel of it.

"I'm Al Babineaux. I heard we were getting a transfer. Sorry I wasn't there to greet you today. I took the day off to prepare for this." I motioned around the ballroom.

"And it paid off if I may say so."

"Flattery will get you everywhere." I giggled. Oh Crap. I actually giggled. What is wrong with me, I never act like this. I am actually giddy. If I didn't know for sure that I had not picked up a drink yet, I would swear I was drunk. The room was actually spinning a little and it was hard to catch my breath. Jeez – get a hold of yourself! I'm a cop – he's a cop. Act like it!

"Sorry to surprise you, I just noticed you looked a little distressed and thought I would offer my assistance." He said with the cutest little grin.

Good Lord.

"Oh, no, it's nothing – really. I just noticed my Aunt walking in and she tends to have that effect on me."

"That gorgeous woman is your Aunt? Wow. She looks like she should be on a magazine cover." Lyle said while staring up at the landing where Aunt Mae was being photographed and adored. Just when I was beginning to get a little jealous he said "But that explains where you get your looks. You look exactly like her – just younger." That's it. Oh crap, I think I just fell in love – just a little.

Before I could explore this idea any further, Colonel and Mrs. Gentry came over to discuss their latest dissatisfaction with the police force. They always felt I would do something about it. By

the time I assured them I would look into their complaint and turned to introduce Carlyle, he was gone.

Oh well, that's just my luck I thought as I headed for the hors d'oeuvres table. Meet the man of my dreams; then he's gone! After filling my plate with all sorts of culinary delights and grabbing a glass of champagne, I found a comfy chair to eat away my disappointment. So I reverted to doing what I do best – observing people. It was particularly enjoyable to watch the crowd around Aunt Mae. She truly had a captivated audience. Most of the gentlemen I knew or had seen around town. But one older gentleman was standing back from the crowd observing Mae with something other than lust. He appeared to be more interested in what she was wearing. Hummn. Funny. He looks very familiar, but I just can't place him. I need to make a mental note to ask Momma who that is. It's not just anyone who can take their eyes off Aunt Mae's face!

Wow, I though as I looked down at my plate. What was that I just ate; flaky, buttery pastry surrounding crabmeat with clove and nutmeg – It was unbelievable!

Aunt Leila Mae was forgotten as I headed back to the hors d'orves table.

After Leila Mae had her fill of listening to and absorbing compliments, she saw Marianne viewing the desert table and made her way over, stopping for more compliments and photographs of course. Along the way, she gorged on more looks of awe and envy. Yummy. If you looked hard, you could see the resemblance to a cat purring after a particularly delicious bowl of high quality cream.

When she finally arrived at the table, she cozied up to Momma to tell her she was heading back to St. Elmo tomorrow, but she would stop by the house and drop off the "borrowed" jewelry on her way out of town, sometime before noon. I saw Momma nod her head as Mae floated off somewhere, presumably for more accolades from her adoring fans.

Ooh creepy. That man I didn't recognize from before is slinking around by Momma. I think it's time I introduced myself.

Momma had just turned and started talking to the mystery man as I walked up beside Momma.

"Hey Momma, are you having fun?" I asked as I gave her a quick hug.

"Of course darling. Everything has turned out exactly as planned. I think the committees outdid ourselves this year! Don't you think it's the best Gala yet?" Her eyes glittered with satisfaction.

"I do have to agree Miss Marianne. This year's production is the best yet. I also must compliment the caterer. The food is divine!" said mystery man.

I tilted my head and did my best dumb blonde imitation "I'm sorry, you look very familiar. Have we met?" I fluttered my eyelashes for more effect.

"Why yes, we have, at BonHaven several weeks ago. I'm Mr. De-Companse from DeCompanse Antiquities. I came over at your Momma's request to perform a valuation on the Art Deco Radio Lamps." He said as he bowed slightly.

Ah ha. Oh Shit. Now I remember. I answered the door half dressed. I could feel myself turning red. I had to make a fast get away.

"Oh right. Very nice to see you again. Oh my, if you'll excuse me, I must go speak with....Carlyle, my co worker."

"Momma, I'll see you later." I pleaded with my eyes giving her that look of "Save Me!"

"Of course Dear." and placed herself between Mr. DeCompanse and myself.

"Mr. DeCompanse, you were saying?"

"Oh, yes. I was just asking if it would be possible to make an appointment to see the lamps again, perhaps tomorrow after luncheon? There is a marking on the bottom of the lamps that I need to verify. It could greatly increase or decrease the value."

"I'm sure that would be fine. I will call you tomorrow if there is any conflict."

As I ran off to hide my shame, I heard Momma agree to an appointment. I was still listening in on the conversation and not paying attention to where I was walking when I walked directly into Carlyle.

"We've got to stop meeting this way." He laughed as he reached out and wrapped his hands around my waist to steady me from falling over. Again.

"I'm so sorry. I'm really not like this. It's this dress." I motioned to the billowy skirt. "I'm used to the uniform or sweats. And my gun. I definitely miss my gun."

"I hope not for me?" he said with THAT grin.

Good Lord. I'm an idiot. "No, not for you, I just meant I don't feel at ease without it at my side." I rambled.

"I know just what you mean." And he lifted his tuxedo jacket to show me his holstered gun.

Man, this guy gets me. I grinned back.

"So, Al. What's that short for? I'm sure Mrs. Babineaux didn't name you Al."

I snorted "Of course not. My name is Alma Sue. It's a generational name." I stood up to my full height. 5'8 with four inch heels and I was still looking up at him. Hmmm. Not a comfortable feeling for me.

As if he could sense my internal struggle with not being able to go eye to eye with him and feeling completely petite and feminine, he stood looking down at me; intently; scrutinizing. Then THAT grin slowly spread across his face, lighting up his sea water blue eyes.

"I'm gonna call you Susie. It fits you better."

My knees crumpled and once again he caught me around the waist, saving me from my destiny with the floor.

The only other person who has ever called me that was my Father.

14

He saw Leila Mae Babineaux make her entrance from across the entry hall landing. He was as stunned as the other onlookers, but for a much different reason. Once he saw the woman wearing that necklace, he had to have it. He couldn't believe it. That necklace and earrings was the very subject of a conference he just returned from in Rome; the priceless jewels of Siena d'Arbia. They were thought to have been lost centuries ago. Having been around Estate jewelry as long as he had, he could spot a fake a mile away. And those jewels around the Babineaux woman's neck were no fakes, no matter how much she protested that she saw a photo in a magazine and had a copy made in Atlanta. He overheard her telling several people who asked her about it as she made her way down the landing stairs, with a dismissive wave of her hands as she breezed by them to avoid further conversation. Now he had to have it. He wondered why she was not wearing the earrings that were part of the collection. He thought he had seen one of the earrings in a dish in the foyer of BonHaven when he was there to value a set of radio lamps, but dismissed the idea as not possible. The earrings alone would keep me for a lifetime on a private island. This was the big one I had been waiting for he thought.

Now he just needed to figure out how to get them. As he stood and stared at Leila Mae, a plan formed. With a lecherous grin, he looked away and pulled out his cell phone to make a call to his assistant.

From across the room he spotted Marianne Babineaux and made a beeline in the opposite direction. He needed to make sure not to accidently bump into her too soon to make his plan work. But he did need to be seen schmoozing with the other guests so he made his way to the buffet table to mingle.

After filling his plate, he made his way to an unoccupied table to eat while he clarified the details of his plan. It was bold, but this was his big chance to finally put this sedate life of his to rest. He had pictured himself to leading a much more flamboyant lifestyle by now on a tropical island somewhere. His bow tie wearing days were almost at an end. He dressed the part, carried a meek demeanor and spoke with the prissy haughtiness of academia. He had to admit, this persona he created has been very lucrative.

His Suisse bank account had steadily been growing over the last several years due to his illicit activities of swindling people all over the world through various schemes, most involving antiquities and fakes; the old bait and switch technique, as old as the bartering system itself. Most people had no idea what an authentic masterpiece was, much less a great reproduction. Once a client had purchased an item and he verified its authenticity as a respected authority on antiquities, no one questioned it value. Of course he had the originals and sold them on the black market for a hefty profit when the timing was right.

But now, this could be the "Big One", the one that finally puts him over the top. He knows the risk, but as he formulates his plan details, thinks he can cover the spread.

He finished eating and mingled a bit more; biding his time for when he could make an exit at the appropriate time. He waited for the auction to begin, then made a few quiet goodbyes and slipped out while everyone's attention was center stage.

On the drive home, he tried to concentrate on the road, but his mind kept coming back to those jewels. "My God" he said aloud. "I cannot believe my luck!" He smiled an evil smile in the darkness of the car as his plan solidified.

Walking through the iron gate that led to the entrance to his townhouse, he pulled out his cell phone and placed a call to his assistant and arranged a meeting for tomorrow morning. After he gave his instructions, he opened the door and hurriedly sat at his antique desk and rolled up the top to reach his stationary. He quickly wrote down his instructions before he forgot anything. It wouldn't do to leave out any details and put his plan at risk. By tomorrow afternoon, it would be done. By next week, he would be gone.

15

A few of Lyci's friends were stopping by for lunch and a quick swim/tanning session before they went shopping for more prom paraphernalia so I invited Sugar over to keep me from killing the teenagers. It was pretty noisy last night as Wallace & Thurman were up to something all night and were pretty loud about it. I heard John yell at them and it seemed to quiet down. Anyway, I over slept and was just rolling out of bed when I heard cars pulling up the drive. That's the plus side to having a crushed shell driveway. You can hear everything. You can't even walk quietly. Every footstep sounds like a canon shot. The bad side is you can't sneak out as my siblings and I found out the hard way. It also takes away the ability to peel out if you're mad 'cause it will wreck your paint job by kicking the shells up!

So I threw on some shorts and a tank and had just walked into the foyer when I heard Lyci's friends asking Lyci when we got the new statues in the front. Sugar had just pulled up as well and was right behind the group of teens. Lyci was herding her friends in as quickly as she could.

"Lyc – where did your Mom get that? It's really cool! I've never seen anything like it!" "It wasn't here yesterday" I heard Ashleigh say. "Like, when was it delivered? Last Night? Who delivers at night?"

"I bet you had to pay extra for that" said Jackson, Lyci's date for the Prom, who also desperately wanted to be her boyfriend.

As Lyci herded everyone towards the French doors leading to the pool, I heard her say "You all know Momma, always changing everything!" as she gave me that secret look of "HELP"

Then the give away from Ashleigh "Lyci, isn't that statue wearing your prom dress? And your shoes?"

Great! Now I knew what all the commotion was about last night.

Thurman.

As I stepped onto the front porch, Sugar had just stepped out of his car and was staring at the "statue". There was indeed a new statue. Of course it was Thurman. His pose was obvious. Thurman was in full out running mode; obviously trying to avoid capture. Looking back towards probably Wallace or John, who were most likely trying to grab him, with a look of evil glee on his contorted face.

Sugar was staring, trying to not laugh.

Thurman was wearing Lyci's prom dress and carrying her shoes. Did I mention yet about Thurman's penchant for wearing our clothes? He seems to particularly like flashy and flowy. He hasn't quite yet mastered the color matching thing; or maybe that's the point. The more it clashed the better. I don't know, and I don't really care. At least the noise last night was explained. It could have been something much worse.

The entire racket last night was Wallace trying to catch Thurman. They were obviously so caught up in the chase that they lost track of time and were outside when dawn broke. Hence his statue form. And that is how Thurman would spend the day until the sun went down. As I went over to the statue, Sugar followed. Together we were able to get Lyci's dress off Thurman. Sugar had a look of deep thought as he struggled to maneuver the shoes from Thurman's stone hands. Sugar had a frown on his face and a look I couldn't decipher.

"What?" I asked him. Sugar just raised his free hand to make a shooing motion. Fine. I'll wait. This should be good. He lifted his sunglasses and stared hard at the shoes in his hand, then dropped the glasses back down on his nose. But he didn't say a word.

As we walked together back into the house, he still was quiet. That's Ok. I could be patient. Kind of.

As he handed me the shoes, he put his sunglasses on top of his head and said "I think we need to rethink those shoes. The color is to matchy-matchy." With that settled, he walked straight to the French doors with a purpose; most likely to find Momma to discuss the shoe crisis.

That's my Sugar.

16

Thinking of "My Sugar" and watching him stride through the French doors to the veranda looking for Momma triggered a memory of Sugar in fifth grade. Once, when we went on a field trip to the Limestone Caverns, we were on the part of the tour where the guides want to convey what the early Indians dealt with on a daily basis by turning off all the lights including flashlights. Back then, no one was that worried with the safety of the students. They were more interested in teaching in their own way. The Cavern was immediately plunged into pitch black darkness, the kind of darkness that you can feel; your ears feel like they are stuffed with cotton; the kind where you can't even see your hand when you hold it up inches from your face. You kind of panic when you can't see your hand, then you think you are deaf because your senses start playing tricks on you all because you can't see all of sudden. Then your brain totally panics, which of course mine promptly, did, causing my equilibrium to go whacko. I thought I was falling, which I actually did! By the time the guides turned the lights back on, I had stood up and was doing a body check, inventorying for anything broken, and came up with blood all over my hands from the sharp pieces of limestone littering the cavern floor.

Sugar was behind me in our group, saw what was happening, and promptly turned ghostly white from lack of blood flow, and fainted at the sight of the all the blood. By the time he had come to, Mr. Jurough, our science teacher, had already passed out band-aides and Bactine to me and was breaking an ammonia capsule under Sugar's nose. The other kids were laughing and ribbing him for being such a wuss at the sight of the blood from my scrapped hands and knees. I still believe they were more relieved that it was Sugar that fainted first before they did. His fainting and the ensuing chaos proved enough of a distraction from the mess dripping down my arms that the other kids forgot about all the blood. That was the beginning of his reputation for being soft, a reputation, which only grew from there. But these kids were dead wrong about him being soft. He has a band of steel inside him. He may be more feminine than most females, but he is one tough MF! He has to be to handle me and my life, bless his little heart!

I also have to say while my life and family may be crazy in a more than the Southern mantra of "if you have crazy in your family, don't bother to hide it but put a cocktail in their hand and parade them on the front porch" kind of way; Sugar's life is extremely entertaining. Take his latest dating escapade with his current "Bear Daddy". His name is Carl, but Sugar always calls him "Bear". He definitely fits the nickname; the man makes Paul Bunyan look delicate. But his profession doesn't represent his appearance at all. A construction worker, Fireman, even a fitness instructor would be plausible, but no, Carl is a florist. That's how he and Sugar hooked up. Sugar was looking for a specific flower for a client he had just signed to a huge landscaping contract and the client wanted a specific flower in the flowering beds. Sugar had never heard of it, which is extremely unusual in itself, Sugar has an encyclopedic knowledge of everything that grows. So when the client couldn't find a photo of said flower, but instead gave him a drawing that looked suspiciously like a hybrid geranium, Sugar promised his client that he would stop by the florist in Mobile to research the drawing. So that's how that meet cute went down.

Leila Mae stopped by later that afternoon to drop off the "borrowed" jewelry. This gave me some relief to know they were off the market-so to speak. Now I still had to figure out what to do with the jewels until I could get them back to where they belonged.

"Love what you've done with Thurman." she drawled as she breezed in the foyer nodding towards the front of the house and stopping in the hall to place the necklace in the dish on the sideboard.

"I know. Too bad he won't stay that way. At least he's out of trouble temporarily." I laughed. Aunt Mae knew how much I disliked Thurman. It certainly seemed like Thurman was a much bigger hit as a statue.

As she turned to walk away, she looked back at the dish. "There are two earrings here. I thought one was missing?"

"Oh, it was. Evidently Thurman slipped it out of Merle's ear the night she brought it back. John saw him wearing it and told Wallace, who chased him down to get it away from him. I heard all the racket the night it happened, but forgot about it by the next morning. Wallace said he put it there."

"Too bad it didn't happen sooner. I would have loved to have had the set for the Gala."

She said with a shrug and gestured toward the doors. "Why don't we go talk out on the veranda?" Mae motioned to the backdoors. "I need to talk with you for a little bit."

Uh oh, this could be bad.

17

By the time we sat down, Sadie appeared with two glasses of sweet tea and some lemon cookies. How she did that, knowing when we wanted something, was amazing. Again, I have learned not to question these types of things too much when I'm not on the clock.

My spidey senses were starting to tingle a little.

"So, I know things have been a little crazy lately" Aunt Mae started. "And I'm sure it's mostly due to Mercury being in retrograde and will last for another two weeks, but I am pretty sure we are in for some nasty goings-on."

I slowly turned my head and stared at her. She was calmly staring out at the water. So I believed her. When Aunt Mae made her predictions in a calm manner, we all stopped and listened.

"Over in St. Elmo's, we've had some interesting things happen." Mae said while still looking straight ahead. "Nothing really out of order, yet, just lots of missing cats, and one missing young boy; but I think he will show up on his own. But there are other…things"

I must have been giving her my skeptical look, because when she looked over at me she said "I'm just giving you fair warning. Something WILL happen around here in the next few weeks."

"Okaaaay. Thanks for the heads up I guess? What exactly am I looking for?" I asked seriously.

"I don't know exactly, but I felt this most strongly when I was wearing Merle's necklace."

"It's not Merle's necklace" I said through ground teeth.

"You know what I mean darlin'." She smiled and reached over to touch my face, rising to leave as she did. "I just want you to be extra careful, O.K.?"

"I know, Aunt Mae, and I do appreciate the warning, truly." I smiled back.

Ever since our special visitor a few weeks ago, I had been carrying around some pretty big existential questions. None of the answers I could come up with satisfactorily solved the problems in my head. A new idea crossed my mind at that very moment and I realized I might be in the presence of someone who could help me solve the problem.

"Mae, do you believe in time travel is possible?"

"Of course darlin'. Time is not linear. Past, present and future all exist at once. You just have to learn how to bend space and time to your benefit. It takes awhile."

I was so blown away by her casual attitude of something most scientists and scholars studied a lifetime just to realize they don't have a clue be dismissed by a wave of her perfectly manicured fingers, I just stared at her. The only response I could manage was to ask her if she wanted to stay for dinner.

"Do you want to stay for dinner? I think Sadie was serving early today."

"No Thank You." She said as she stood up. "I have dinner plans in St. Elmos and friends are waiting. But I'll be away for awhile again, so give everyone my love." She said as she kissed my cheek. Then she walked out down the steps of the veranda and around to the front drive and was gone. As I got up shaking my head, I had to wonder whether everyone was smarter than I was or just crazier? I opened the screen door from the screened in porch when Wallace pops in front of me and follows me into the hall badgering me.

"You know, Leila Mae is correct in her thought process. How do you think we move around? With the death of your humanity comes knowledge. Knowledge that everyone carries locked away within themselves and is given the key to open after each life is completed. Some figure out how to pick their internal locks while they are still living in this world, but few are able to use the knowledge they discover."

With his soliloquy completed, he promptly turns his head towards me, sticks out his tongue, wiggles his eyebrows and passes through the wall beside him.

Figures. That pompous ass.

Just as I closed the door behind me, Uncle Howard walked through the foyer heading for the dining room. "Did you just call me a pompous ass?"

"No Uncle Howard, I was speaking to Wallace." And I didn't realize I said it out loud.

"Well then, that's makes perfect sense. Was that Mae I heard outside? Will she be staying for dinner?"

"No, she just stopped by to warn me of an oncoming storm." I said with a laugh.

"Oh boy." Uncle Howard said with a straight face, perfectly serious. "Better batten down the hatches!"

Later that night, Al is rudely awakened. Then again what other way is there to be awakened when you find your face hitting the ceiling? As she had an early shift tomorrow, she tried to go to bed fairly early and had just drifted off to sleep, when she slowly came out of her light sleep to feel her bed being shaken roughly and heard the tell-tale giggle. But when she looked over the edge of the bed expecting to see Thurman, the bed was four feet off the floor. By the time she crawled to the edge to look over and see that it was Wallace levitating the bed, her face was already to the ceiling.

"God damn it Wallace!"

At that exact moment, Lyci was passing her door. She did a double take then came back to stick her head in the door frame. "Good Lord Wallace. Put her down this minute!" Lyci started to walk past the door, but stopped and narrowed her eyes at Thurman who was gripping the edge of the bed and swinging his feet with glee. "Thurman, the buttons go on the front. However did you manage that?" She said while shaking her head and grinning, referring to Thurman's outfit of choice for the night – consisting of a sparkly sequined blouse; most likely pilfered from Mae's room and a disco beret from who knows where.

Thurman let go and dropped to the ground, rolled and took off running while Wallace looking embarrassed, gently lowered the bed to the ground. Lyci stood in the doorway with her arms crossed while she waited for Wallace to leave. He did so with a nod to Al and a bow to Lyci.

"My apologies ladies." And promptly disappeared into thin air.

Sadie had just brought in two glasses of iced tea and some small cakes to the parlor for Miss Marianne and their neighbor, Miss Betty from across the way when she decided she wanted to steam some shellfish for dinner. She narrowed her decision between a Jambalaya or just steamed and served over rice with maybe some lemon and butter when she realized she needed another large pot. She had a huge pot reserved for the crawfish, but she still needed something else for the clams and mussels; and she would need something for the pinto beans to soak in too. Miss Marianne liked to order from the internet and always made sure the kitchen was well stocked with the latest gadgets and gizmos, but Sadie swore that most of them were about as handy as a back pocket on a shirt. She was pretty sure she had put the extra pots up in the attic last winter in an effort to neaten the cabinets in the butler's pantry when she was bored. Although the cabinets were now neat as a pin, she avoided the butler's pantry most days as it had been taken over by an unwanted resident. Some type of beastie or maybe just a really cranky ghost. Either way she just didn't feel like dealing with him most days. Uncle Howard was usually on his own to go in and get a can of potted meat for his favorite sandwich; at least until someone did something about the crank pot that invaded her space. She had been meaning to speak with Wallace about intervening, but every time she ran into him and started to tell him to do something about the situation, he seemed to know what she wanted and disappeared.

Literally.

"Well, I'll swan" she said out loud. "I guess I'll just have to climb up to the attic and go a hunting".

Once in the attic, she made a beeline straight for where the pot was; exactly where she left it.

But something that wasn't there before caught her eye. Three small boxes were neatly stacked in front of the old chifforobe the pot had been placed on. She had to move the boxes to get to the pot. After she had placed the last box on top of the other two she had moved, the lid dropped to the floor. As she was placing it back on the box she noticed two pieces of jewelry on top of hand written papers. She looked more closely and saw Alma Sue's name on the top of the papers. They looked very old and had the feel of something important. She had a strong feeling Al would want to see these. She put the pot on top of the boxes and brought them all downstairs. Once back in the kitchen, she left the boxes stacked by the kitchen door leading to the screened porch. She would have to remind herself to tell Al about them when she got home later.

At that exact moment, the door to the pantry slammed open and a can of potted meat came flying out of the panty.

Sadie casually ducked, then went over picked up the can and held it up in the air yelling "This is MY kitchen and if you want to stay, throwing something at me is not the smartest thing to do. This just proves what I knew all along. There are tree stumps in the Louisiana swamps that have higher IQ's than you!" then threw the can as hard as she could back into the pantry and slammed the door.

18

As I arrived back home from my shift, all I could think about was my waiting bed; all fluffy with crisp linen sheets. The house was dark, with everyone still asleep. I came in the side door into the mudroom on the back side of the screened in porch. I promptly tripped and ended up ass over tea kettle. I was exhausted from the adrenaline of a last minute car chase of a robbery at the local wash and dry. We caught the guy red-handed with two bags of quarters and four boxes of laundry mat detergent; another genius thief. The marble floor was so cool and soothing; I considered staying put on the floor for a quick snooze. A nice little siesta would be great!

Just as I was actually dozing off, I heard the giggle. Great! Thurman's around. Of course he is, where else would the little brat be? My guess is that the boxes I just tripped over were moved in front of the door just for me, for Thurman's amusement. Wait, there's a sticky note stuck to my pants. I got up and acted like I was smoothing the crease on my jeans and pocketed the sticky note, which I saw had my name on it and casually moved the boxes to the side of the doorway, and walked off. No way was I gonna give the little guy any satisfaction to see me angry. On my way to the staircase, I saw a blur run by the dining room with his tongue sticking out at me. Then I heard a thud and a muffled blue streak of cursing. Best guess is Thurman ran into the wall on the other side of the dining room as he was too busy looking back at me with the whole sticking out his tongue show. I did a fist pump of victory and ran up the stairs. Yay me! I actually won a round. Uh oh, this will mean payback. Whatever, it was worth the win. They are few and far in between for me around here.

It didn't occur to me until I was laying on top of the covers with the overhead fan turning lazily, its humming lulling me to sleep, to wonder what the boxes I tripped over were and why the sticky note had my name on it.

When I woke up the next morning, the sticky note with my name was the first thing I saw as it evidently stuck to my T-shirt as I slid into bed. During the night it had migrated to the collar of the shirt. So, it was literally the first thing I saw when I opened my eyes! Instantly my curiosity was stoked. I bounded out of bed and pulled on some yoga pants and a zip up and headed downstairs. Everyone seemed to be gone or at least somewhere else in the house, the kitchen was empty. Sadie had left some cinnamon rolls on a plate for me! Yaaa! Sadie's rolls have actually won awards. After I found my favorite mug and poured my coffee, I took the plate of rolls to the dining room to devour. As the rolls were up to Sadie's usual par, the eating went pretty quickly. I decided this was a great time to look through those mystery boxes that make a better storage container than a door mat as evidenced by my graceful entry last night, and headed to the screened porch. I bent down to lift the two boxes by the door to bring them into the library. As I was squatting down to pick them up, I heard angry buzzing. And yes, there is a difference in buzzing sounds – thank you very much. There's the buzz of an appliance or florescent lighting in a quiet room and then there is the distinct sound of insect buzzing. There is the tranquil buzz of a bee or fly lazily inspecting the spring flowers or summer air and then there is the sound of that same bee or fly being pestered or denied that very same act. I looked up and out the screen door. Sitting on the last step from the porch to the rear garden was a child sized statue. Interesting…..I opened the door and stepped out onto the first step. By the next step I figured out where the buzzing was coming from. A large June bug was flying in circles around the statue. Not because it wanted to or was curious about the statue, or even because it was checking out the wonderfully fragrant honeysuckle vine that wound its way up the brick wall on the back of the house. No, it was flying in a circle because it's rear leg was tied with kite string and attached to the now stone finger of the statue also known as Thurman. Obviously Thurman heard momma and Aunt Merle talking about their childhood antics the other night when we were watching the storm roll in from the Gulf in the screened Patio. He must have been having so much fun with his new pet that he lost track of time as usual, hence the stone child statue. I reached to pull the string in so I could untie the poor June bug, but stopped. I know it's wrong and all sorts of bad on sooo many different levels, but I just couldn't stop myself from reaching in my pocket for my phone. Just one quick pic. And maybe a video. Maybe I'll even let Thurman watch it later.

After I set the June bug free, I went back inside, picked up the boxes and carried them into the library. I put the first box on the table and started sorting through it. The first box had mostly what looked like ledgers or journals. I sat those aside and opened the second box. The box has several journals also, but appeared to be newer. There was also a small jewelry box, handmade of Rosewood with inlaid mother of pearl panels. It was beautiful workmanship. I carefully opened the lid to find a small ring and a brooch. The ring was very delicate. It was made of yellow gold with small panels of white gold with a very tiny ruby in the center. Again, the craftsmanship was amazing. The details were so fine and obviously worked by hand. The brooch was a similar design, but had a large Ruby with several smaller diamonds surrounding the center stone. Hmmm. A mystery. Why would the jewelry be in these boxes?

I opened the journal that was with the jewelry. Holy Cow! It's dated 1814. The first line is:

NO WAY!

The first line: "I cannot believe I have actually been driven to speaking out loud as I dip my pen into the ink to place my thoughts onto this paper! Due to the nature of the things that are occurring in my physical surroundings, I believe it would be prudent to begin keeping an accurate record of such things in the instance it shall be necessary for the future."

Signed,

Alma Sue Babaneux

Good lord! This is written by my namesake, my great –great- aunt.

I pick up the ring and place it on my ring finger of my left hand. It's a perfect fit.

I pack up the other journals in the box to read later, but keep out Alma's diary and the brooch. After I finish my coffee and put away my dirty plate, I tuck the box under my arm to bring upstairs to read later.

As I pass through the entryway heading to the staircase, I decided to put the brooch on the side board to ask Momma about later. As I placed it in the dish I saw the necklace Mae had borrowed, I remembered she had returned it. That's good, now we can figure out what to do with it!

19

When Jimmy-Don was done editing his film, he thought he had the perfect submission for Ghost Hunters. With this "evidence" it was guaranteed that he would be invited to come join their crew. He was sure of it! This was definitely his ticket to the big time. He felt it was important to keep the film under wraps until he was ready make a big public showing. He couldn't believe his luck in capturing those fourteen seconds on film. He knew there was something hinky about that big ole tree. And the funny thing about it is it was a total accident. That new guy, Vic Torres, was pointing the camera in the wrong direction when they were rolling.

He was supposed to be shooting towards the tree, but for some reason that idiot was shooting in the direction of BonHaven. Everyone is fascinated with that place. "Shoot" Jimmy-Don said out loud to himself. My place is just as nice. Oh well, he thought to himself, it worked out pretty well for me! Jimmy-Don may have flunked out of every program he was in at school, but he wasn't a complete fool.

What Jimmy-Don didn't know is that Vic was filming in the wrong direction on purpose. The only reason he was working with Chaser's was to get close to BonHaven. His real boss was paying him good money to get into BonHaven and this job was the perfect cover.

Vic Torres could care less what Jimmy-Don thought he caught on film. He did not believe in ghosts or the paranormal. He lied his way through his Chaser's interview with ease. It was actually fun coming up with stories and reasons why he wanted to be a part of Chaser's crew. Jimmy-Don and his buddies bought every word!

As it was, Vic couldn't believe his luck in getting on with the Chaser's crew so fast. It was only three days ago that his boss called him and told him what he wanted of him this time. Vic had been doing small jobs for his boss, known only as Mr. D for two years now. Usually it was just small time petty theft. Sometimes he got to be a goon and work some-one over. It was these jobs Vic preferred the most. But this latest job for Mr. D was a big one. He had to get into BonHaven. He had not yet been told why, but Mr. D promised to let him know tomorrow. He said he was waiting for confirmation first. He wouldn't tell me confirmation of what. Whatever – It paid well.

Vic pulled into the entrance of the Randy Road Recreation Park and drove through the large iron gates in the shape of twin pink flamingos on each side. The pink painted on the gates had long since faded in the relentless southern sun and humidity, but you could still make out the shape of the birds. Why someone would bother to put so much detail into a trailer park entrance was beyond him. It seems highly unlikely that someone would grow up with visions of building the greatest trailer park ever made, but hey, most people don't grow up wanting to be the best criminal they can be either, yet here I am he thought. Yeah, here I am he chuckled to himself as he pulled under the carport of space #55. He turned off the ignition and stared up at the mobile home in front of him. It once was a happy shade of mint green with bright white trim, probably in the 1970's, but the relentless southern sun had baked it to a baby puke green. The once crisp white trim was now rust-colored beige thanks to the humidity. Another ten years and it will be a perfect addition for the scrap metal heap at the county recycling plant; but for now its home. He walked up the six steps to the front door trying to balance his small bag of groceries and grab his keys from his front pocket at the same time. Not being as agile as he thought he was, the Piggly Wiggly bag tipped over and apples spilled from the top rolling everywhere. One fell onto the platform and rolled off and under the steps to rest somewhere under the trailer. He finally got the lock undone and pushed open the front door. It constantly stuck as it was perpetually swollen from the humidity, but he had the trick to open it down pat now. He had been living here almost two years, always paid his rent on time and was quiet. He was very aware of remaining under the radar. In his line of work, standing out in someone's memory was not a good thing.

Putting the grocery bag down on the kitchen counter, he reached for the TV remote and turned on the set. He wanted to catch the weather report for the week. He was very through on his work and wanted to be ready for any situation for the whole week. As he still wasn't sure what the job Mr. D wanted him for, he had to be prepared for anything and knowing whether he would be in the pouring rain or heat could make a difference between doing a good job or ending up in county lock up. Been there, done that; he was not a brilliant man, but he did learn from his mistakes. After putting away his meager grocery purchase, he wiped down the small kitchen counter. Even though it was already spotless, he couldn't help himself from doing it. He was a little OCD about being clean; most likely from habitually wiping away his fingerprints.

He just caught the tail end of the weather report and made a mental note to himself. Rain was only expected for Wednesday night, and that was just a small shower, so he should be fine no matter what the job was. No extra precautions had to be taken. As he sat in the worn recliner, he looked around the small living room. The mobile home had come furnished, so nothing was to his taste. Actually he didn't really know what his taste was if he was truthful with himself. He had never stayed in one place long enough to buy anything of his own. The furniture looked to have been bought when the trailer was new, again, probably 1977 or '78. The only personal item in the place was a photo of his younger sister who was kidnapped when she was eight years old and never found. He was seventeen at the time and was devastated. He was very close to her and treated her like a princess as did his parents. The incident tore apart his family and scattered his father to the wind and sent his mother into a depression she has never recovered from. He liked to blame that part of his life for sending him down this path he was now living. Well, if you could call this living. Maybe he would take this payday from Mr. D and take off. Move to somewhere tropical. Try to get a real job. He was good at fixing things. Maybe get a job as a handyman.

Just as he was thinking of how he would spend his pay on something constructive this time, his cell phone rang.

"Vic" he grunted into the phone "Oh, hiya Mr. D. I was just thinkin about the job."

As he listened, his face scrunched up as he tried to process whatever he heard on the line. "Yeah, OK. I'll pick it up tomorrow. I know. I know. Tomorrow- ten o'clock- Library on Main street." He hung up the phone looking satisfied. Soon he would know what his target was.

20

Torres was sitting on a bench in front of the library precisely at ten o'clock as requested. Vic was prompt as usual. That was one of the reasons Mr. D kept him on. In Mr. D's mind, being prompt for appointments was equated with doing a good job. Considering what Mr. D usually asked of Vic, it was pretty ironic. Vic was a thug. Plain and simple. Maybe even more than a thug if the job called for it. Mr. D was pretty sure 'ole Vic could handle a shovel in the dark. Every now and then, Mr. D's thoughts drifted to his dark "what if?" space in his off kilter mind and he wondered if on some dark, sultry night, he might find himself on the wrong end of that shovel.

Regardless, he always got the job done.

He was still sitting there twenty minutes later wondering where in the hell Mr. D was. He suddenly felt the hair stand up on the back of his neck and had the feeling he was being watched. He was sweating lightly in the sun with no breeze to cool him off. He looked around and saw Mr. D across the street across at the opening to an alleyway between two storefronts. He was holding up an envelope making a production of exaggeratingly placing the envelope in a crack in the bricks in the alleyway wall. Vic gave him thumbs up to show he got it.

Jimmy Dons' idiot friend Buster happened to be in the library where Vic was sitting waiting in the heat on a bench outside. Buster had been sent on the wild goose chase of finding a book for Jimmy Don's "research" on a case. The idea of Buster in a library was in and of itself a wild goose chase. No one thought he could even read; much less locate a book with the walls of a library.

Buster had been looking for the book for over fifteen minutes and was extremely bored. Finding the book at this point was not going to happen. He happened to look up and out of the large picture window overlooking the front lawn of the library just as Vic was giving the thumbs up to Mr. D. Buster did not recognize who the old dude dressed in the prissy clothes was, and almost gave himself a stroke wondering why he was making fun of the old guy because that was just mean, M-E-A-N. Buster may be stupid, but he didn't go for mean, especially to old people. He prided himself on that principle. But he did not like Vic, not one little bit. He didn't seem like a true good 'ole boy and he certainly didn't seem like a real ghost hunter.

"I need to remember to talk to J.D." he whispered to himself remembering he was in a library. He then went back to hunting after the book "Alabama Ghosts and their favorite haunts" with a renewed fervor.

Vic opened the envelope to find a handwritten note of instructions on Mr. D's personalized stationary; the old fashioned kind. Thick creamy paper written on by a quill type pen with an ink cartridge substituted for a dipped ink pen. It gave the letter an old fashioned quality that lent substance to the words. Mr. D and his details.

The instructions were simple. Meet at Mr. D's office building at noon today. Two hours. Not much notice. What he didn't know is by giving such short notice; Vic also wouldn't have the opportunity to blab to anyone. The short notice was not an over site by Mr. D, far from it. Vic walked down the block to grab lunch at Maude's Café. As he walked in the door, bells jangling brashly, he was in deep thought as to what he should order. Should he eat light in case whatever he was going to be doing for Mr. D was some kind of strenuous exertion? Or should he go big in case it took all day and he would be late for dinner? As he slid into an empty booth, he decided to err on the side of a late dinner. He had a blood sugar issue and didn't want to have a problem with being hungry.

As the waitress walked over, order pad in hand, he waved away the menu and ordered "I'll have the chicken fried steak with gravy, biscuits and a side of okra."

The waitress, Jamie according to her name tag, popped her gum and put the menu back under her arm. "Sweet tea?"

"Yeah. Large." Vic said as he stared at her. She was cute. Young, but cute. "Thanks."

"No problem." Jamie said backing away. This guy looked mean, and she had had enough of mean. "I'll be right back with your tea." She had no intention of bringing back his drink; or anything else. As she turned in his order, she told the other waitress she was taking her break. Hopefully his food would be up and delivered by the time she got back.

Vic didn't even notice who brought his food. He was too busy spending his future paycheck for the job today. Now he could walk away from this town, and it couldn't be soon enough! It was spooky. He always had the feeling of being watched. He had never been one to be afraid of the dark, but he'd had the heeby jeebies ever since he joined up with Jimmy-Don and his crew. Maybe it was all the effort in trying to produce a ghosty. He really couldn't wait to tell Jimmy-Don he was quitting. He didn't know if he could keep a straight face as he told him ghost hunting just wasn't for him. But he needed to keep up appearances and not stand out. It wouldn't do to leave a trail. Mr. D. wouldn't like that. And he wanted to keep Mr. D happy, at least long enough to collect his pay.

What Vic didn't know is that he WAS being watched. Ever since that day he filmed BonHaven and Bastian, John had seen him and periodically followed him around. John knew he was up to no good and decided to check up on him from time to time. John hated leaving BonHaven at all anymore, so the fact he was following someone around in town was significant. John didn't want to discuss his apprehension with Wallace or Al for that matter until he had something concrete to bring to their attention. In the mean time John just vowed to follow this man around. He decided it couldn't hurt. Besides, John thought, it was kind of exciting, like he was a spy in some movie. Except he was a ghost. And ghosts can't exactly make a big splashy chase down and crash cars in a big finale. What was he going to do if he caught the man in the act of something heinous? Say BOO? Hopefully it would not come to that John thought to himself and starting wringing his hands together nervously. He was just about to talk himself into leaving when the man got up to leave.

Vic finished eating and glanced at his phone. He had better get going to make it downtown in time.

21

Thursday nights were my favorite night of the week. It was my last day on shift for the week, at least during this schedule rotation. It was a quiet night at the station and I was done at midnight, and I usually worked seven to seven, so I felt it was the middle of my day so to speak. Needless to say, I needed something to do, but the rest of the house would be in bed, so I really didn't want to head home yet and have to tiptoe around. I finished up my report on the third DWI of the night for a Mr. Bradley Mahoney; three DWI's on a Thursday night, go figure. I guess I wasn't the only one whose favorite night of the week was Thursday; or maybe it was their least favorite night, hence the DWI's. As I robotically filled in the reports, I found myself thinking about Officer Baveras. After we met at the Huntington Gala, I had only worked one shift with him, so I didn't really get to know him yet. The strange thing was no one seemed to know anything about his background, not that I asked around... much. Hmmm, maybe I need to run a background check on him myself. Wow, that's a little stalkerish I thought and shook my head a little. But I have found my thoughts sneakily wandering to him since last week. There is no denying he's hot, that's not up for debate. What is up for debate is the fact that I haven't found anyone even remotely attractive in a while. After I spent eighteen months, eighteen wasted months of my life that I will never get back, with David, I have been reluctant to even think that way about a man. Any man.

Of course Momma was already planning a wedding after my third date with David. Maybe that's what doomed the relationship. No, that's not fair to Momma; David is what doomed our relationship. Our sex life was great; adventurous but within bounds, my handcuffs never found their way into the bedroom. The problem was evidently other women had the same sex life with David. At the same time I did, hence the problem. You would think the fact that I carry a gun would deter him from cheating, but obviously not. He knows I love my job too much to throw it away by cutting off his balls and putting them in a coke bottle, as much as that would give me some measure of satisfaction. The truth is even more simplistic than his cheating. A few months into our relationship, David and I were painting his new townhouse. The paint had just dried and I was helping put the electrical plate covers back on over the outlets. The flat blade screwdriver I was using slipped and went into the electrical outlet. In short, I was electrocuted. Not deadly obviously, but electrocuted never the less! The impact actually lifted me and threw me three feet across the room where I landed none too daintily on my backside. Rather than run over to check on me as I sat dazed and confused, and possibly smoking a little, David burst out laughing. Tears streaming down his face, full guffaw laughing! I never really forgave him or trusted him after that. The cheating was just a tangible excuse.

But back to the subject at hand, Carlyle Baveras. I know it's all kinds of wrong to be attracted to a fellow officer, especially being a female. We are under a microscope all of the time. The old guard doesn't want female officers on the force at all. They think we are too soft; our God given feminine feelings will not allow us to be as hard as we need to be, blah, blah, blah. I faced the same discrimination in high school and even college on a smaller level while I was involved in wrestling; until you proved yourself to be capable at least. Maybe everyone faces that feeling of discrimination and just attributes it to their sex. Sometimes it makes a girl just want to pull out her Glock and boom. Oh wait, was that a God given feminine thought? Makes you think, doesn't it?

But Carlyle, there is definitely something different about him. He says he was born and raised around here, but his accent doesn't fit this area at all. Actually, I can't peg his accent from anywhere. It's almost as if he learned to speak English as a second language. His diction is perfect and his words end with a lilt; like he is caressing the words and almost making a question of every sentence. It's very fluid. Almost like words spoken under water, but without the reverberation. Very unusual; I would say strange, but as we all know, strange is very relative around here. I know he's hiding something. It's more a feeling than any actions. He hides it well. He seems so open yet secretive at the same time. Most people probably wouldn't pick up the vibe, most regular people: which means my family would feel it immediately. They would ask him right off the bat after talking with him for two minutes. Maybe ten seconds with Lyci.

I understand secrets. There are secrets and then there are SECRETS. The regular secrets most people feel compelled to keep under wraps usually always come out; like the truth. The truth will always present itself at every opportunity it gets. This is part of Nature. Most good cops know this, but usually attribute it to good detective work, but it's actually just Mother Nature asserting herself. Everyone has a life path and when someone veers too far off of that preordained path, Momma Nature usually steps in and corrects it in some way; some good, some bad. But even good and bad is relative depending on perspective. But SECRETS, now that's a whole different animal. SECRETS are usually best kept that way. Even Nature agrees. Maybe that is why I'm drawn to Lyle. He gets it. Then again, maybe he's a serial killer. Now there's a cheery thought. Good Lord! What's wrong with me? Nothing that a Moon Pie wouldn't fix.

But being the hour it was, there's really nothing to do but go home, but I WAS hungry and really didn't want to wake anyone at home by banging around in the kitchen. Too bad Lum's wasn't open as a Moon Pie and a RC would really hit the spot now that the thought popped in my head and wouldn't go away, but Lum's opened and closed with the Sun. They never had posted hours, but everyone knew. I could go by a Krystal off the interstate, but that wasn't what sounded good at the moment. Oh Well, maybe Sadie had left something in the fridge. At this point even a bologna sandwich would do. I vowed to try and be quiet.

I pulled up the drive and parked on the side of the house under the Porte cochere. When I walked into the mud room and onto the screened in porch, I saw Lyci sleeping in one of the two oversized swings that were hung from the wooden slat ceiling. The porch was originally designed to be a sleeping porch after all; used as a respite from the Southern heat and humidity that frequently hung around all night making the upper sleeping floors unbearable during the summer. It wasn't that warm tonight, but we all loved being on the porch and frequently fell asleep in the swing from the gentle rocking motion. It was easy to imagine previous generations of our family sneaking out of their beds at night in mid-summer to try and catch any breeze that might come up off the water. As I crept across the porch as quietly as I could so I wouldn't wake Lyci (which is a feat in itself as my leather service belt creaks with every move), and continued on to the entry hall, I heard whimpering coming from the dining room.

I froze in my "let's be qwiet, very, very, qwiet", comical cartoon exaggerated high stepping tip toe move I was doing and quickly went into cop mode.

I poke my head through the open double entry doors, but I don't see anything. As I was turning to leave, I heard the whimpering again and pinpointed the sound to be coming from under the dining table, but it was too dark to actually see anything. I pulled my flashlight from my belt and instantly spotted what was causing the sound.

Cooper, Momma's beloved dog, was tied up to several chair legs and had a red bandana through his mouth so he couldn't bark.

"Poor Baby. It's alright Coop, I'll get you free." I baby talked him as I climbed under the table and pulled the bandana from his mouth and started untying the line. It looked like the line that was outside on the old clothes hanging rack. Cooper was licking me furiously as I untied as quickly as I could. "Well, too bad you can't talk, but it doesn't take a detective to figure this one out, huh?" I murmured quietly to him as I rubbed him behind the ears. Thurman. He was gonna be in huge trouble when I told Momma tomorrow what happened. I wonder how Thurman got to him. Momma usually kept her door locked after she went to bed and Cooper was always with Momma. Good Lord! If Thurman figured out a new skill of picking locks, we were all in big trouble.

I scooped up Cooper and headed towards the stairs. Thurman rushed past me and ran up the stairs without a look back. When I got to Momma's room, he was there waiting for me blocking the door. He was on his knees in a begging position; looking up at me with huge liquid black eyes. I knew what he wanted. He never begged anything from me. This was a new position to be in with him. Our standoffs were usually more of an OK Corral variety. Hmmmm. Maybe I can use this to my advantage.

"OK Thurman. I'll make a deal with you. I won't tell Momma of this latest transgression, if you promise two things." Thurman cocked his head to the side prepared to listen. What a brat! He had to consider? He was the one begging, not me. Figures, he still thinks he can manipulate me. The scary thing is he probably can.

Still acting like I had the upper hand, I held up one finger. "One; No more playing rough with Cooper, you can hurt him. Momma made that clear last time." Thurman was solemnly nodding his head yes.

I held up another finger. "And two; you leave me alone." To this demand, he cocked his head to the other side, locked his hands behind his back and just stared at me. I could tell he was thinking hard. He was weighing his options and deciding if he wanted to give in to this demand or face Momma's wrath. I knew instantly when he arrived at his decision, but I was worried by the grin that accompanied his nod of yes. I had a feeling he had beaten me again.

I opened Momma's door, which I realized was unlocked, and placed Cooper inside the door and nudged him towards the bed. Cooper scampered over and hopped on the chest at the foot of the bed then onto the bed and snuggled up at Momma's feet. I closed the door and turned to grill Thurman about the unlocked door, but he was already down the hall and heading for the stairs. But just as he was about to slide down the banister, he turned and gave me that evil grin again. He also pulled his left hand from behind his back to show me his crossed fingers. In his mind he only agreed to one of my demands. As I headed towards him, he snapped off a perfect salute and slid down the banister backwards, holding the salute in place as he disappeared from sight.

Good Lord! I definitely just got beat. Again. Dammit!

22

The reluctant sun rose higher and higher in the sky, already resigned to being cursed by millions of beings below before it even hit mid morning. Dauphin Island in spring was like a sauna, the humidity was so high it was tangible. It was humid, but nowhere near what it would get by mid- summer. This humidity was like a pleasurable Sauna you choose to take for relaxation. Carlyle wiped the sweat from the back of his neck with the shirt he had just stripped off his body and tossed it on the deck chair. He would swear you could see steam rise from the crumpled and now wet shirt. Even though he has a townhome in Mobile, his family home here in a gated community on Dauphin Island was where he grew up and still considers home if anyone asks. Most people assume the building is what is referred to as home, but it's actually the location. He always feels the call of home like a whisper on the waves and usually gives in and answers that call with growing frequency these days. With three large steps he reached the water's edge and dove gracefully into the warm water, skirting the sandy floor with his chest, and with a powerful kick dove even deeper under the waves, heading for Alassi; his real home.

Carlyle leads a secretive life; by necessity, not choice. He is fairly certain Al knows; maybe not what exactly, but that he is definitely hiding something. Now he just needs to figure out if he can trust her. Trust her with the biggest secret of his life; not just his life, but his family as well. Actually even more than that; his kind. His secret is that he is Baov-veche, a merman. Yes, they are real. And yes, they do still exist. There are not many colonies left anymore, Global Warming has taken care in helping evolution along. What the warming of the current didn't change, the pollution of the humans completed. The ocean has a very finely balanced ecosystem; each individual ecosystem supporting another. The amount of carbon dioxide to the oxygenated air has to be exact for some creatures, both sentient beings and Vvundren (Earth or hard rock and coral reefs), to thrive or at the very least survive.

One of the remaining colonies is Alassi; an underwater oasis just off the southern coast of Alabama, about ninety miles South East of Dauphin Island, a barrier island at the mouth of Mobile Bay. It is rela-tively secluded and not a common place for divers. As beautiful as the southern Gulf Coast of Alabama is, it's not the first place chosen as a dive destination. The waters are warm, but have the protection of large land masses all around. Open water is accessibly close if needed. There is a natural underwater cavern that is disguised as a dangerous looking coral reef which keeps all but the most adventurous of divers from exploring. The opening to the cavern appears to be a deep sea trench, which most divers know to avoid. The opening to the cavern is actually quite shallow, only two hundred feet below the surface. This allows quite a bit of natural light to refract through the water to light the cave. This area is known for its limestone caverns throughout the area, and un-der the water's surface is no exception. If anything, they are even more spectacular. There was a colony off the coast of eastern Mexico, but too many divers created the need to move a little further south where there were less people in the water.

The roof of the Alassi, this particular cavern, has many crystallized stalactites, called dripstone, that were formed in a different period of time, soon after the birth of the world. They hang in different lengths along the ceiling; over thirty feet from the floor of the cavern, appearing to be chandeliers hung in a specific pattern. These dripstones are home to the phosphorescent phytoplankton, microscopic sea creatures, who wrap themselves around the crystalline structures. They secrete illuminating chemicals that have a chemical reaction with the carbonate ions of the stalactites, which in turn, give off an unearthly glow and bathe the interior of the caverns in a soothing blue effervescence. The effect of the glow through the water is something that must be seen to be believed, as there are no words to truly describe the vision. There are no human words because no human has ever seen it, well, with the exception of one. It is one of Lyle's favorite things about coming home.

The main entrance to the cavern is called the Ballroom. Despites its massive size, it has a cozy feel. Most events are hosted here, including the Clan gathering that is held every four years. The Ballroom being near the front of the cavern is an advantage in that it keeps the living areas private. Along the sides to the opening of Alassi are cenotes, natural shallow pools formed by the collapse of limestone deposits that overlap each other and fan out from just inside the large opening to either side of the entrance, creating the illusion of scales. As the pools are of varying depth, the colors of each pool are slightly different, ranging from deep green to the lightest of turquoise blues. They are quite beautiful and look as if they were designed by a great landscape architect by plan rather than by nature. Then again, maybe Nature IS the greatest architect.

Further back into the cavern are many chambers including sleeping rooms and specific purpose rooms. Most storage is outside the main cavern in a series of smaller connected caves. The rear of the main cavern is elevated and has a unique design that had been excavated over tens of thousands of years to create three chambers that are giant air pockets. Due to the elevation, one chamber actually has an opening to the surface like a giant sun tunnel that allows light an air into the room. It reflects off a shallow pool that forms in the center from the crashing waves and natural rainfall.

The smallest of the three chambers is used to hold valuables that are best preserved dry. These days most monetary items are stored in the bank vaults all over the world that have grown with each generation to create the vast wealth that the Bavares family controls. Lyle's mother currently handles all of their holdings as she has shown a talent for all things requiring timing and instinct regarding anything monetary.

The last of the three is furnished as a small apartment and is currently occupied by the only human to ever see Alassi. The presence of a human has caused numerous arguments within the Clan as to the wisdom of allowing the location to be known and required compelling arguments as to why it was a necessary risk. In the end everyone on the governing council agreed it was for the best, well all but one, but Joran disagrees with most all ideas that he doesn't create himself, so his dissent was to be expected.

It is this chamber that Lyle wishes to visit. He loves conversing with this human housed here in Alassi for the last two years. In particular, just through stories, he has fallen in love with his daughter. Nothing will ever come of it as this human is being hidden and protected for a reason. No one must know he is here and that secret must be kept at all costs. Now that the Baovveche are involved, their survival is also at stake. Lyle understands that, but he has had a taste and the only way to satisfy his craving is through talking with this man. Carlyle's mother doesn't really understand his obsession, but is just happy to have Carlyle visit so often when he was away for so long prior to this new situation. What his mother doesn't understand is his obsession is with this man's daughter. He knows he can't take things further with Al until the issue that is keeping her father here at Alassi in this for lack of a better name, Cosmic Witness Protection Plan, is resolved.

As Lyle enters the chamber of the guest, he must first enter the antechamber to allow the oxygen to regenerate the air of the small cave. When he is breathing with his lungs, not his gills, he knows it is safe to continue in to the main cavern that houses their guest.

"Hello Fraser!"

"Hi Lyle" The tall man who has just stood greets back.

"I'm sorry it's been so long since my last visit, but I have a respectable job now you know." Lyle grins.

As Fraser grabs Lyle in a bear hug he laughs "Yes, and that's why I'm not angry. Knowing you are checking on my Susie, how could I be upset? And speaking of, how is everything at BonHaven?"

"Well, I haven't been there yet. But I haven't heard of any problems, so I'm assuming all is well.

"I so regret what this must be causing everyone, but until whatever is happening in Palisphor is settled, the Elders there felt it best for me to stay put. We are forever in your debt for allowing me to stay here. We understand the danger this puts your family in as well." Fraser said with feeling.

"Think nothing of it." Lyle said with a wave of his hand. "We understand the danger to us all. But the danger of doing nothing may destroy everyone, especially those of us with secrets to be kept from the world that threaten our very existence."

"I'm afraid that is very true. That is what makes this even worse. If it was just my family, that is one thing, and we could handle it. But it appears it is much bigger than that, so I thank you again. But I am not sure how much longer I can keep this up. I miss my family. The reports you bring are helpful to keep me informed, but now I think we may have a bigger problem." He said with a grimace.

"More problems?" Lyle said sitting down

"Well, maybe." Fraser answered. I have known for awhile that Lyci knows I am alive. I think she has sensed it from the beginning, but I also know she is staying quiet about it for the most part. I'm not sure why. Maybe she understands it is part of something important, or maybe just out of curiosity. But I know she can't keep quiet about it much longer. But more worrisome is Mae. She is up to something. I can feel it. She has put out some kind of feeler. She's looking for me, and I think she is trying to find out on her own what is up with the Elders. She can be loose cannon sometimes. I had told Wallace to try to keep her in line.

And I know he is trying, but when Mae gets an idea in her head there's no stopping her. No one can control Leila Mae. Never could, even as a child she was unpredictable. We need to figure this out quick so I can go home and deal with everyone. I actually though Lyci would have confided in everyone what she knew to be true. She must have her reasons."

"I am planning working more closely with Bobby so when we get called out on a case, I can tag along and hopefully get more intel." Lyle said while running his hands back and forth through his hair. "I didn't want to just show up at BonHaven. With all that you have told me, someone will most likely blow my cover."

"You're right about that." Fraser laughed. "And who knows what form it might take. No, its best you avoid that as much as possible. Unless it's necessary, and I have a feeling it might be soon."

"I'll get word to you soon if anything comes up. But as always, it's been great talking with you." Lyle said as he stood to go.

"You too, Lyle." Fraser said with a slap to Lyle's back. "I wish I could say send my greetings, but we both know that's not possible right now." He said with such sadness Lyle's heart broke a little. "But soon. I feel it."

"For all our sakes, I hope so." Lyle said as he walked through the antechamber.

23

Mr. D was waiting for Vic in the car with the engine on and the AC going full blast. When Vic opened the door to get in, he was hit with an arctic blast. He had walked from Maude's in the moisture laden heat and the sudden change in temperature was disorienting.

"Isn't it a little cold?" Vic asked with a shiver.

"Just get in and close the door." Mr. D ordered.

"What's the rush?"

"The rush is I made an appointment with Mrs. Babineaux for one o'clock and its now twenty till. I like to be prompt." Mr. D looked at him and raised an eyebrow, starring until he felt Vic got the point. He then put the car in drive and pulled away.

"So, you're sure this is going to work? I mean, in broad daylight? She wasn't suspicious?" Vic had read the detailed instructions, but he still wasn't quite sure.

"She doesn't suspect a thing. I had paid a visit to her several weeks back to authenticate and value some art deco period radio lamps. I told her I had an interested buyer and she thinks I just wanted to have another look to officially authenticate the value to complete the offer."

"But I just don't understand why we're going in during the day. Wouldn't it be much easier and a hell 'ova less chance of getting caught if we did the heist at night?" Vic had looked at this at every angle, and he genuinely did not get it.

"It is a necessary risk. I overheard that the necklace would be dropped off before noon. I can't take a chance that it might be put into a safety deposit box at the bank. That would be a much greater risk for you than this small time home break in, don't you agree?"

"Well, when you put it that way." Vic shrugged.

"We're almost there. The driveway is directly ahead, you should probably get out here just in case there is someone around." Mr. D pulled the car off to the side of the road. "Do you remember what you are to do?

"Yeah. I got it. See you after." And with that Vic slipped out of the car and hopped the fence that ran along the road following the property line; bee lining for the big white house. Being back in the heat after the arctic iciness of the car slowed him down pretty quickly; like watching a fly in molasses. Funny how you think you are in such great shape, but the first time a really strenuous task is put before you, you poop out pretty quickly. Maybe he should have skipped the chicken fried steak at Maude's. Definitely should have skipped that last glass of sweet tea.

He walked towards the house with a now leisurely pace. Looking for all- the -world as if he belonged right where he was, doing exactly what he was doing. Anyone that saw him would think just that. At least that is what he kept saying to himself. He walked up the stairs to the rear entrance which led into the mudroom and onto the screened porch. "Wow!" Vic whistled under his breath. This place was pretty cool. What he wouldn't give to crawl up onto one of those swinging beds and grab a nap! He had spied in the house from afar and had heard stories of Bon-Haven, but to see it in person was really something! He waited on the porch until he heard Mr. D's voice talking with Mrs. Babineaux. When he heard the footsteps on the hardwood floor heading to the east side of the house, he knew they were heading into the front parlor. From the diagram he was given, he knew this was where the lamps were. He also knew this was his cue to head to his destination. He walked through the entry hall which ran the length from the back to the front of the house, then hid behind the dining room French doors until the footsteps stopped and the voices were muffled. Vic had that distinct feeling of being watched again. The hair stood up on the back of his neck and his arms. He felt a slight breeze and looked back over his shoulder. Of course, there was no one there.

But that wasn't exactly true. What Vic didn't know is that John had been following him since he got out of the car. By the time he took the first stair on the back porch, John was a nervous wreck. Wringing his hands and moaning so softly it couldn't be detected. It was obvious the man was up to no good. But what to do? Should he sound the alarm somehow? Scare him? Just appear and say "Boo?!"

But John did not of those things. Where was Wallace when you needed him? Probably chasing down Thurman. Actually, considering it was midday, Thurman was probably frozen in the act of something he had no business in when the sun crept over the horizon this morning and surprised him in said act. Someone really should teach Thurman how to tell time. Or at least make him wear a watch with an alarm. Now there's an idea; an alarm on Thurman; or maybe a collar with bells. Like a cat. John went back to following Vic.

Vic crept into the entry hall and went straight to the sideboard where he was told the jewelry would be in a heavy cut blue glass crystal glass dish. Sure enough, there it was, just as Mr. D said it would be; except there was more than just a necklace like he expected. Should he take everything or just the necklace? Maybe if he took it all, Mr. D would be so pleased with his quick thinking; he would get a big bonus! He picked up the dish and dumped all the contents into his jacket pocket. Bonus indeed!

John knew when the man picked up the glass dish what his intentions were. He was robbing them! Of all the nerve. In broad daylight! And BonHaven; doesn't this guy know where he is? John was about to appear and show himself and/or give the man a swift push when he realized the necklace the man was stealing was the necklace Al was upset about. Al wanted it out of the house. Maybe this would be a good thing. Then Al wouldn't have to worry about what to do with it. Pleased with his thinking, John turned to walk through the dining room wall thinking he would discuss it with Wallace later. Unfortunately he went through the wall and into the kitchen where he scared Cooper who yelped, which startled Sadie who was holding a big ladle which she dropped and clattered to the floor. It was just on the edge of his thought to wonder why the man seemed to know exactly where he was headed when he walked into the house when John was positive he had never seen the man in BonHaven, but the commotion he caused sent that thought floating off to the air.

The noise startled Vic, alerting him to the fact that there was someone in the next room, reminding him he was dawdling as he stood there mentally congratulating himself on being so shrewd.

Having accomplished what he set out to do, Vic quickly walked back down the entry hall and onto the screened porch. He carefully slipped out the back door and retraced his steps in getting to the house. He went back to the spot he got out of the car, hopped back over the fence and leaned back and waited for Mr. D to conclude his business. While he waited, he realized he had a grayish white dust on his pants; almost like an ash. He tried brushing himself off as he tried to figure out exactly what it was that he was coated in. To John, who had followed Vic outside and was currently watching him, it looked like a dog trying to catch a flea biting his hind end. Before Vic could put too much thought into what the substance was, he heard the approach of a car.

Within ten minutes, Mr. D's big black Mercedes rolled to a stop in front of Vic. Vic opened the door and the black Mercedes swallowed him whole leaving only dust and white ash trailing down the road.

24

The car ride from BonHaven back to DeCompanse Antiquities was a quiet one. Mr. D was obviously deep in thought with the ghost of a smile on his face. Vic knew better than to interrupt his mood. He had seen him go from what appeared to be happy to snarling in a split second and did not want to be on the receiving end of that today. In the quiet of the car, he let his mind stumble along without any guidance. He was glad he had lunch before he met Mr. D for their excursion today. He knew from past incidents that a rumbling stomach and burglary did not go well together; he had fourteen months in county lock up to prove it.

He had the jewelry in his jacket pocket and as he shifted in the car seat, the weight of it reminded him that he was excited to share the other piece he picked up from the sideboard dish. He glanced over to see if Dr. D was still smiling, but at that moment he realized they had arrived. As they pulled into the back alley of the imposing brick building that housed DeCompanse Antiquities and Holding Company, Vic sighed; the moment had passed. The brick building was formerly a cotton mill and had been registered on the national historic register as a historical treasure. Vic had to admit it was a pretty cool building. He always thought Mr. D should sell it and turn it in to lofts for all the yuppies moving down south. He would make a killing.

Mr. D continued down the alley to the rear entrance of the building and parked in his reserved parking space. As they stepped out of the car and started into the building a small gust of wind blew white ash across the parking lot's asphalt.

"What the hell is this stuff? Huh. Looks like snow doesn't it?" Vic questioned. Being from Arizona he wasn't used to the stuff.

"That would be the reason it is referred to as Alabama snow." Mr. D stated in his prissy pretentious voice. Oh No, Vic thought, here comes a lecture. You can see it on Mr. D's face. There's not much Mr. D likes more than showing off how much he knows to those less fortunate, and in this case that's Vic. Mr. D went on; "During sugarcane harvesting season, the earliest stage of the harvest is the burning. They found out that by burning most of the stalk, they had less to dispose of and were left with the best part of the cane to produce sugar and more recently ethanol." He was on a roll now. "Unfortunately for the rest of us, the byproduct is this ash that blows all over the region. It coats our cars and homes and even the greenery. It's a nuisance is what it is." He said as he lifted his nose in the air and brushed some ash off his suit jacket as he unlocked the door and started to enter the building. He turned to Vic looking down at his feet, "And for God's sake, make sure you wipe your shoes before you come in. That stuff just smears over all my rugs." He sneered and turned up his nose again as he too wiped his shoes on the sea grass mat before stepping inside.

Vic dutifully followed directions and wiped his shoes before he stepped into the room. Mr. D gestured towards a display case near the register.

"Please place the jewels here." He motioned to a velvet display board the shade of an overripe grape.

Vic took the handkerchief that held the jewels from his jacket inner pocket and carefully unrolled it. He lifted the necklace and earrings onto the board. His calloused hands and fingers made a scratching noise as they brushed against the fabric of the display board. Then he reached for an additional item and placed it on the board as well.

"Oh my goodness!" Mr. D said while taking a sharp breath. "Both earrings are here. I thought the other was lost!" he exclaimed. He actually started trembling from excitement. "I wonder why the Babineaux woman did not wear them the evening of the Gala? These would have been marvelous! Spectacular! The woman is a fool!" He was speaking out loud, but to himself. Vic was forgotten in his excitement. But he realized he was not alone and gathered his wits about him. It would not do to give anything away to Vic. No, it would not do a 'tall.

Vic deflated like a balloon. He thought Mr. D was excited because of the brooch he picked up. He was so proud of himself for thinking so quickly and secreting the items into his pocket without being discovered. Little did he know he was discovered. John saw everything. The question would anyone else ever know. John had not said a word to anyone yet.

Vic was still hoping Mr. D would give him a bonus for being so smart and picking up the brooch. He assumed it was as priceless as the Jewels he was told to take. It looked old, so he just assumed. Maybe it was and Mr. D. just hadn't gotten around to taking a good look at it. Didn't he need to use that magnifying thing; what's it called…a loop, that's it! A jewelry loop or something like that. See, he thought to himself: I'm just as smart as the next guy; maybe even smarter!

Mr. D finally noticed the other piece of jewelry on the board. "What is this?" he asked mostly to himself as he examined the piece closely. He didn't really expect an answer from Vic.

But Vic did answer. He launched into his story about why he took it; thinking it was valuable and wasn't that a great idea. But Mr. D held up his hand mid sentence to have Vic stop talking.

"It's not worth much, the jewels are too small. But the workmanship is very fine. But that was very enterprising of you." He said with a grin. "I'm sure someone will purchase it if I add a story for a background." Mr. D carried the brooch to the front counter and placed it atop a display. He returned to the register and pulled out an envelope from beneath the register drawer.

"Here you are" he said as he handed the envelope to Vic. "Payment in full. I think that will be all for now." Mr. D. said dismissively. He was anxious to examine the D'Arbia Jewels and wanted Vic gone.

After verifying the contents, Vic pocketed the envelope back into the same hiding spot that held the priceless jewels moments ago.

"So, no bonus for the extra pieces I got?" He figured it was worth a try.

"Now Vic" Mr. D explained patiently. "You know how I conduct business. We agreed on a contracted price that matched the scope of work. Just like any other business would. We mustn't go changing the specifics at the end of a job now must we? That would earn us both a very disreputable reputation now would it not?"

At this point Vic knew he was not getting any more money out of the boss and really didn't want to sit around being lectured like a child. He just wanted out at this point. He wanted to go home and take a nap.

"OK then. You have my number. Call when you need me." He snapped off a salute and walked out the back door.

When the door closed, Mr. D walked over and turned the lock. "Oh, I'll be calling you alright." He turned and walked back to the display case and pondered his next move.

What that might be, even Mr. D himself wasn't sure of. All that he was sure of was that the jewels now in his possession were incredible! The complete set at auction could bring well over twenty million. Maybe more if he could create some kind of frenzy on the black market. The collectors that bought on that market had the money, but could not purchase on the authentic market as they had to show the money provenance. Most couldn't. Mr. D didn't care where the money came from. His Bon Mot was if it was green, real and in abundance it that worked for him.

The real problem now was Vic. He was a liability; even if this was not the last job he wanted from Vic. He had no choice. The minute he saw the "Have you seen this man?" poster with a very good likeness of Vic's face, he knew what he had to do. But since Vic was his guy for dirty jobs, it looked like this dirty job had to be handled alone. With an evil chuckle, Mr. D settled it in his mind. Now he just had to figure out the details. How he loved the details. He scurried into his office to begin writing them down on his stationary then realized he left the jewels on the back counter. Not wanting them out of his sight for even one minute, he went back and scooped up the case to bring them with him. On his way back to his office, he had the strangest feeling of being watched. His hair stood up at the nape of his neck and he shivered slightly. Maybe he needed to turn down the air. It did seem positively frigid in here. As he sat down in his desk chair, he gently laid the jewels on his desk and placed a glass dome over them to keep them dust free. Even though he planned on a through steam cleaning later, he was treating them with the reverence they deserved. He planned on putting them in his vault tonight for safekeeping, but for now just wanted to admire them. As he gently lowered the dome his eyes came to rest on a small framed piece of art. A replica of another piece he had copied from a previous customer. Actually he had the original, the customer had the copy. But the art gave him an idea. As he furiously started jotting down the details, a small crash from the front room gave him pause. He stilled to listen and called out "May I help you?" thinking it was a customer that had wandered into the shop. But there was only silence. There was a slight flicker of his desk lamp and a ripple in a glass display case reflection. As John stood to the side of the case, he wrung his hands nervously, but was not noticed. John doubted Mr. D would notice the building imploding around him such was the abundance of greed exuding from the man's body solid enough to be touched.

25

Friday morning found me wandering around the house on my day off. As I had nothing planned for the day, I felt out of sorts, but as I meandered through the dining room, I smelled the distinct aroma of cherry pipe tobacco. Following my nose, I was lead towards the rear of the house. As I neared the French doors to the screened in porch, I was in for my first shock of the day. Notice how I say first, as I know more will follow. I'm used to it.

There was a storm rolling in from the Gulf and everyone had gathered on the rear porch to watch the lightening on the bay. This was nothing unusual as the whole family always liked to watch the show of a spring thunderstorm from the relative safety of the screened in room, as it barreled up from the Gulf. You could always feel it coming in, just from the atmospheric pressure. In the south, you don't need to watch the weather reports, you can feel it! Especially in your joints. And your ears. It was like blowing out while holding your nose. Or being underwater, that weird pressure feeling. Hard to describe, but once you've experienced it, you'll never forget.

As I walked into the room, I almost couldn't hold in the laughter that threatened to explode from my chest. I managed a cough instead as I tripped into the room. Uncle Howard, Granddaddy, Aunt Merle, Lyci and Momma were all seated around the room enjoying a cup of coffee and looking out over the bay, watching as the sky illuminated everything through the gloom of the oncoming storm. That was perfectly normal.

Not normal were our Uglies, well, in all honesty, normal around here is relative. But even so, this was a new one. John & Wallace were laid out on chaise loungers wearing smoking jackets, ascots and holding ornate old fashioned pipes carved from whale bone with delicate wisps of smoke drifting from them.

That explains the tobacco smell.

"Oh Al, we were wondering when you would come down." Aunt Merle said as she looked up when she heard my cough. She patted the sofa cushion next to her.

"Come here. Lyci was just telling us of a vision she had. She said she has been seeing my necklace that Mae borrowed. But it doesn't make sense." She said furrowing her brow.

Since we discovered our theft yesterday, we have had many group discussions on the correct way to handle the situation. Obviously involving the police were out of the question. As we could not prove provenance and didn't have anything insured, what could we claim. Actually, I was more upset that the brooch I had only just discovered was also missing along with the D'Arbia jewels.

"Go on, Lyci" Merle prodded. "Tell Al what you see."

Lyci rolled her eyes and began again. "I was just saying I had a flash of the jewels being held in a man's hands and again sitting on what looked to be like a jewelers display case." She shrugged her shoulders as if it were no big deal. But I also saw Daddy reading in a big room that looks like the Caverns we visited last summer.

"OK. Good." I said as I rubbed my hands together ignoring her comment about Daddy. She always says little things here and there since the day Daddy disappeared. While we knew he was not alive, evidenced by the fact that two years later, he still was gone, Lyci refused to believe the facts. We knew there was nothing that could keep Daddy away from BonHaven and his family. He simply loved Momma too much. Lyci just used this as a coping mechanism and we all allowed it. Whatever lets her deal with her grief, we agreed to let her have, but lately it was getting harder and harder to ignore. But I tried.

"What else do you see?"

"I don't know." She answered; bored to go through this again.

"Well." I pushed. "What did the man's hands look like? Were they big or small, white, black, in between? Anything you can remember is a good start."

"Definitely a white man. Kind of rugged. You know, like he worked outside or something."

"That's great!" I praised. "What about the jewelry case? Anything stand out?"

"Well, actually, now that I think about it. The necklace was on a velvet board. I thought it was cool because it was a deep purple color. Usually those things are black right?" She asked now excited. "And it was under a glass dome. Like the one in the kitchen Sadie keeps over her pies."

I had started writing down the information in a notepad that was lying on the wicker table in front of the small sofa I was sitting on. I looked up to give Lyci a smile.

"The thing I can't figure out though is the room he's in. It reminds me of the room in a bank where they keep the big money." She said with a look of confusion.

"You mean like a vault?" Momma said helpfully.

"Exactly!" Lyci clapped her hands.

"But why would someone steal the jewels and put them in their own bank vault? It doesn't seem like the thing a thief would do." Merle said.

"How would you know what a thief would do?" Uncle Howard said with a shake of his head.

A half hour later, I had a pretty good description. Merle was a pretty fair artist and had drawn a pretty good rough sketch from Lyci's description. I planned on making a few copies and passing it around town quietly. I couldn't very well explain how I got the description now could I. It would just be tagged from an anonymous source like always. I would run it through the data base at the station when I went back on shift. I was hoping to get a chance later to read some more of the diaries found in the attic, but my mind was now stuck on the description Lyci had just given me. Maybe I should call Bobby and see if the description rings a bell with him. Just as I got up to call him, the storm arrived with a vengeance. The skies lit up and jagged bolts of lightning crashed down into the bay where it met the water with a deafening noise and a small sizzle; always spectacular to watch, but also dangerous. On the tails of that thought, the power flickered twice, then went our completely. The phone call to Bobby was forgotten amid the chaos to find lanterns and candles and the fun of planning a weenie roast for dinner over an open fire.

26

After Lyci's premonition, I had been expecting something. What, I didn't know, but something; especially after I posted the flyers around town. The more I looked at the flyer, the more something pulled at me. I'm sure I have seen that face before. But where? Who knows! Maybe it was just becoming familiar because I was looking at it so much as I gave the flyers out around town. But thinking back on Lyci's vision, I didn't figure a crime on my property. Definitely did not see that coming. I wasn't on duty today, but Corporal Purvess called me to the scene, since the scene was basically in my back yard. Purvess said the tip came in after 11:30 and it was now quarter to midnight so I said I would be right there. Being that I was literally three minutes away, I didn't think that estimate would be very far off! I threw on jeans and a light windbreaker jacket with POLICE stenciled huge Day-Glo orange letters across the back. I hated wearing that jacket, Besides making me a target, I felt like I was an extra in a cop show; pretending to be a cop. Wow, did I have some kind of deep seated chip on my shoulder or what? As it was still 82 degrees outside, the jacket was for identification purposes only, but since I wasn't in uniform, it was a necessity. Oh well, like ii or not was a moot point. I shrugged into my holster, tucked in my Glock and pulled my hair up into a tight bun from its usual ponytail. Outfit complete!

As I was clicking my seatbelt into place in the SUV, it occurred to me that I could walk to the crime scene, but since it was pitch black outside and would be even darker where I was going, the headlights of the SUV may come in handy. I put the SUV in gear and rolled down all the windows to catch any breeze that might come along; I was caught by surprise by the large dirt clod that hit me in the ear.

"Thurman, Damn it!"

I saw a flash of white child sized shorts run towards the house at the same time I heard the high pitched glee of laughter. Considering that I had an ear full of dirt, I'm surprised I heard anything at all. I hit the brakes and put the car back in park so I could get out and shake the dirt off. That kind of accomplished, red dirt doesn't just shake off, I got back in and drove down the driveway, the sound of the crushed granite soothing in the cotton stuffed night air. Then again, that could just be my ear clogged with dirt. Good Lord, I hope Thurman just got lucky. It would be terrifying to think he has been working on his aim!

Two minutes later, I pulled off route 48, the country road that literally divides my Aunt and Uncles property from ours. Our property line turns at a 90 degree right angle from the road. I parked the car at the same angle as the property line, shining the car headlights onto the crime scene and, wait for it, right on Bastion. Yep, Bastion, the very same tree involved in Jimmy-Don's "incident". (Incident meaning his self proclaimed ticket into the inner circles of Ghost Hunters; the "14 seconds of infamy" also known as "The Tape"). I was climbing over the fence, when a police cruiser pulled up and parked, adding their headlights to mine.

"Hey. Since it was your day off, we thought we would bring the crime to you." Bobby said with a mock bow and a tip of his ball cap.

"Gee, thanks Officer Taylor', that's awfully thoughtful of ya'll". Al grinned into the darkness as she recognized Bobby's voice and kept walking towards the large shadow of the tree.

She had known Bobby Glen Taylor since grade school. They had gone to high school together and found fame and glory on the wrestling team together. He was the one guy who had taken her seriously and gave it his all when they had a practice match. He didn't freak out or make jokes; or even start with the "I refuse to hit a girl" speech. He gave her the benefit of the doubt from the get go. After she pinned him with a perfectly executed Fireman's Carry takedown move, he respected her in a way the other guys never did. It was funny that there was never anything romantic between them, but they became great friends. She was truly one of the guys to him. He went away to college at Tulane and went into the academy down there, but the call of Alabama got him and he came back home. He transferred to the force in Blakely and had been with them three years now. Professionally, she trusted all her fellow officers on the streets. He was one of the only officers she truly depended to have her back in her personal life. He even knew most of the secrets of BonHaven. Most – not all. And he still came back. That earned him her highest respect.

"So, what gives?" Al asked as Bobby caught up to her.

"Call came in at 11:35. Caller used fake Mexican accent and said you want to go to that big, ugly old tree out on route 48. You're gonna find a body and it's not pretty."

"How do you know it was a fake accent?" Al asked with a grin.

"Well, not many people of Hispanic decent really talk like the Taco Bell Chihuahua." He said as he scrunched up his face.

They arrived at the base of the tree just then and Bobby raised his maglight to shine the beam on the tree. Tied to the trunk was a body of a man, well, probably a man, most likely a man. There was a lot of blood from an obvious head wound to the left side of his head that made the answer questionable. The skin of his face hung in flaps and tatters to his chest. Large gaping holes resided in the area of eye sockets. Although that was even hard to discern as the optical orbits were shattered. The head was bowed down at an unnatural angle. There were symbols carved into the trunk of the tree with what appeared to be blood. CSI could determine that tomorrow in the daylight. There were several candles spread around the body, giving the appearance of a sacrifice on an alter, which was maybe exactly what it was supposed to look like. Al saw crime scenes and bodies all the time, so it wasn't really upsetting. But the worst part of the scene, and definitely upsetting to Al, was the grotesque head of one of those damn sheep she had to drive past every day, placed between the splayed out legs of the body.

Detective Taylor and Al looked at each other, then back at the body.

"Wowwwww." Bobby said drawing out the w for what seemed like forever. "This reminds me of a case we caught down in Shreveport. Some kid wanted to get into dealing and crossed the wrong dude. Some mid-level dealer wanted to raise his rep for being scary, so, he threw around Voodoo symbols everywhere he went. It mostly worked because people though he was nuts, so pretty much left him alone. But when he came across the chance to prove he was a Voodoo high priest AND get rid of the kid on his turf, he took it.

"So, what happened?" Al asked while leaning in for a closer look at the symbols carved into the trunk and snaps a few photos with her cell phone.

"Oh, he was fingered for it immediately. Since he was always trying to be scary and act nuts, he was always swiping his big switchblade across his tongue. It was the same one he carved initials and symbols on the kids body – had his DNA all over it; still serving the rest of his 15 to life in the LA State Penn."

Lights and sirens came blaring down route 48 just then.

"Well, it looks like CSI is here. They can preserve the scene and we'll figure this out tomorrow. I was just getting into bed when Purvess called" Al shrugged while turning back toward the road. "Our power was out for most of the day due to the storm. We can't get a good look at things till daylight anyway. Let me know if you ID the vic before I get to the station tomorrow, OK Bobby?"

"Alright, I'll pass along any info in the morning, Night."

"Thanks Bobby. Night."

"Oh, and Bobby, I know where you can get info on that sheep's head; call Lamar Jureaux and see if he is missing any of his demonic herd." She yelled as she climbed into her car quickly so she could repress her shudder until she was hidden by the darkness of the car interior.

Al was thinking to herself that this was an unusual case for their area. All she knew for sure was Bastion had nothing to do with this. He knew to stay out of the limelight. But one thing she did knew for certain, and that was Bastion was gonna be one pissed off tree!

27

Bleeh! That is the only way to describe how I feel walking into the station today. I wanted to be sitting by the pool this morning. The weather was perfect. Late April in Alabama is beautiful; as long as the tornadoes stay away. The humidity is just starting to come on, the trees are in bloom and the smell of honeysuckle is really cranking up. There is nothing better than the smell of honeysuckle wafting around on the breeze, especially in the evening. Sweet Home Alabama indeed! Maybe I was just hoping to erase the memory of what I just had to deal with and the laying poolside thought was the quickest way to calm me down. It's a visualization trick the Officers Union shrink taught me once when I had to see him after a justified shooting. Another story for another day, but whatever, the trick works for me. I just think of a pleasant memory and when I clear my head, the bad memory fades a little, not completely, but enough. As I left the house this morning and got in my car, I had a bad feeling; then again, after the crime scene last night, who could blame me right? Rather than think about it too much before I got to the station, I pushed the start button to turn on the engine, crank the radio, and lose my thoughts to some great 80's tunes. A gift from Daddy; he was constantly listing to classic rock and singing the lyrics where ever he was; didn't care if anyone heard him or not, just kept right on singing. If anyone had a problem with it, he considered it their problem, not his. God I loved that about him. His quiet confidence in whatever he did. He was just comfortable in his own skin.

That's rare. I think most people don't even realize how UNcomfortable they are with themselves until you're around someone like Daddy. That's probably for the best! But Lord, how I miss him. Every day brings some new reason to miss him even more. But the car wouldn't start. Figures. My SUV was only two years old, I couldn't believe it! Maybe it was the battery; I did leave the lights on for quite awhile last night at the crime scene shining on Bastian. I was cursing myself as I got back out of the car and went around to open the hood of the car. Once I found the latch after a lot of fiddling around and popped the hood, I realized it was not a battery problem. It was a Thurman problem. How in the hell did that little brat get the hood up? He must have had help. My money would be on Wallace. As I gazed over the detached spark plugs and finagled which ones went where to reattach them, I realized it could have been worse. He could have taken the distributor cap and hid it somewhere. It was probably best if I kept quiet about this one rather than open the discussion and give him more ideas.

But this morning, Jeeze, THAT situation was a new one, even for these parts. When I finally got back in the car and it successfully started right up, I headed down the drive to hit the main road. Just as I reached down to blast the radio, I came around the small bend to the portion of the road that ran alongside the fence shared with Jimmy Don's property and had to slam on my brakes.

Good Lord!

The SUV skidded a little to the right, which was a good thing as to the left was a row of lawn chairs filled with the behinds of some of the townsfolk. With them were assorted coolers and shade canopies all placed alongside the crime scene tape which had been placed alongside and around Bastian last night after the body was removed to the county morgue in Blakely. I reached over to grab my radio in the passenger's seat and called in to dispatch.

"Dispatch, this is Officer Babineaux. I'm at the crime scene off route 48 from the homicide from last night. We're gonna need some officers here ASAP to protect integrity. Over."

"Copy that Officer Babineaux. On route. Over." crackled back dispatch.

I pulled over father to the right and threw the car in park and hit the on button for the siren horn a few times. That got their attention. I reached under my seat and grabbed the bubble light and placed it on the roof of the SUV as I got out and slammed the door. As I looked over the scene, I zeroed in on Jimmy Don. He was standing on a wooden crate and addressing the crowd.

"Now the history of this tree is known to most of ya'll, but not the whole history, if ya know what I mean. Our government don't want us to know all they know. They think we can't handle the truth. Well, I'm here to tell all ya'll right now the whole truth and nothing but the tru.. tru.. truth." He stuttered while thumping his chest and looking around to make eye contact with every person he could. He musta learned that move from some evangelical preacher in a drive through tent revival from his childhood. It was a pretty good move, I must admit.

But one that needed to be stopped immediately.

"Jimmy Don you all need to back away right now. This is an active crime scene; hence this here bright yellow tape that states "Crime Scene Stay Back" is to protect the integrity of the scene. This ensures nothing is missed in finding out who did this. "I said as I lifted a piece of said tape up in the air to a chorus of oohs and aaahs. This was better than Friday night CSI on television for most of these folks. "A man was murdered here last night and it would be wise to be respectful of that." I placed my hands on my hips and forged on. "Now there will be more officers here in a few minutes and I would suggest you disperse right this minute if you don't want to be placed in custody for impeding an investigation." I nodded to Jimmy Don and then motioned to the rest of the crowd.

"But I am on my side of the property. I know my rights." Jimmy Don said authoritatively.

"You're right on that, but an active crime scene means it doesn't matter whose property it is on. Until the CSI is done here no one steps past that barrier. Are we clear?" I lifted my eyebrow for emphasis.

Just at that moment several squad cars turned off the main road and started down the drive. The crowd stood and started milling about now that I had reinforcements. Some started packing up their chairs and coolers. The sun shades were quickly dismantled. There was grumbling in the crowd; some protests of harassment and stifling their God given rights. There was so much noise I couldn't make out individual conversations, but I did catch Jenny Katherine's nephew saying something about the carving on the tree. I headed over towards him, but was cut off by Wiley Carmichael looking for trouble and getting in my face.

"What you gonna charge me with, huh? I ain't done nuthin." He huffed as he stood almost nose to nose and dug his hands into his pockets.

"To start with, unlawful assembly, No permit and how about tampering with evidence on an active case? Those three will stick; at least enough to keep you away from Blo and Mo's. How'd you like to lose two days pay while you're on a 48 hour hold while we sort out the details?" I knew he needed his landscaping job as he worked the contracts when Hollis needed more help around BonHaven. Wiley may be stupid, but he wasn't a complete fool. I could tell when he decided to back off in his eyes. "And if you don't back away from me right now and get your hands out of those pockets where I can see them, you're getting a pair of cuffs thrown on them."

Wiley had already taken two steps back before I even finished my sentence.

I turned away from him looking for the boy who was talking about the tree carvings, but he was lost in the crowd. As the officers finished helping everyone to their cars and restrung the barrier tape, I had a sinking feeling I had just missed out on something important. Maybe I should look this kid up later and make sure he doesn't have any info we need; Lord knows it can't hurt; we need a break. I pulled my notebook out of my shirt pocket and made a note to contact Jenny Katherine later to find out where to reach him.

28

As the Station door closed behind me with a whoosh and the air conditioning rushed over me, I was still smiling to myself as I heard counting, loudly, from the EOC room. The emergency operations center was our largest meeting room, with large viewing screens and enough tables to accommodate the whole on duty force. The situation room is used for many things other than emergency ops coordination. We hold community events there, including our Citizens Policy Academy. It's actually an awesome program that enrolls twenty or so citizens who attend a twelve week mini-Policy Academy. It is a great way to reach out and educate the community on what the police actually do! We cover everything from policy and procedures (boring, but important), to drugs (everyone loves seeing the drugs that have been apprehended), gangs and domestic violence and sentencing, to the crowd favorite – SWAT night! Also a fan favorite, Driving While Intoxicated demonstration night. One officer volunteers to drink a six pack and several shots at specific intervals, then they take a breathalyzer. It's pretty entertaining. I think we officers enjoy it as much or more than the citizen cadets. On the night the simulation training trailers for driving and situational confrontational learning are brought in, most officers can be found in the driving simulator fighting for a turn! If we lose the fight for a turn, then we race over to the other trailer, the confrontational situations training lab. Here you are given a service belt to wear and handed a taser and gun. It's a real taser but the gun shoots pellets. Different scenarios are played on the oversized video screen at the end of the trailer and you have to react in real time to choose what level of force to use. It is pretty eye opening for the average citizen when they are shown a young mother sitting on a park bench arguing animatedly with her eight year old daughter. Seems fairly easy to choose right? But on the screen the child is trying to tell you something, but in a foreign language you can't understand. She seems scared. As you approach, it is up to you to say what you think is appropriate. Beforehand, you are given a basic script and can go from there. On the video screen the mother stands and approaches you, agitated and shooing you away. There is no sound, but you can clearly see her mouth say "Go Away". As she approaches you, most citizens reach for their taser, feeling they may be in danger, but again, she is just an upset young mother probably embarrassed to be caught arguing

and yelling at her child; at this point, whatever officers are standing around start giggling like little girls at a tea party. This is our favorite part.

The safe looking mother pulls a gun from her purse and shoots you at close range. The child was saying "She has a gun." Did I mention real pellets are fired at you from the screen? They hurt like you wouldn't believe; and leave a bruise. Well, you do have to sign a release to participate. I know it's all kinds of wrong, but we get a kick out of it!

"THREE!"

The counting and loud laughter drew my attention back to the present. I hurriedly push through the door to the EOC, not sure what to expect.

"FOUR!"

Jeez, I definitely didn't expect this. Knowing this group, I shoulda, but I didn't.

Eight guys from SWAT and one dispatcher on a break were watching the TV screens.

"Now, Meow, What are you laughing at? Do you think this is a laughing matter?" came from the TV screens.

Then "FIVE!"

Joey Matthews, Corporal Matthews, that is, fell off his chair laughing.

The idiots were watching "Super Troopers" on the big screens. The screens placed there for use during emergencies and large briefings. The screens bought and paid for with hard earned tax payer money. The thought process being they were better off being used than just sitting there. The officers on break were watching their favorite part of the movie where two officers made a bet at a traffic stop on whether or not one officer could say the word meow instead of now ten times by the time he writes up the speeding ticket. It is pretty funny. Stupid, but funny. Personally I prefer the repeat game which shows how mature I am.

I just shook my head and slunk out the door quietly. I had paperwork to finish up.

29

"Hey Bobby, what did we find out?" I asked as I walked through the locker room door. Having arrived at the station early for my shift, I was anxious to find out if the CSI team had discovered any new facts in the Bastian murder case. Well, at least I was calling it the Bastian case, since it involved Bastian.

"On the Bastian case?" he said looking up from the file on his desk.

Ha, it wasn't just me! "Yeah, anything?"

"Nothing yet, except for the obvious we saw last night. They're running the prints for an ID, and checking the rope the body was tied up with to look for fibers to see if they can pull any leads that way. The rope itself may be significant too."

"It's a good thing CSI started last night. The scene might have been compromised this morning. You heard about the group of idiots Jimmy Don gathered around the crime scene this morning?"

"Yep. Classic Jimmy Don. Did he do any damage this time?"

"I don't think so. It looked like everyone was pretty far from the tape. Jimmy Don was literally standing on a soap box looking pompous spouting whatever nonsense was rolling around his head that day. Ever since that tape he acts so smug; like he has something on me. Which he does, but he doesn't need to know that." I said with a smile. Just then what Bobby said earlier caught up to me.

"Wait, why do you think the rope might be significant?"

"It's the size. Didn't you notice the diameter?" He continued as I shrugged my shoulders. "It's really thick, more like you would find on an old fashioned sailing ship."

"No. I was more interested in the carvings. They kinda looked familiar to me."

At just that moment, Carlyle was walking through the hallway and passed the main room doorway "and it smells funny" he said. While Bobby and I looked at each other Carlyle clarified "the rope, it's old and smells funny" and kept walking. OoooKaaaay.

"You mean not something you would pick up at Sam Spade's then." Sam Spade's was the local hardware and lawn and garden center and Momma loved to check out the flowers once a week.

"No, definitely not" said Bobby "Oh, I called Jureaux, but no one answered, so I left a message. Maybe we can find a lead from the sheep angle; wow, that sounds weird."

"Yeah, well the whole thing with the sheep IS weird." I said shaking my head and repressing a shudder again. "I hate those sheep. What about CID, anything other than the obvious?"

"They are pretty scary looking." Bobby said with a shrug looking at me and winking his brow. Nothing yet on Cause, I sent some photos to that Voodoo High Priest we pulled in on the case down in Shreveport. Maybe he can decipher what the carvings mean, if anything."

"I took a lot of photos last night, do you want me to email them to you and see if there are any you can use?" I asked. "I haven't really looked at them yet, it may have been too dark to pick up the details of the carvings, but I can forward them all to you and you can view them yourself." "Yeah, thanks, that'd be great. The ones I took are all too dark. I'm sure CSI took some, but I haven't gotten them yet". I took out my phone and was in the middle of forwarding the photos to Bobby when the Captain stuck his head out of his office and yelled for us to come in his office. At least I think that's what he yelled. With that Cajun accent of his sometimes I wasn't sure, but it was a pretty good guess as Bobby had started walking in that direction. I looked over at Bobby and at the same time said "SUTU" and headed into the Captain's office. But before I put my phone away, I noticed the photo showing on the screen. It was a close up of where the victim was tied to the tree. I noticed the rope. It was unusual. Very thick and was wound with multiple strands for strength. Maybe it would tell us something.

Walking into Captain Joe Sampson's office was a little like time traveling, specifically to the mid to late 1970's. A huge promotional poster of the band Blondie hung on the back wall, with the phrase "One way or another…..I'm gonna getcha" across the photo of Deborah Harry, with her classic platinum blonde over black look. He said he thinks it should be every cop's mantra.

Chief Sampson is a great cop. He may be a little crazy though. He was originally from New Orleans, born and raised in Cajun country, in a little town called Beaux Bridge, complete with swamps, gators and Creole cooking. His black eyes always have a twinkle, as if he is one step ahead of you and is slightly amused by how long it's taking you to catch up with him. He joined the force in the Big Easy and saw some pretty hard times with the force during the big IA cleanup. It definitely made him a better cop, but he is so by the book, sometimes we think he shits SOP. But we always know he has our backs on patrol and any other time. That goes a long way to another officer. We would follow him through anything. Blindly.

"Sit". He points to the chairs in front of his desk. Even with the accent, that was clearly understood.

We both sat. Every time I sit here, my eyes are drawn to a framed 8 x 10 photo on the Chief's desk of Sammy Hagar. It's autographed to him. "Joe, to my favorite cop, Remember, I can't drive 55, don't arrest me, Sammy". Chief Sampson, resident rocker. Although, to give him his due, everything does have a police theme. All that is missing is a poster of Elvis Costello – Watching the Detective.....

"Do you have anything new to report on the Bastian case?" He asks as he breaks me out of my revere.

I couldn't help myself "you're calling it the Bastian case too, Captain?"

"Why not? We don't have an ID yet on the vic, and we all know Bastian. Makes sense to me."

Okay. Makes sense to me too. "No Sir, not yet. We were just going to look through our personal photos from last night since we don't have the official ones back yet."

"CSI thinks the victim was drugged first, and then tied to the tree before he was murdered. Lab report won't be back for three days. So for now, it's just a guess."

"I want you to follow up on the carvings on the body and tree. See if that leads anywhere."

Bobby finally pipes up "I emailed my contact this morning. We worked a case involving Voodoo a few years ago. If there's anything to know, they'll know it".

"Good". He said while standing up and herding us out the door. "Oh, we did get something on the rope fibers. You were right. It is old. As in antique old. It's evidently what was used mostly on big mast ships; you wouldn't find it in marine shops today. That may be a big break; it definitely narrows down the suspects who would be in possession of any length of it. See what you can find on that." He added as he was closing the door. "And the Sheep"

Oh No, Oh No, Oh No. He's gonna say it, then it's real and then I have to follow through. Oh Jeeze, Please no.

He yelled as he stuck his head out of the doorway. "They may bring you some info; look into it." With that he ducked his head back inside and closed the door.

At the mention of those sheep, I shuddered again. What is it about those damn sheep!

Good Lord!

30

I was lying by the pool having finally found some sun soaking time, reading one of the diaries from the box that was discovered last week. I had been meaning to get around to it, but something always came up. So far, it was full of personal things. Daily routines, who came around to visit, that sort of thing. It was definitely not boring though. There were so many parallels to her life it was scary. The details the previous Alma Sue chose to include were amazing. The escapades of Wallace were especially interesting. Wallace didn't seem as stuffy then as he is now, although it could just be that everyone was stuffy, so there was not as much distinction.

I was interrupted in my thought process when my cell phone rang.

"Hello?" she said as she slipped the phone against her neck to hold it so she didn't have to put down the journal.

"Hey, it's Bobby."

"Oh Hey Bobby, what's up?" I asked as I turned a page. I was just getting into what happened on May 28, 1878. It looked like there was a big storm coming in up from the Gulf and they were making preparations. Sadie had just sent the handyman, Burlie, who happens to be related to Hollis (big surprise), down to the basement for the storm doors for the windows.

"I just had a message on my phone from that source in New Orleans. You know the Voodoo guy. He said he would meet with us if we would come to him. Well originally that's what he said until he started interrogating me for details. I explained a little about what we wanted to question him about and that you would be coming with me. When I said your name, he asked if you were Babineaux from BonHaven and when I confirmed it, he said he would meet us there." He shrugged.

"Where? BonHaven?" This was interesting. I put down the journal. Now he had my full attention. "Who is this guy?" I asked. "Is he reliable, or just a nut job who gets lucky?"

"His name is the Honorable High Priest Grady P. Glawan; in the Voodoo world he's legit."

"I know I shouldn't be surprised by anything, but for some reason this is weird to me." I said with a laugh.

"I know, but he was a real help in our investigation a while back. He really is the real deal. He takes his practice very seriously; comes from a family of high priests. You should see his website. He has qualifications and testimonials. He offers guarantees on most of his services." I could almost see Bobby shaking his head in my mind.

"What kind of services does he offer?' I asked. Now I was curious.

"His website offers pretty much anything and everything. If you can think it up, it's covered; money spells, protection spells, enemy, revenge, bad day, health, beauty, and of course love spells." I made a mental note to check out his website as soon as I got off the phone. More entertainment,

I switched my phone to the other ear. "Why does he want to come to BonHaven? Wait, better yet, how does he even know about Bon-Haven?"

Bobby snorted. "Probably the same way everyone south of the Mason- Dixon line does; by reputation."

"You have a point. I'm fine with that if you are. When does he want to come?"

"Tomorrow. Once he found out it was BonHaven, he couldn't get here fast enough!"

"Well, maybe we can use that to our advantage." I said

"Maybe being the operative word; it seems like every time you say that it always backfires. Remember the time we had to arrest that lady for check fraud and the only place we could find her was at her gym?" Bobby was already laughing so hard he could barely get out the last word. "You said, and I quote, "That's my turf, I practically lived in a gym for eight years during wrestling training in high school and college. You can wait in the squad car if you want, I'll have her cuffed and in the back in less than five."

"Why do you have to always bring that up?" I groaned. "She just got in a lucky punch when she slipped out of my hold! Why would someone be wearing baby oil to work out? That's just stupid!" A year and a half later, and I'm still indignant about the whole thing.

"Jeeze, sensitive much? Sorry I brought it up. My point is, just because he's coming to us doesn't necessarily give us the advantage. Hopefully he can shed some light on the case."

"Hey" I sat up in the chaise lounge as a light bulb went on over my head. "Maybe we can take him by Bastion and let him look over the crime scene. Maybe he will spot some detail that means something to him that we overlooked as meaningless."

"I was thinking the same thing" Bobby said. I could tell by his tone he was grinning.

"That can be a test. If he truly is some Voodoo Hoodoo High Priest, he should be able to pick up on Bastian's vibe. If he acts as if it's just another tree, we know he's full of shit." I said, now firmly seated on my high horse.

"All right. I told him to be there at ten tomorrow. So I'll see you then?"

"Hey, wait. You already agreed he could come to my house?" I dropped the phone as I was talking so I grabbed for it and missed but luckily it fell onto the towel at the foot of the lounger. "Did you hear me?" I garbled into the phone.

"Yeah, I got it. And I said yes because I knew you would say yes because A) You wouldn't want to lose him as an expert and B) because you are curious to the point of getting yourself in the same situations as the cat of same curiosity."

"Hmmm. You know me well O Obi Won." I retorted back with a laugh. "O.K., I'll see you and Mr. Honorable tomorrow. Call me if anything new comes up. Otherwise, I am going back to working on my tan. Oh, and I was thinking about that rope. Maybe we can swing by De-Companse Antiques tomorrow. Maybe the owner can shed some light on its origin. He was out at BonHaven to talk with Momma about some antiques. He seemed to know what he was talking about. A little uptight, but acted like he knew what he was doing. It can't hurt right?"

"Sure. You're right; can't hurt. See you tomorrow."

And then it was just me and my journal. And a cocktail. Can't forget the important parts.

31

The next morning arrived with thunder in the distance and the occasional flash of lightening along a heavy promise of the real show to come later in the day when the heat came in. I puttered around the house and finally ended up on the back porch with another cup of coffee. Well that's simplifying my morning. Before I ended up on the veranda, I ran into Col. Farragut as I was coming out of the kitchen with said cup of coffee; which means Col. Farragut walked through the kitchen door as ghosts tend to do, while I ended up wearing the coffee and subsequently having to go back upstairs and change.

Everyone seemed to have left the house for the day already which meant I wouldn't have to worry about introductions to the Voodoo Priest. Not that it would be a problem, but my family would be so interested in him, they would keep him busy all day answering their questions. Bobby Glen and I would never get a chance to question him about the case.

At eleven-thirty when the doorbell rang, I jumped up to get the door, but Sadie beat me to it. I was just walking down the hall when Bobby Glen came in with the new detective, Carlyle, trailing behind.

"Hope you don't mind, but Lyle wanted to come along for the questioning. He brought up some good points this morning at the station." Bobby said motioning his thumb behind him.

"Hey Al, hope its OK that I showed up without an invitation." Carlyle said with a wave. It was funny how he spoke with a formalized version of the Southern language. Not perfect English, but a colloquial version. I liked it. A lot.

"No problem." I said. "The more clowns, the merrier. This could end up being a circus anyway." I gave him my best smart ass grin.

"Speaking of clowns, I came up with a sure fire invention!" Bobby snapped his fingers at me as we walked through the foyer. "You know those fold up car shades you put in the front window to keep the sun from heating up the inside of your car? Well, we make them with big clown faces. NO ONE is going to break into a car with clowns. No one fucks with clowns. They just don't. We could even branch out into home alarms with those little stickers you put in the window. It could have a clown face and the slogan "Don't F*** with a clown"

I rolled my eyes and was fixin to tear into him, but really, where would I start, when I had second thoughts. Maybe he was on to something. He was right, NO ONE messed with clowns.

Just then the doorbell rang and once again Sadie appeared out of nowhere to open the door.

All three of us had turned back towards the door from the hallway. So we all saw the sight at the same time. Sadie had the giant man with the tall hat standing in the doorway in a huge bear hug.

"I'll swan!" Sadie exclaimed. "I never expected to see you again in a thousand years!" she said to the finely dressed black man stepping into the house.

"Nor I you." The man answered back with a beautiful smile. He really was very handsome. His skin was deep ebony, but creamy looking; as if he used the world's best moisturizer. His eyes were almond shaped and the clearest of green. The color of a budding leaf just unfurled in the bright clear sunlight in the infancy of spring.

Sadie stepped back to allow him to fully enter the room. He was very tall and ducked slightly as he entered the doorway. The entry doors on BonHaven were over fifteen feet high, but his actions looked automatic as if ingrained from a lifetime of being overly tall. He was dressed in very fine clothes, complete with a waistcoat. He was carrying a black bag, like an old fashioned doctor's bag, made of very fine calfskin leather with an unusually colored alligator trim. If it were a handbag, it would be in the designer section. Do they have designer bags for specific professions? I'll have to make a mental note to ask Momma. She'll know. But the truly arresting thing about him was the top hat. It was what I had imagined for a Voodoo priest to be wearing. It was almost comically cliché. But it was very incongruous with the rest of his dress. The shoes he was wearing were $1,200 loafers or I would eat his hat.

Oh, Good Lord. Where were my manners?! Momma would have a hissy fit. After I collected my jaw from off the floor, I stepped forward, pushing my way between the two men in my way.

"Hello, I'm Alma Sue Babineaux." I said as I extended my hand.

"But of course you are." The man said as he took my outstretched hand, but instead of shaking it, raised it to his lips and kissed it. Whoa. "And I am the Honorable Percival G. Glawan. Most of those who know me well, intimate or enemy, call me Grady. I do foresee you to become a close friend, I hope."

Hmmm, how do I properly respond? First, I need to stop staring. Then figuring out how to make my knees work correctly, as they seem to be wobbly at the moment, would be a close second.

"Nice to meet you Grady. Thank you for taking the time to help with this case. Officer Taylor has briefed me and tells me you could be quite helpful in answering some of our questions. Especially in your field of expertise which he tells me you quite renowned for."

Grady made a praying hands motion and bowed his head in acceptance of the praise.

"What precisely did you need my help with?" He asked as he cocked his head to the side, seemingly very interested in whatever I had to say. It was very disconcerting to have his attention so focused entirely on whatever was coming out of my mouth. It made me nervous. It reminded me of someone, very strongly. I was having that classic déjà vous feeling. Some important connection was staying just out of reach. The more I concentrated on it, the more the connection danced just outside my comprehension. Grady was staring intently at me, looking me directly in the eyes, with a slight smile on his face. It was almost as if he knew what I was grasping for and was silently egging me on to make the connection. It seemed important.

Bobby cleared his throat just then to get my attention back on track and Grady sat back, the connection broken. "It may be a real lead or it may just be gibberish made to look like a voodoo connection to distract us and lead us in the wrong direction. I figured you would be the best expert to make that distinction." Bobby said to Grady. "From what I saw on the last case you helped with, the carving and symbols look real to me. But what do I know, that's why you're here."

"And here you are" Sadie said setting down a tray with a small assortment of finger sandwiches and tall glasses of iced tea so cold sweat was already running down the glass. "I never thought to see you again, especially here, at BonHaven. How's your grandfather?"

Grady smiled as he picked up one of the glasses from the tray and moved to sit down on the closest chair. He tipped the glass to his lips and took a long drink. "Perfect. Thank you. Grandfather is doing very well. He will be so excited to know you are here also."

The rest of us moved into the parlor to sit as well while watching the interplay between Sadie and Grady. But Sadie just smiled and said "Give him my best" over her shoulder as she left the room.

As they quiet settled over our little group, Grady leaned forward with his arm extended to shake Lyle's hand.

"I'm sorry, I forgot to introduce you" I said with a thump of my palm to my forehead. "Grady, this is Officer Carlyle Baveras. He is helping out with the case."

"Yes." Grady said as he shook hands. "I know of Officer Baveras."

After a stare down of a few seconds between the two, they seemed to communicate with their eyes and apparently come to an understanding. Grady turned to face me, Lyle dismissed from his thoughts.

"I am willing to help however I can, but before I agree, I must meditate and receive the blessings of the spirits. Can you give me a basic run down of the facts as you know them? Then assuming I am granted the spirit's agreement, we can meet in the morning."

I must have been staring again as he cocked his head at an angle willing me to give him an answer. I also must have been slow in doing so as Bobby threw a balled up napkin with a crust of a finger sandwich at my head.

"That would be fine. Will you be staying here at BonHaven? We have plenty of room."

"That would be very gracious of you. Wallace mentioned you would not be adverse to me staying."

All of us stared at him with our mouths open.

Then bombarded him with questions at the same time.

"Wait, you know Wallace??!" from both me and Bobby.

"Who is Wallace?" from Lyle "And why is that strange?"

Sadie appeared in the doorway at that moment with fluffy cream towels on her arms and beckoned for Grady to follow her. "Come with me Grady and I'll show you to your room. I got it ready yesterday afternoon for you." She shot me a smile.

As Grady stood to follow Sadie, he turned "I have business to attend to in the area, so will not be available until this evening if you need me. Thank you again for your hospitality."

And with that statement, both he and Sadie were gone.

As we stood and stared in shock at their retreating figures, Wallace popped through the wall, raised his eyebrows and wiggled them Like Grocho Marx or John Belushi's classic Animal House move. He laughed at our stunned look then gave a gracious bow before turning and gliding up the stairs to follow behind Grady and Sadie.

A quiet fell over the room again.

"Wow that was weird." I made a face at Bobby. "So, how long have you known this guy? And why does he seem to know my family? And Wallace? What's that about?"

Bobby stood and shrugged "Beats me. I just met him the one time we worked that case in Baton Rouge. He was polite, but distant. He seems at home here. Maybe you should tell me."

"Wait, who's Wallace? And why is this so weird" asked Lyle who looked amused.

Bless his little heart. He wasn't weirded out by any of this. And come to think of it, he totally looked at ease sitting on the chaise, not in awe of the house like most that enter for the first time. He also went right into the parlor as if he knew the layout of the house. Something to file and think about later. My Think About Later File was starting to overflow. It was due for some serious cleaning, but who has that kind of time?

"Never mind, let's get to the station and see if anything else has come up yet." I said as I herded everyone outside.

Thank God, they both just did what I asked. After that exchange, I don't think I could handle any more questions.

32

Grady had agreed to help in the investigation so after returning from a quick trip to check in at the station, we headed back to BonHaven. This was starting to have too much of a Scooby Doo feeling to it and was getting under my skin, but I had to admit it was fun. Bounding through the front doors, Bobby and I laid all the evidence and photos we had from the crime scene across the dining room table. The room was perfect as the floor to ceiling windows allowed for plenty of light and the long trestle style table made an excellent layout board so you could see the storyline unfold. Well unfold as much as it could with the facts on hand. We still were missing the biggest pieces of the puzzle.

Grady had relaxed and was walking around the table examining everything. He was carrying a large opened bag of Pork Rinds, munching as he studied the photos. He must have felt me staring at him. "I know" he said. "These" he said as he shook the bag, "are a disgusting habit, but I love them. I'm addicted. Would you like some?" he asked as he held the open bag towards me then Bobby.

"Uggh. No way. They're gross!" I scrunched up my face as Bobby took a few and popped them in his mouth, gave them a chew then held his mouth open wide so I could view his work. "Now give me a bag of Sour Cream and Onion Lays and you'd have to wrestle me for them" I smiled.

"Alright, I get the photos, but I don't feel them. I need to feel them; get a vibe. Can we go to the site? I may be able to pick up something from the tree. Living objects give off vibes. Plant, animals, humans; they all feel." He looked at me and Bobby as he said this. I think he thought he would have to convince us of this basic fact. Ha. Wait till he met Bastian.

"Sure." I said with a smile. "We have you listed as a consultant, so you could walk onto the crime scene no problem."

"Plus" said Bobby. "It's on Al's property."

"No shit." Grady exclaimed.

"Yep. Although, after you see the crime scene and Bastian, I think you might have even more questions." I said cryptically.

"Well," he said as he rolled up the bag of Pork Rinds and slipped them into his doctor's bag. "Let us go a larkin and find some truth!" He said while popping the last pork rind into his mouth and licking his finger. I really liked this guy – his coolness was off the chart.

As we were walking out the front door, Sadie came running into the hall carrying three bottles of water. "I figured you'd be thirsty after that nasty snack you insisted on. I could have fixed you something tastier than those!"

"Thank you for the trouble Sadie, but those "nasty" things hit the spot. I truly believe it sharpens my thinkin'" Grady said with a sly smile and a slight bow as he took the water from Sadie.

Sadie smiled as she shoo'd us out the door.

Grady climbed into the back of patrol SUV while Bobby and I had a brief skirmish for the driver's door. I decided it wasn't worth it, so skulked over to the passenger side, threw myself into the car and belted in. When Grady's chuckle started to turn into a guffaw, I silenced him with a finger pointed at his face, but I couldn't stop the corners of my mouth from turning up, so I turned around and faced the front as Bobby started the car.

"So boys and girls, where are we headed?"

"Just down the drive and halfway down the road you came in on." I pointed past the entry gate.

"That, is not only convenient, but might be meaningful" He said with a raised brow.

"We thought so too, but I'm leaning towards it just being convenient. I think someone knows the lore behind the site and is just capitalizing on it. But at this point, we just don't know." Bobby said with a shrug.

As we pulled off the road alongside the fence, Grady sat up and leaned into the front. "No way." He opened the door and threw himself out of the car, stumbling and catching his balance at the same time until he regained his fluid graceful stride and leapt over the fence to stand by the large tree.

"Grady, meet Bastian." I gestured.

Bobby and I stood and watched as Grady stood and stared. Then just as suddenly, he reached out to touch the imposing tree, but pulled his hand back just as quickly.

"He doesn't want to be touched." Grady said slowly as he turned to us with a look of awe.

"Yeah" Bobby said with a shrug of his shoulder. "He can be like that with strangers."

I nodded in agreement.

"So you both know about this?" He said and motioned to the tree.

"Most everyone knows there is something up with this tree, just not how much. If they had any idea of the truth, they wouldn't be able to handle it." I explained

"Yeah, you know, the whole "We are not alone thing"" Bobby added.

"Doesn't this play into the murder investigation?" Grady asked while crouching down to open his black bag.

"Yes and no." I said. "No, in that no one else on the force knows what Bastian really is. Yes in that we are hoping something "else" may crop up. We also were hoping that by bringing you in, you may pick up on more than just the symbolic aspects of the carvings. We are pretty sure this is not truly a ritualistic killing."

"You are right on that. He said while pulling out a fancy digital camera and fitting a custom lens on the base. "The carvings on the trunk" he paused as he fired off a few shots "are describing a plea to the underworld for success in a relationship. Unless the victim was dating a mythical Greek goddess, than I'd say this was all just for show." Grady smiled as he took a few more shots and walked around the trunk. "Either someone has a great sense of humor, or is just really stupid. In my line of work and I'm sure yours as well, experience leads me to lean toward stupid when referring to those on the wrong side of the law. Also whoever did this is not very original."

"What do you mean? Bobby asked.

"This particular drawing was used in an art exhibition awhile back. It made the local papers in the Sunday section on taboo art. It generated a lot of interest in people that really had no idea about art, but liked the idea it was "taboo". You would think they would dig a little deeper and do some research if they wanted to fool someone."

We all looked back and forth at each other grasping what this truly meant. The killer was staging the scene; and apparently not very well. This could be a huge break.

Bobby looked across the land and gestured towards Jimmy-Dons' house. "Has anyone talked to him yet? Maybe he saw something."

"He was out here mucking around Bastian a while back. Maybe he did."

"Probably not, knowing Jimmy-Don. If brains were leather, that boy wouldn't have enough to saddle a June bug." Bobby said with a grin.

I looked up just in time to catch that grin and Grady staring with a raised eyebrow followed by a grin of his own as he pulled more items out of his black bag he had placed on the hood of the cruiser. "What was this Jimmy doing with Bastian?"

"Jimmy-Don" I corrected. "He had decided his professional calling is being a ghost hunter and not a very good one I might add. Obviously." I gestured back at BonHaven. "He and his "crew" were filming him for some hair brained scheme to be a Ghostbuster. I was driving past on the way home from the station and saw the bunch of idiots. So, I stopped and casually told them to run on home as they were blocking the road. He said they were just finishing up and packed up and left. At the time it made me nervous because they gave up so quickly when I shut them down. I just recently learned why."

"And?" Grady motioned with his hand.

"Last week in the Piggly Wiggly I overheard the town gossip saying she saw a tape of "that tree" that briefly turned in to a human face, an evil scary face." I watched as both Bobby and Grady hung their heads and both laughed and looked freaked out at the same time. "I know. So I quickly shot the story down and laughed it off and told Miss Ethyl Jimmy Don faked it and she would lose her credibility if she spread it around town as the truth."

Bobby looked at me sideways "Did she buy it?"

"Have you heard anything?"

"No."

"Then I would say she bought it." I said smugly.

33

The next shift found me at the station sitting at my desk letting the information on the Bastian case rattle around in my head. After speaking with Grady more last night, I am pretty sure everything at the murder scene was a ruse. It was definitely meant to send us in the wrong direction. Why? Usually when someone tries to make you look the other way it's because something is happening right under your nose. So…what is right in front of me? I sat tapping my pen on my desk. I also started to smell a very strong floral odor. In our family a premonition was preceded by a smell; usually flowers or smoke. I concentrated on picking up on the vibe.

"Hello. Earth to Al." Jaynie, the staff records clerk, was trying to hand me a folder. That explains the smell. Her perfume. Oh well.

"Sorry" I said as I looked up and took the folder. "Just thinking"

"Too hard if you ask me. Someone can get hurt thinking that hard." She grinned and walked off.

She might have a point. But I know the answer IS right in front of me. I can feel it. If I could only put two and two together I thought as I stared down at my hand. I was admiring the ruby ring I found in the box with the diaries. I had been wearing it since I found it. Too bad the brooch was stolen – it matched perfectly and was probably worth quite a bit too. Not as much as the necklace that was also taken, but...

"Oh Good Lord." I slapped my forehead. "What if they're connected" That's what was right under my nose. I had a fortune in jewels stolen from my home. Where were they? Was someone expecting the police to look for them? As I got up and pulled out my cell phone to call Bobby, my spine started to tingle. I was on to something.

By the time I got to my car, I had already talked to Bobby and told him to meet me at Maude's for lunch. I could go over everything for him and maybe he could see what I was missing. I started the car and turned the AC on full blast. As the air turned icy, so did my thoughts. I really hadn't had time to dwell on the jewels being stolen as the murder case was dropped into my lap at the same time. But now that I took a second, I felt myself getting really pissed. Someone in my house, taking something from me.

By the time I got to the café, steam was coming from my ears. I walked in and headed to the booth where Bobby was waiting and threw myself in.

"O.K. then" he said looking at me. "Who licked the red off your candy?"

I had just opened my mouth to get my anger off my chest, when Lyle slid into the booth next to Bobby and across from me.

"Hello Susie. Hope you don't mind. I was with Bobby at an accident scene when you called him. I heard Maude's and wanted in." he wagged his eyebrows at me as he picked up Bobby's menu.

Bobby shrugged. I shrugged. Just like that my anger was gone. The waitress came and took our orders and left quickly. It seems cops in uniform freak most people out. Makes you wonder what skeletons they have in their closets.

"Wait" Bobby pointed at Lyle then me. "Did you just call her Susie? No one's called her that since her Daddy. Weird."

Lyle quickly looked down and fiddled with the menu the waitress left on the table in her rush to get away. He hadn't meant to call her that, it just slipped out. Hopefully she doesn't push it because he doesn't think he can lie to her.

"I know. I know. Whatever. You have to hear this. I'm pretty sure the Bastian case has something to do with the theft at my house."

"Wait, you mean Merle's necklace?"

At the look I gave Bobby, he held up his hands "I know, I know, it's not Merle's. You know what I mean" he said.

Lyle sat up straighter "Do you mean the necklace your aunt wore to the Gala?"

"Oh that's right. You were there." I nodded. "That necklace and an antique brooch were stolen from my house last week. The day before the murder. Or actually, the afternoon of."

"Maybe this is connected. Pretty big coincidence."

Bobby, Lyle and I looked at each other and said "And you know how I feel about coincidences" at exactly the same time and burst out laughing.

The waitress brought out our food at that moment and we all spent the next ten minutes with eating and small talk. Lyle talked a little of his previous department, but I found myself mesmerized by his voice. He and Bobby were talking about the Jubilee coming up at the end of the summer when Bobby threw his napkin at me.

"Hello. Are you even listening?"

"Would you stop throwing napkins at me! When did this become your new sport?"

"Wow" Lyle sighed. "You guys are like brother and sister, the way you fight all the time."

"Well," Bobby said as they all got up to leave putting money down on the table. "We pretty much are."

"So" Lyle said with a tilt of his head. "Are ya'll going to the Jubilee this summer? I hear it's predicted to be one of the largest on record due to the unusual tides this year."

"We never miss it. There was that one summer…" he said as he lowered his neck and looked up at me like I was a naughty student and he was my stern teacher.

"Now why do you always have to bring that up? I had nothing to do with it. You know it was Wallace. He thought he was being funny putting blue dye in my shampoo. He saw it in a movie and thought it was the perfect prank. There was no way I was going out in public, especially to the beach for the Jubilee, with blue hair. Long blue hair; like a mermaid. Can you even begin to imagine the grief I would have got on that?" I was still a little perturbed about missing that year.

Lyle coughed up the drink of sweet tea he had just taken. It actually spewed a little.

"There, see what you've done. You almost killed our new officer." I said with a laugh.

"A mermaid?" Lyle asked. "You looked like a mermaid?

"Well you know, the long blue hair. It's just what everyone would assume I was trying to look like. With the sea creatures basically beaching themselves for no good reason, it would kind of make sense."

"And what's wrong with that?" He asked. "I bet it's a good look on you." He said with a lazy grin.

I caught Bobby watching the interplay between the two of us out of the corner of my eye. The last thing I need is getting harassed by him about what I may or may not feel towards Carlyle.

"Knock it off, both of you. End of story. No mermaid."

Lyle must have decided it was time for a change of blue hair subject as well. "Have you ever really looked into the history of the Jubilee phenomenon? It's pretty amazing really."

Bobby laughed. "Most people don't think about it too much. Looking a gift horse and all that since it's an easy free meal. It doesn't seem fair to all the crabs and fish really does it. They just keep coming into the shallows acting all dazed and zombie like. It is literally fish in a barrel"

"Why do they act like that? I never really thought about it. Just that it's a fact that every year around the same time the sea creatures wander into Mobile bay and act crazy. Everyone comes down to the beach, scoops them up in buckets and has a great seafood dinner." I said.

"You know" Lyle said bending over the table and pointing his finger at me and Bobby with eyes wide open "I have even seen people pull pickup trucks to the water's edge and literally fill the truck bed with crabs. It's kind of disgusting" He sat back and we were all quiet for a minute. "They act drugged because they are. Something happens to the tide and the water loses its oxygen. They can't breathe. So they head towards shallower water where the water is more oxygenated."

"So it's like altitude sickness then" I surmised.

"Exactly." Lyle said putting his finger on his nose.

"Wait" Bobby threw a napkin at him. I gave him the exasperated look. Enough with the napkins. "Why do you know so much about it?" He asked.

"I suppose you could say I have a fascination with the sea." He shrugged.

"Well, all I know for sure is its too bad that it always happens right before dawn." I stated emphatically.

"Why does that matter?" They both said at once.

"Because, it means Thurman can move around then and he always heads down to the beach. Last year he ended up being stuck on beach road with crabs hanging off him and spilling from every pocket he had. He must have walked into the water to play with the animals and they attached themselves to him. The mayor was on the hot seat for months about the new statue dedicated to the Jubilee that just showed up at the end of Beach Road without Council approval. Nothing is allowed to happen in this town without every elected idiot having his say and rubber stamping everything in triplicate. Oh, let's not forget the costly studies required before anything can even be put forth as an idea. I know, I know, shut up about my politics. "I said waving my hands. Bobby knew I harbored a secret of giving Missy Hurlihy a run for her money for her council seat one day. We had a rivalry since high school and one day, I swear… "Anyway, everyone wanted to know where the money came from and why was it removed the next day. Who had it now and so on."

Both Bobby and Lyle were in hysterics by then. It was pretty easy to imagine the little boy statue covered in seaweed and crabs.

"I'll bet he was pretty pleased with himself, huh?" Bobby chuckled.

"You cannot imagine. He went down to the beach every night for two weeks and couldn't understand where the sea life went. He acted like he was the last pea at picking time. Even I almost felt sorry for him. Almost. Then he tied my shoe laces together and I remembered I don't like him."

Both Bobby and Lyle stood up to go while I slid out of the booth.

"It's that time. Gotta head back to the station." Bobby said. "Where're you headed?" He asked Lyle.

"I was thinking of heading over to the antique store on Main. I wanted to ask some questions about that rope."

"Do you mean DeCompanse Antiquities? I was gonna run by there too."

"If it's the one in the big brick building, then yes." He said with a shy grin. I kept forgetting he was new around here.

"Okay, how 'bout I meet you there in half hour." I said as I counted out tip money and left it on the table.

"Deal." Lyle said and headed out the door.

As they went their separate ways, they agreed to meet back at Bon-Haven later that evening to see if Grady came up with anything new, Carlyle secretly sighed to himself and relaxed a little. If Bobby and Al thought of each other as brother and sister, he could ask Al out. He stopped himself from doing a fist pump before he got to his patrol car. Barely.

"So." Bobby said grabbing Al by the arm as we walked down the steps from the café. "What was that all about?"

"Oh Good Lord! Who are you my father?" I said with a laugh. The laugh died on the air as I realized what I said. I'm not sure why it hit me like it did. Just a careless saying, but it made it seem more real.

"Hey, I'm just kidding Al. Carlyle seems like a stand up kind a guy. You could probably do a lot worse. He's no David."

"That's one way to cheer me up. Thanks a lot."

"You know what I mean." Bobby lightly punched me on the shoulder. He really did treat me like one of the guys. I loved him even more for that.

"I know. Thanks. So are you really going back to the station right now?" I asked.

"Yeah. Grady called and said he wanted to see the CSI photos that just came in. He has a hunch, but wants to see the photos first before he tells us anything. He also wants to stop and see Bastian again. Said he has something to talk to him about; go figure right?"

"OK. Cool. I'll swing by the antiques store and visit with the uptight weird little man and see if he can tell us anything. Meet you back at BonHaven later, K?"

"K, see you later." He said as he threw himself into his patrol car.

34

I had just arrived at the antiques building and parked in a space in front. It looked like Carlyle hadn't arrived yet so I thought this would be a good time to take advantage of my free few minutes to call Sugar. I had not talked with him in a few days which was unusual. We had both been so busy with our own busy little lives; we were missing our "us" time.

Sugar answered on the first ring. "Hey. I'm just closing up shop. I'll call you right back." And promptly hung up on me.

Nice.

Just then someone rapped on my window and scared the crap out of me. I looked up into Lyle's big seawater colored eyes. Hmmm, what would you call that color? Turquoise? Blue? Green? I put my money on turquoise. I tried to regain my composure by leaning down in the seat to search for my phone that I had dropped when he knocked on the window. When I sat back up, I caught a glimpse in the rearview mirror of John sitting in the backseat. Lyle didn't seem to see him, so I ignored him for the time being. But what the hell was he doing here? And in my backseat? He usually doesn't follow me around. Actually I can't think of a single time he has shown up in my car. As I got out of the car, Lyle took a step back so he wouldn't crowd me.

"Hey. You beat me."

I looked back into the car. Yep still there.

"Everything OK?" Lyle asked with concern. "You look like you've seen a ghost."

Ha.

"Yep. No problem. I actually just had to make some calls and make some notes for a report I need to file tomorrow, so I just moved my car down here from Mimi's and waited with the AC on."

"Multitasking. I like it." He drawled.

"Hey, I may talk slow with a drawl and use a lot of prepositions, but that don't mean I'm stupid." I said with a smartass grin.

'No maam. Wouldn't ever imply it." He said back with his own matching smartass grin. "Shall we?" he motioned towards the door.

The closed sign was just being turned over as we walked up to the door. The nattily dressed little gentleman looked us right in the eye then turned away. Ummm, I don't think so.

Lyle knocked on the glass. Hard.

When the gentleman turned around we both were holding up our badges.

Dare you.

You could see he was seriously thinking of not letting us in. You could also tell the instant he decided that would not be a prudent decision and turned the lock in the door. He stood back as we pushed the door in and entered the building.

"May I help you officers? As you can see we are closed. Perhaps you could come back tomorrow during business hours? I really must be going. I have several appointments I must attend to this evening. I do so despise being tardy. My clients have come to rely on my promptness." He said prissily.

Wow. He really is uptight. Even more so than when he was at Bon-Haven and I wouldn't have thought that possible. He was breaking out in a sweat across his brow and took out a cloth handkerchief to gently mop across his brow. Jeeze, could he really be that distressed about being a little late for an appointment. Funny man.

"No Sir." I stated. "We really need to speak with you tonight. It shouldn't take very long. We really just have a few questions relating to a case the Blakely Police Department is involved in and hope you can share your expertise on a particular subject."

"Oh. Very well then." His said and relaxed instantly. Well this is interesting. "I am Mr. DeCompanse. Welcome to my antiquities shop. What can I possibly help with?"

Carlyle stepped forward and began asking questions about the rope while I walked around the display cases.

I could hear them discussing the rope and Mr. DeCompanse explaining what the rope might be and what its uses were. Yes indeed, it was used on the antiquated large mast ships of days gone by, but you would never see it used today due to its weight. New rope was made of commercial manmade fibers that were stronger, much lighter and more durable in the elements. But he had never seen anything recently.

When I looked up Carlyle had a funny look on his face as Mr. De-Companse kept on with his story. He was on a roll now quoting dates of ships that passed through Mobile Bay and what their cargos were.

I'm not sure what prompted me to look at the front windows, but I did. What I saw was John standing outside with his nose pressed to the glass staring down at an object in the front display window. He then began some kind of a dance; or a spasm of some kind. He was stamping his feet while alternately pulling at his hair and wringing his hands together. He was a champion hand wringer. It made me wonder what his occupation was during his lifetime. Huh. Mental note. Also standing there was a child of about six. Staring at John. He obviously could see him, but his mother and older sister who were walking behind the little boy did not. The mother grabbed the little boys hand and dragged him along obviously asking what was so interesting in an antiques shop. The little boy protested, but was dragged behind the frazzled young mom who walked right through John which caused the little boy to scream. You could tell from the distressed look on the young woman's face that she was embarrassed of her child's apparent tantrum. What she didn't know was the little boy was gifted. He could obviously see John standing right there in broad daylight. Well obvious to me that is. Most anyone else would just see a child having a fit and give the woman a dirty look for not being able to control her child.

At that moment of the woman passing through him, John looked up and made eye contact with me. He just stood there looking so forlorn. Then he pointed at the display case and faded away.

What the hell?

I really don't have time for John's theatrics. Just then I glimpsed a velvet covered display board.

"This is beautiful." I said loudly pointing to the empty display board propped up on a counter. I had said that in what I hoped was a voice meant to interrupt.

"Do you mean the empty display?" Mr. DeCompanse said with a raised brow indicating he thought he may be dealing with a mentally unstable person.

"Yes" I said. "I so love the color purple. I've never seen a jewelry display case this color. Aren't they usually black?"

"Why yes. You have a good eye. I prefer to have items with originality. I have these specially made for me by a seamstress in New Orleans." He said with pride.

"Well they are beautiful and must have cost a preeeetttty penny." I said with exaggerated admiration. And knowing he has a reputation for being frugal made it even more interesting. Actually it has been said he squeezes a quarter so tight the eagle screams.

"Officer Baveras, do you have the information you need?" I tried to send him telepathic thoughts for him to pick up on, but it wasn't working. He just stared at me kind of squinting.

Then all of a sudden he got the hint. "Yes, I believe we do have everything we need." He said while closing his notebook and putting it back in his shirt pocket.

He turned back to Mr. DeCompanse and shook his hand. "Thank you for letting us in and answering our questions. I know we have kept you."

"Yes, thank you." I said while turning to also shake his hand goodbye. "I hope we haven't kept you too long for your appointments. I'm sure your clients will understand when they hear how you were of service to your community." I said with a sweet smile

"Think nothing of it." He said. "I always want to help whenever I am able. I am glad I had some knowledge that could be of use." He said puffed up with pride.

Lyle and I turned to leave and realized we were still locked in the store. Evidently the proprietor locked the door behind us. Mr. DeCompanse was reaching between us to place the key in the lock before we had a chance to question him about it. The lock made a clank as the tumblers fell into place unlocking the door. I pulled the door open and we stepped out into the twilight, thick humidity and a huge cloud of gnats.

The only downfall to living in the south, at least that I will admit to, are the amount of bugs constantly present; drives me nuts.

After we both start waving are arms to clear a path to walk through, we turn to face each other at the same time and say "He's lying; or up to something."

"Okay." I say. I think we both picked up on the same vibe.

"And what was John doing on the sidewalk?" Lyle said with a chuckle.

"You saw that?" I said and started to freak out. "You can see him?"

"Why wouldn't I? Oh wait, you mean because most people can't? I'm not like most people; not by a long shot."

I was starting to get that. "I'm not actually sure what he was doing. I think he might have been trying to get my attention. For what I have no clue, but I intend to find out as soon as I get home tonight. But what do you mean you think Mr. DeCompanse was lying back there?"

"Not think he was lying." Lyle said adamantly. "He was lying."

"How could you know that? I know he is weird and extremely uptight, maybe that is what you were picking up on." I suggested.

"No Susie, he was lying. He said he had never had that rope in his shop. He was lying."

"Don't call me that. And how do you know he was lying?"

Why can't I call you that? It suits you. And I know he was lying because I could smell it."

"Huh?" I said dumfounded. And not just because of the Susie thing.

"Smell it?"

"I know that sounds weird, but I have an unusually sharp sense of smell; kind of like a dog." He said smiling sheepishly.

"But how would you know that?" I asked trying to stay professional, but it was becoming a losing battle.

"I smelled it when it was brought in to the station for processing into evidence. It actually reeked. I could smell it even after it was put into plastic and put into storage."

"That's right! You walked by and said the rope smelled funny the morning we booked the evidence. I just thought you meant at that moment."

"Yes. And I could smell it the minute we walked into his shop just now; which means it was here fairly recently. So I know he is lying about the rope."

"And if he's lying about the rope, what else is he lying about. And why?" I said with a frown. I pulled out my phone to call Bobby who picked up on the first ring.

"Hey, what's up?" He asked.

"Hey, Lyle and I just left the antique dealers. Something is definitely up here. I don't think the uptight little man could have done it, but he is involved somehow. When we first got here he started sweating and was as nervous as a cat in a room full of rockers. Lyle picked up on the smell the rope had and John was standing in front of the store window while we were there AND Lyle saw John!" I rambled.

From the other end of the phone Bobby didn't miss a beat "So Lyle can see John and has super smelling capabilities like Aqua Man and the antiques dealer is quite possibly a bad guy. Did that cover it all?"

If I hadn't known him forever, I would think he is being sarcastic. But I have and he isn't, he is just putting his thoughts in order. "Yep. That about covers it." I said looking at Lyle who was nodding his head as if he could hear the whole conversation. Who knows, maybe he could; another mental note to file later. Good Lord! I have got to clean out that file.

"Yeah, you got it" I said into the phone and gave Lyle thumbs up. "We can discuss it more tonight O.K.? We'll see you back at BonHaven but I wanted to give you a heads up so you could be thinking about it."

"Thanks. Grady is meeting me here at the station soon, so I'll pass it along to him. Maybe he can think of something we are not looking at."

"Great. Good idea. We'll see you later." As I put the phone back in my pocket I realized I was just assuming Lyle would be there, but I never asked him. I was suddenly shy with the thought of asking him. What the hell??! He is a co-worker. Yeah I might find him interesting and maybe even hot, but he is still a coworker. Jeeze Al, shake it off. You're a professional; act like one.

"Hey Lyle, you gonna come by BonHaven? Bobby and Grady are meeting there after shift and we can go over all we know" I said nonchalantly; or at least I hoped it sounded nonchalant.

"Sure. I think that's a good idea; use a fisherman view. If we come at it from four different directions then we'll have a better chance of nothing escaping from the net, right? At least that's what my uncle says is a fisherman's view."

Hmmm. There was that unique thing again. It made sense, but the wording he uses is just...off.

As we were walking back to our cars, I kept trying to grasp at something that was just out of reach, but to many thoughts racing through my head and not enough cans to catch them and examine them closer. I needed to use a fisherman's view. Good Lord! It was starting to make sense.

"Hey Suze, You OK" He asked touching my shoulder.

I spun around to face him "Why do you keep calling me that?"

My question seemed to catch him off guard. He was genuinely surprised at my reaction.

"I don't know. It just seems to fit you. Why? Is it a bad thing to call you a nickname? Have I breached some form of official protocol? Is it because we work together?" He actually seemed upset.

"No, it's not like that." I said hesitantly. "It's just that...only Daddy ever called me that name. Since he died no one uses it, so it just kind of came out of the blue. Even Wallace, who loves to torment me, used to jokingly call me that with a sneer of course, but still used the nickname. He hasn't called me that in two years, so it's just a shock." I explained.

"I'm sorry." he said and reached out to touch my arm again. I felt that slight tingle again. I felt it every time he touched me, but I just shrugged it off as my imagination. But this is not my imagination. It's real. I know he feels it too because his eyes widened a little when he touched me. So I know it's not just me. This is nuts.

"No." I said with a shrug. "It's fine. Actually I like it. Like I said it's just a jolt to my system and reminds me of Daddy. But don't sweat it." I gave a small smile to let him know I really meant it was OK.

"So, I'll meet you back at BonHaven after shift, OK?" he said with a nod as he got into his car.

"OK. See Ya." I answered back and climbed into my car as well.

35

As it was just after seven, Al figured this would be a good time to catch everyone at the house in the same place. Dinner was usually at six thirty so it was a good bet. As she dialed the home number, she was deciding how to word her demand. Should she be official or ask sweetly? The wise sage who penned the adage "You can catch more flies with honey than Vinegar" never met the group living at BonHaven. They would respond to the vinegar just to be ornery. Well, except Thurman, the honey would definitely work better for him.

Lyci answered the phone with "Good idea. I will have everyone in the front parlor at eight thirty. See you soon" and hung up.

I didn't say a word.

I guess that settles it.

Since Al wasn't sure in what form the notice had been given to the family including the Uglies to meet promptly at eight thirty in the front parlor, she wasn't really sure what to expect; but obviously everyone knew she meant business as they were all gathered and waiting when she came in the room. Even Aunt Leila Mae was there. Sitting on the sofa looking perfect; not a blond hair out of place in her chignon. Her eyes glittered with excitement. Wonder why? I had better talk with her privately and see what she's up to now. So everyone was actually there, well, with the exception of Wallace she noticed. Just as she was getting ready to yell his name he came sauntering through the wall to stand by Uncle Howard. His posture and attitude said everything one needed to know about his feeling for being summoned for a mandatory family meeting. As she walked further into the room, she made eye contact with everyone and placed her hands on her hips; the leather of her service belt creaking as she was still in uniform as she rushed straight from the station. John was looking worried as usual, although he had not started with the hand wringing yet, so there was that.

"Alma Sue" Momma said. "Please stop trying the police intimidation tactics, they don't work here. Please just get on with whatever this is about please."

"Momma, just hear her out. This is actually important." Lyci said sitting up straighter and leaning towards Al.

Hmmm Al thought I must really be on to something if Lyci is interested.

"Where's Thurman" I asked as I looked around the room. Everyone looked around the room also like they could spot something different. Wallace even looked up. That was a frightening thought; Thurman skittering about on the ceiling. I shivered. Great now I would have nightmares about that; at least it would take the place of the sheep's heads. Although I'm not sure which is worse? No, Thurman is definitely worse; he lives here!

"I will find him" John said already out of the room.

"John, wait, you need to hear this" I said to thin air. He was already gone.

Wallace starting making rolling motions with his hands indicating get on with it.

"So I am sure you would all like to know the meaning of this impromptu family meeting." I was met with curious stares. Except from Wallace of course, who managed to look bored and perturbed at the same time; no small feat.

"It actually has to do with a case I'm on."

"You mean the Bastian case right?" Lyci piped up.

"Well yes and no. I also mean our theft here at BonHaven."

"Whatever would that have to do with the Bastian case?" Momma asked.

"I'm not one hundred percent sure yet. It's just a feeling I have. Bobby, Carlyle and."

"I do like that young man Al."

"Momma, please let me finish."

"Well, I do. And that's all I will say about it."

"I thought he was very handsome." Mae chimed in. "And a gentleman."

"When did you see him Aunt Mae?" Lyci asked.

"At the Huntington Gala; and he looks marvelous in a tux."

Momma was nodding her head in agreement. Uncle Howard was looking at the floor and laughing.

I definitely did not care for where this conversation was going. "May I please continue?"

Everyone murmured their I'm sorry's and I went on. "So, Bobby, Carlyle and I" I narrowed my eyes and looked around the room daring anyone to interrupt me again. "were at Maude's for lunch earlier and we were talking things through when it dawned on me that our theft happened the day of the murder and wasn't that a coincidence and how we didn't believe in coincidences. It just hit me they were connected."

"Did you order the French dip?" Uncle Howard asked. "That's my favorite. I order the same thing every time I go to Maude's; with onion rings. They have the best onion rings. They remind me of Shoney's. Remember Bob's Big Boy? They had they absolute best onion rings; especially with a chocolate shake. Remember Merle, they were real thick like homemade." Everyone was staring at him like he was nuts. "What? Doesn't everyone miss Shoney's?"

"You're right you know." Lyci looking at her nails as if everyone should know that.

That brought the conversation back to the subject at hand.

"About what? I asked Lyci.

"The two cases being connected. They are." She said with a shrug

"A little help here?" I was thinking of yelling at her, like I would my sister, but I figured I should treat her like an informant.

"I can't be specific. What I see isn't always linear. Just glimpses really. But you are on the right track. I can definitely tell you that."

"Alright. Fair enough. So let's go over what we know."

Just when we were getting down to the details Sadie escorted in Bobby and Grady with Carlyle on their heels.

"Hey everybody.' Bobby waved.

"Good evening all, sorry to interrupt." Grady said politely while he put a finger to his mouth and sat on one of the side chairs.

Lyle just stood beside Bobby and gave an embarrassed wave. He obviously didn't like being the center of attention.

I had already briefed them at the station about this family gathering and said they might want to be present just in case anyone said anything that might be useful in our case. Besides, we were meeting after to discuss whatever Grady wanted to discuss.

"OK ya'll. So what we know. Merle brought back a priceless set of jewelry. Mae wore said jewelry to Gala, where it was seen by a million people."

"I only wore the necklace Alma Sue." Mae said with a dismissive wave of her hand. "And it was not seen by a million people as you say, there were only 857 persons in attendance. I checked. And I returned it the next day. I put the necklace in the blue cut crystal dish on the table in the entryway."

"Right. I stand corrected." I said seriously. "So yes, the necklace was in the dish, I saw it myself. One earring was with Merle the morning she woke up."

"I put that earring in the dish on the sideboard in the entry hall myself. Merle said.

Lyci raised her hand "and I put the other earring in the dish. Thurman had it. Wallace and John took it away from him and gave it to me and I put it in the dish with the other one."

"Right. I saw that. So the necklace and both earrings were in the dish on the sideboard in the entryway. I also put a brooch in the dish. The one from the storage boxes Sadie brought down from the attic. I was going to take it in to the antiques store to be valued for insurance."

"I have been meaning to get over to that antiques store myself. I heard they carried memorial rings and wanted to buy one for a friend as a gift. They are so hard to find these days. The collectors snap them up the minute they come on the market." Mae said.

"What's a memorial ring" Bobby asked.

"Mae turned to face Bobby in the back of the room. "They are pieces of jewelry from the Victorian age, usually rings that memorialize someone's death. They can be from other time periods, but the Victorian ones are the better collectable items. They are usually very simple but beautiful. Some can be quite morbid with bits of the deceased person's hair or ashes made into some part of the jewelry."

"Pardon me maam, but that seems pretty disgusting." Bobby grimace.

"Well to each his own". Leila Mae shrugged off the comment.

I was losing control again. Just as I puffed out my chest to make some kind of ridiculous statement, Wallace stated the obvious.

"So who was the thief that came into this house and stole from us?"

John came floating into the room carrying Thurman by the suspenders he was wearing at the moment creating the sensation of Thurman floating in midair; at least until he gave him a toss so Thurman rolled into the room and came to a stop at my feet.

I just pointed at the sofa next to Momma and Thurman quickly slunk over to sit.

"So? Any ideas who could be the thief?" Wallace repeated.

"The thief?" John repeated. "Do you mean that brute of a man who stole the jewelry from the sideboard last week? Can you believe the audacity of that man?!"

"John!"

"You knew??"

"All along, you knew? And you didn't say anything"

Wallace had materialized right beside John and was now throttling him. It was a good thing he was already dead. With three police officers in the room, it could have gotten ugly.

The shouts were coming from everyone; all around the room. It was chaos for a few minutes until Bobby got everyone's attention and Grady and Carlyle tried to pry Wallace off John. This was pretty difficult considering you can't really grip a ghost.

Lyci was just watching with a giant smile on her face. She was really enjoying this. Actually so was Uncle Howard.

It was at that exact moment that Sugar walked into the room.

"Ya'll didn't tell me you were having a party. My feelings are hurt." He said with a grin.

"Sit DOWN Sugar, don't make this worse than it already is." Momma said exasperated and more than a little embarrassed.

Sugar went and sat down on the other side of Thurman who was sitting with his hands folded. Thurman was just happy to not be involved at this point. It's usually him that is causing this kind of ruckus.

Wallace finally lets go of John and walks to the other side of the room disgusted with the turn of events.

John glides over to Wallace quickly and starts wringing his hands. "I did try to tell you. Don't you remember the evening I was looking everywhere for you but couldn't find you. You were gone all day and all through the night. I looked everywhere for you. Remember Howard, I even asked you the next morning if you had seen Wallace." He looked at Uncle Howard with a pitiful expression.

"He's right, I remember that morning." Uncle Howard confirmed.

"Wait." I said. "I remember that too. Remember Uncle Howard, I said I was looking for Wallace and you mentioned John was also looking for him, something about having to discuss a very important problem.""Yep. That's exactly what I said." He nodded.

"Where were you anyway?" I asked Wallace.

Wallace looked sheepishly away and glanced at Carlyle. Why the hell was he looking at Carlyle?

"Well?" I pushed.

"I was away on business. You do realize I have a life other than hanging around BonHaven. You know what I mean" He clarified as I gave him a withering look at the have a life comment.

"OK. Whatever" I said. "But John, why didn't you tell someone else what happened?"

All eyes were now on John. "Well." He started while wringing his hands in an even more agitated manor if that was possible. "I saw the man come in through the screened room at the rear of the house and I followed him. I wasn't sure why he was here but I thought I should keep a close watch on him. So he snuck down the hall and into the entryway. He seemed to know exactly where he was going and what he was doing. He walked right over to the crystal bowl and picked it up and dumped the jewelry into a handkerchief and put it in his pocket."

"But John." Momma questioned. "Why would you tell me or Alma Sue?"

"Well Maam, At first I was worried, but then I remembered how upset Miss Al was when they jewels showed up and how worried she was someone might find out. So I thought maybe the necklace being taken was a good thing and Miss Al wouldn't have to be upset anymore."

There was a collective "Oh, how sweet."

But then there came the grumbling. "But John, Some stranger was in the house. What if he was dangerous?" This from Aunt Merle.

Sugar broke the tension as only he could. "Was he handsome?"

Of course we all broke out in laughter after that. Sadie brought in a cart with glasses and a pitcher of sweet tea and cookies and coffee for those that wanted some refreshment. After we all had taken a break, the questions flew.

"So, would you recognize the man if you saw him again?" "Did you try to stop him" "How did he get away?"

"Of course I would recognize him again." John said indignantly.

"And what the hell was that you were doing earlier at the antiques shop? It looked like you were having a fit. And you do realize that little boy walking by with his mother totally saw you right?" I asked John

"No. I did not notice that. I was too busy trying to get your attention, not that you noticed, Thank You very much. See what happens when someone tries to do you a favor? He said putting his hands on his hips for emphasis.

"And what pray tell were you trying to get Al's attention for? And since when do you go into town? You always say you are afraid of being noticed." Wallace asked John.

"I just thought Al might want her brooch back. She had only just discovered it and I thought it was unfair to lose it so quickly."

"What brooch? Do you mean the one that was in the boxes from the attic? The same one I put in the crystal dish and was stolen along with Merle's necklace?" I asked. I was dumbfounded at this point.

"I thought you said it's not Merle's necklace." Bobby said across the room with a smirk on his face.

"You know what I mean. Don't be a smartass. We may be on to something here."

All of a sudden Granddaddy was awake; he had been dozing in a chair tucked into the corner. "Did you say a brooch from the attic? Was it with some old boxes full of ledgers?"

"Yes. Sadie found them a few weeks ago. Do you know anything about them?" I asked excitedly

"I know there are boxes and boxes of family ledgers and diary up there. It's always been a family tradition to keep a personal diary and ledgers regarding the properties. I thought Fraser discussed them with you and Bug."

The whole family was looking at him like he had grown horns. He never discussed anything with us anymore. We just assumed he was a little senile, or a lot.

"No, he never told me anything. Maybe he talked about it with Bug. I'll have to call him tomorrow and ask." Another mental note. I hated to bother my brother. It seemed he was always busy with something or other up at the capitol. For all I know he could be Governor by now. I snickered out loud. Everyone looked over at me and I pretended a cough to cover it up. Lyle was staring. Oh Good Lord! I started blushing again.

"Ollie, is there something in the household ledgers we need to know about? Momma asked.

""No, No, probably not. But Alma Sue should be readin those diaries. That's for sure." He stated solemnly. "And I'm glad you found that brooch. It belonged to my great aunt and she was known in here day for being a real firecracker. A lot like you." He said pointing at me. "There was a ring too. They were supposed to have been kept together."

"I have it." I said holding out my hand where it had been since I had found it in the box and placed it on my finger. "I just put the brooch in the dish so I wouldn't lose it. Funny huh?"

"Yes" John said. "Now do you understand why I was trying so desperately to get your attention? And you were more interesting in critiquing my dance moves." John said with a curt nod.

"OK. I apologize for that. I should have taken you more seriously. I knew when I saw you in the backseat of my car something was up. I just had a lot on my mind and didn't really think it through, so again I'm sorry." What I couldn't say was that I had Lyle on the brain and couldn't think straight; especially with him standing in the room. I made eye contact with him at that exact moment and blushed. Jeeze, get a grip.

Bobby caught the look and a small smile formed on his lips. I shot him a dirty look while my family watched in amusement. "So why would an antiques dealer have a piece of stolen jewelry on display right in the front window?' Lyle asked

"Because maybe he doesn't realize its stolen." said Grady being the voice of reason.

"That's right. Mr. DeCompanse is known to purchase trinkets to resell. We do not have a Pawn shop in Blakely as our town council feels that they are distasteful and tend to invite a more undesirable sort and therefore refused to allow one to open in town; so rather than drive in to Spanish Fort, some people choose to sell their lesser pieces of jewelry or things they no longer wear to the antiques dealer" Aunt Mae stated with authority. "The same thing is true in St. Elmos."

"OK. Makes sense so far. So we go and ask some more questions of Mr. DeCompanse tomorrow. Who's in?" I asked.

Before anyone could answer John chimed in again. "You know, it is interesting that we are discussing Mr. DeCompanse as he was here the day that brutish man snuck into the house and stole the jewelry." He mused while rubbing his chin in thought.

"Wait. Were they together?!" Bobby and I said at the same time.

"No, I don't believe so." He answered. "But I couldn't honestly say. I was too busy watching the other man who came walking up the drive alone. That was what caught my attention in the first place. I had just walked by the kitchen window and spotted him out of the corner of my eye. I thought it unusual to be walking up the drive. Even the looky loo's who come to see the house are in a car. Why would anyone be walking in the midday heat? "

"What were you doing in the kitchen?" Sadie asked as she had just stepped back in the room to collect the cart she had brought in for the snacks.

"I was in the pantry speaking with"

"Don't you dare even say it John! Why do you speak with that thing? It looks like it fell out of the ugly tree and hit every branch on the way down and is meaner than a stepped on snake." Sadie said.

"Well" John stated "That is where I was. I am just trying to tell the story. Shall I continue?" At everyone in the rooms shouted yes, he went on "As I was saying, I saw the man walking up the drive, alone, and I was suspicious. I looked for Wallace, but like I said before he was nowhere to be found. So I decided to follow him. I met him at the rear stairs. He walked in through the screened porch and through the mudroom into the hallway. He seemed to know exactly where he was going. He waited just outside the kitchen. He must have heard the voices of Miss Marianne and Mr. DeCompanse. Mr. DeCompanse had just arrived and he said he was here to re evaluate the radio lamps for a potential buyer." "Yes, that's correct." Momma said nodding

"Then what?" I urged him on. Bobby and Lyle had both taken out their notebooks at this point and were taking notes. Grady was intently listening.

"Well, after Miss Marianne and Mr. DeCompanse went into the front parlor, the man tip toed through the hall to the front entry. He walked to the sideboard straight to the crystal dish and emptied the contents into a handkerchief and put them in his pocket. Oh, he did wipe the dish with his sleeve before he left. He obviously did not want to leave any fingerprints behind."

"Then What?' Wallace was starting to look angry

"Then he went back the way he came and out through the screened porch. He walked back down the drive and that's it."

"But I don't understand why you didn't follow him." Lyci asked "I think you dropped the ball there dude."

"But I explained all that" he said in a whiny voice. "I thought Al would be happy the necklace was gone. I didn't know the brooch was in the dish. Had I known I would have followed him. I know you wanted that brooch Al, I'm sorry." He said as he looked at me eyes brimming with tears. Can ghosts cry? I've never paid attention. Hmmm, another mental note.

The family meeting broke up shortly after Granddaddy dropped his bombshell. The family was pretty much left speechless after he had his say; whether from what he actually said or just due to the fact that no one has heard him talk that much in years is up for debate. Either way, I think the family was done for the night. It was very informative though. John was just a font of information. Why he didn't tell someone sooner was beyond me; but in his head, the matter was resolved. I stopped Sadie as we were all heading out of the front parlor. I had questions.

"Sadie, what made you think of bringing me the boxes from the attic in the first place? I mean why not Momma? Did John say something?"

"John? Lordy, if that man had a thought on his own it would die of loneliness! No, it was Wallace that mentioned you had started keeping a diary. When I saw the boxes with your name on them."

"Not actually MY name, remember it was another Alma Sue." I interjected

"Well right. O'course. But still it did say Alma Sue. So I opened them to see if it was something you might need and as I was already up there it made sense that I just bring 'em on down. But when I saw what was in them, I thought for sure you would want to take a look see through them." She said walking out of the room with a shrug of her shoulder.

Okay something new to be concerned with; why was Wallace spying on me?

Bobby, Carlyle, Grady and I had moved to the library to discuss what we knew. Sugar followed behind quietly. Actually he had been pretty quiet ever since Momma had chastised him earlier.

36

We were all pretty quiet for awhile. I think we were just trying to digest everything. We had a lot put in front of us in the last hour.

Bobby spoke up first "So. Where do we begin? I wish we had the victims ID back. That would be a big help. But until then lets hit what we know."

"I think it is a really big coincidence that the thief was here the same time as the antiques dealer." I said

"I agree." Lyle said

"Me too." Grady added.

Bobby just nodded his head. We all knew how he felt about coincidences. We all felt the same way and it wasn't just a hunch, but based on our collective past experiences.

Just then there was a huge crash in the dining room and a ruckus coming from the other end of the hall. Before we could even react, Thurman came skidding into the room and weaved in and out from every chair in the room with Cooper following closely on his heels barking as loud as he could. If dog barks could communicate feeling his definitely did. If the bark was vocalized it would probably sound like a child complaining his favorite toy was taken away from him. He would have good reason to feel that way as Thurman indeed had his favorite toy. A combination platypus and duck which was dangling on a rope that Thurman had tied around his waist. There was just enough slack that it dragged behind him on the floor to tease the poor dog into chasing him. Which of course, Cooper did.

Thurman ran up the wall like a race car banking on a high turn at Talladega and ricocheted back into the hall. The barking quieted as they got further away.

No one said a word or missed a beat. See what I mean by normal being relative around here?

"So, the rope; let's start with that" Lyle said I'm sure we were all thinking the same thing because of the Thurman incident being fresh in our minds. "I am absolutely one hundred percent that the rope our victim was tied to Bastian with was at the antiques shop at some point in the very recent past."

"And my brooch which was stolen from BonHaven along with the necklace and earrings is, according to John, at the antiques shop at this very moment." I said matter of factly. "Which we will verify tomorrow of course."

"The fact that the antiques dealer himself keeps popping up is pretty telling" Grady said

"Yes, but that little man is so uptight. I can't for the life of me picture him getting his hands dirty." I laughed at the mental picture that popped into my head at that moment; a cartoon version of Mr. De-Companse dressed in his bow tie looking down at his dirty hands with a bubble above his head saying "Oh my Gaaawd."

"Yes and Ted Bundy would never have been pegged to be a serial killer is we just used his looks as the only criteria" Bobby said making the mudge face.

"Touché. Point taken." I agreed

"Alright. We all agree that we need to take a closer look at Mr. De-Companse as a suspect; but a suspect as what, the murderer or with the theft?" Lyle asked

"Maybe both." We all looked at Grady, surprised he added that.

We were all quiet for a moment trying to absorb that idea.

"But why?" I pointed out "What do they possibly have in common?"

"Well the obvious connection is the jewelry. One of them stole them from BonHaven and the other had a piece of it in his shop."

"I know Bobby." I said. "But what if he just was on the receiving end of the fence? Whoever stole it knew they could use him as a pawn and just got rid of the brooch quickly. They probably figured they could make big money selling the necklace and earring set on the black market. There's no way they could sell it at auction. They can't show provenance. A reputable auction house wouldn't touch it with a ten foot pole. It's the same reason I didn't want it around as I couldn't insure it; I couldn't show where it came from. Even if I could, no one would believe me." I said throwing up my hands. "And why aren't you freaked out about any of this? Either one of you?" I said with exasperation looking at both Lyle and Grady. "Sugar and Bobby have lived with it long enough so they don't get weirded out by much, but you two...You should both be running for the hills screaming."

At exactly the same time they both said "Believe it or not, I've dealt with weirder." They both laughed while I stared at them with my jaw on the ground. This was definitely getting weird and not in a relative way.

"OK, whatever. My original point was I don't want to go in tomorrow accusing an innocent man. I think we need to be subtle until we get more info. I also think we should keep this to ourselves until we know more. Agreed?" I looked around to make sure we were all in agreement.

Grady clapped his hands together and started to rub them back and forth like he was going to perform a healing ritual. "Hot Damn! This is exactly what I was hoping for when you called me to BonHaven." Then promptly threw himself into an armchair draping his legs over one side. "But I have been thinking about something all day. Why didn't Bastian just do something to prevent the murder? Why would he let himself get defaced with the graffiti? Aren't you curious about that?"

Sugar was interested in that answer "Yeah, why would he just allow it to happen? I mean it wasn't like he could speak up or anything, but he could have, I don't know, maybe dropped a branch on the guys head or something."

"Fair question" Lyle said looking at me.

"I don't know; why are you looking at me? What am I? His best friend? Why didn't you just ask him? You were out there today." I said throwing it back at Grady.

"I did. Wanna know his answer?"

We all just stared.

"His response was ask Al."

"What?!" I was dumbfounded. Again.

"Yep. He just kept saying ask Al. And I swear to God, he shrugged."

Sugar giggled then shut up when Grady gave him a look.

"What did he mean by that?"

"I don't know Grady. How am I supposed to know what a centuries old human turned tree thinks?"

"You must have some idea. Think about it a minute." Bobby pushed.

"I really don't know. I mean I know he has done things in the past and I." I stopped mid sentence and slapped my forehead. "And I told him to keep his mouth shut no matter what and stay out of trouble. I told him if he caused any more problems or even attracted the least bit of attention I would drag out Daddy's chainsaw."

Everyone in the room groaned. "Don't blame me for this. How could I know a murder would be involved? He usually just scares people. Oh, poor Bastian. The one time he really needed to do something and he was scared of my reaction!" I felt terrible. What if I really could have prevented a man's death?

Lyle, Sugar and Grady all came over to give me a hug. Lyle let Sugar go first but pushed Grady back. Grady just held up both hands and walked away. Interesting.

"It's not your fault." Sugar said. "Of course there was no way to know something like this could happen."

"But you need to go talk to him. Maybe he can tell you what we need to know." Bobby pointed out the obvious.

To change the subject Lyle said "OK. What else do we need to look at? Al, didn't you say you needed to talk to someone who showed up at the crime scene?"

"I did." I said regaining my composure. "Jenny Katherine's nephew. He's a sixteen year old punk that spends a lot of time trying to prove he's tough. He was parked by Bastian with his truck full of other punks piled into the bed of the pickup. He was standing on the tailgate yelling something about the carvings on Bastian. I couldn't hear it very clearly, but I'm pretty sure he said he knew what those carvings were. He said he had seen it before. I meant to call and get his number from her today, but when we had to respond to that accident on the turnpike, I forgot all about it."

"Alright" Bobby said writing it in his notebook. I will take care of that in the morning. Actually, I might give her a call tonight to get the number. I've got Wiley's phone number at home. We used to play poker together sometimes. He always cheated at Texas hold'em so I backed out of the group. Cheating makes me crazy." He said with a grin. "Anyway if I can find out how to reach him tonight, I can get a hold of him first thing tomorrow."

Bobby stood up and put away his notebook. "I'm done. Too pooped to pop. I say we call it a night." As he looked at his watch, he was genuinely surprised how late it was. "Wow, it's after eleven. I gotta go." He said walking out of the library. We all followed him down the hall and into the front foyer. As he opened the door there was a huge rumble of thunder. We all stepped out onto the front porch. The humidity was still really high as the storm started to move in from the bay. A large bolt of lightning came down to hit the water. It was still some distance away, but you could feel the electricity in the air.

"Looks like a good one" Lyle stated as he stepped down the stairs.

"Drive safe guys. Talk to you in the morning. Maybe once of us will get an epiphany while we sleep." I waved as they both got into their cars. Grady, Sugar and I walked back inside.

Sugar wrapped his arm around my waist and steered me towards the back veranda. He knew our family's ritual of watching storms from the rear of the house.

"If you will both excuse me, I have some phone calls to make. Good night and thank you for an exhilarating day." Grady said as he turned for the stairs.

"This late?" I asked.

"In my line of work, the hands of a clock make no difference." and turned to climb the stairs. He stopped and turned back to ask me "I know this may be an imposition, but would it be possible for me to stay a while longer? I seem to have found myself in a personal situation that would behoove me to stay out of sight for awhile." He looked at me with a sheepish grin.

Sugar had to ask "Does it involve a woman?"

"Of course it does." He said

"He had to ask" I said with a laugh. "Sure, it's no problem. I'm sure we will still be working the case for awhile. You can use that as an excuse."

You will have my perpetual gratitude. And, more importantly, I will owe you a favor." He said looking me directly in the eyes. "My favors have been known to come in handy." With that cryptic statement he turned and finally climbed the stairs.

"He's a pretty cool guy, huh?" Sugar said.

"The coolest" I agreed.

As Sugar and I turned to walk through the French doors onto the veranda I realized something. The house was quiet. Quiet here is bad. Just as I was about to comment on it we stepped onto the veranda.

Wallace and John were sitting in chairs facing out towards the water. The quiet was like a velvet caress compared to the usual explosion of noise usually present in the house. Wallace and John liked to watch the storms roll in with the family but they especially liked lightening storms. Especially before the rest of the front came in. Most people don't know it but sometime lightening produces sprites. Lightening sprites are reverse lightening that can happen over water. Well anywhere actually, but more commonly over water. They are fifty times more powerful than regular lightening and appear red in slow motion. To regular humans it takes a slow motion camera to catch it, but "others" can see it. John and Wallace love to watch as they say it reminds them of spirits "evolving". Whether that's true or not I don't know.

But tonight's show has them spellbound. Besides Mother Nature's show of force gearing up, the liquid moon hovered above the waterline as if trying to decide to fully rise and demand all of the attention or if perhaps it should remain low in the velvety darkness and allow the emerging night stars to grab some of the Glory. Fireflies were still flitting about to and fro in their nightly ballet.

Sugar and I slip quietly into the room to join them. As we are all sitting quietly Thurman goes screaming by the room then noticing we are all on the veranda, heads back towards us and skids into the room. He looks back and forth between Wallace and John, and then looks at us, then out to the water trying to figure out what we are watching. He hears Wallace each say aaah and sigh when there is a lightning strike, but he doesn't get it. Then he sees it. His first sprite. He literally falls on the floor in a fit of giggles. Then he creeps up between Wallace and John and settles in. I have never seen him this still; finally something that stopped Thurman in his tracks. Too bad I can't harness lightening.

37

I was actually off the next day so I thought I would drive over to St. Elmo's in the morning to visit with Aunt Leila Mae.

I had some questions.

I didn't want to be too far away in case something turned up on the case. DeCompanse Antiquities was not open for business until one tomorrow, and that would my first stop on the way back.

Sitting on the veranda having my coffee was one of my favorite parts of the day; today was no exception. It was gonna be hot again today. The ceiling fans all along the veranda were lazily twirling around keeping the heat at bay. Only the slightest sheen of perspiration was allowed to form on your neck or brow before the blades of the fans did their job.

It was great catching up with Sugar last night. It seemed like we hadn't seen each other in forever. But it was good to know his relationship was going well with Karl the Florist. That still makes me giggle for some reason. Yes, I'm immature I wrote down. I had been ignoring the diary entries for a while. I've been busy, but this morning was a good time to play catch up. I've been giving a lot of thought to what Granddaddy said last night. There had to be something to me getting those diaries of the previous Alma Sue. Regardless, I had to be more diligent about keeping a record of this time period for the next Alma Sue.

Going through my mental notes has proven difficult as well. I did try to call Bug this morning, but he was out so I left a message; but I'm not going to hold my breath. He always likes to keep me in suspense. When we were kids he was so mean to me. He was always threatening to kill me for some reason. Well, I'm sure I probably started it, but that was no reason to want to kill me all the time. That's probably why I became a cop; some deep seated need to be able to protect myself.

I have to admit he had some great lines though. A few stuck with me. One of my favorites was "I'm gonna knock you in the head and tell God you died." The other was "keep it up and I'll cancel your birth certificate."

Gosh, I hadn't thought about that in a long time. He was pretty funny. Obviously my smart-assed-ness is come by honestly. With that thought I made my final entry in the journal and closed it up until the next time I remembered I forgot to make an entry. I took my empty cup to the kitchen and went to get ready when I was hit in the shoulder with the kitchen door.

Guess who?

Dammit Col. Farragut! "Don't you have somewhere else to be?" He disappeared without saying a word, so he must have sensed I meant it.

It was almost seven and I wanted to get on the road. If there was no traffic it would only take me about 45 minutes to get to Aunt Mae's. I probably should call first, but I wanted to surprise her. Lyci said she would be home, so I trusted that to be true. But Lyci also had a funny look on her face that I couldn't read when she said it, so that might be a problem, but I was willing to risk it.

Once I was on the highway I was able to relax and let my mind wander. I cranked up the radio and just drove. I think I came to a decision last night about Carlyle. I want to get to know him. So after this case is resolved I think I will casually ask him out for a drink. That's OK right?" Just a drink. Then we'll see.

Luckily she was at her exit so she had to stop contemplating disaster on a date.

As she turned off onto Mae's street, she was assaulted by a wave of energy. She actually had to hold on to her steering wheel to control the swerve. The engine sputtered but kept running.

"What the hell is she up too?'

As I pulled down her private drive, I noticed several cars parked along the entrance.

I parked and walked up to the front entrance. I stood and listened for any unusual noises but heard silence.

I rang the doorbell and waited for what seemed like an eternity before someone I did not recognize answered the door. But they recognized me.

"Oh hello Alma Sue." The woman said brightly and ushered me in.

"I'm sorry, do I know you?"

"Well, no I suppose not. But I know you from your Aunt. I've seen you in her memories."

Well, that's a new one.

"Oh." was all I could think of to reply with.

We continued our walk towards the rear of the house where she led me into a large bright room. The huge floor to ceiling windows filled the room with bright morning sunlight. Seated around a large wooded table scarred with age were six women, one being my aunt with one empty chair.

"Hello Al" Aunt Mae stood and walked towards me. "This is a surprise. What brings you to St. Elmo's?"

"You. I think we need to talk."

'Well this is not really a good time. As you can see I have company. I know you came all this way, but perhaps we can meet tomorrow. I will come to BonHaven. We are in the middle of something very important that cannot be delayed." She gestured to the table and the other women.

"Mae, maybe she should stay. She might be helpful. She is a Babineaux after all" The woman who ushered me in said to Mae.

Mae seemed to consider this.

"You may be right. Alma Sue, meet my friends." She introduced the six women and in turn Alma Sue.

"I'm sorry. I don't mean to be rude, but what exactly are you doing and how would I be helpful?"

"So many questions" Aunt Mae said as she ushered me to the table and pulled another chair from against the wall for me to sit in. "I will explain the best I can."

The other women just watched patiently as if I were a small slightly mentally irregular child that needed careful guidance to complete a basic task. It was not a good feeling.

Mae began explaining that they were all seven Guides. She briefly explained their purpose and the governing rules that they all must abide by.

"So, you are all witches?" I asked with my head cocked to the side. After the explanation I just received there was no other way to describe the women. The very definition of that noun covers the explanation I just heard perfectly.

"Oh Heavens no." One of the women whose name I had already forgot trilled with a smile.

"No, nothing of the sort." another woman confirmed.

"No no." Mae went on. "We are Guides. We guide people to their correct destinies. "We may do a few other things here and there, but mostly just Guide."

"OK. I'm sorry. You're right. This is a bad time. I'll just take off now and talk with you later Aunt Mae." I stood to leave.

"Don't you want to know what's going on with your Daddy?" She asked me with a smile.

She said the one thing that could and did stop me in my tracks. That's not fighting fair.

"Daddy is dead."

"No. No Dear I don't think so." Mae said while motioning for me to sit back down.

I sat.

I was stunned. Was she crazy? I felt the world tilt. I pushed back my chair and put my head between my legs and took deep breaths. In. Out. In. Out. In. Out. Mae put her hand on my back and I felt better. I sat back up only to have the women staring at me with those same patient expressions.

"So, do you want to know what we are doing or not?" Mae asked me

"Yes."

"Good. Let us begin" They all answered as one.

The woman named Leonora spoke "Your father Fraser is an Elder on the Council of Elders in Palisphor. You do know where that is yes?" At my nod she continued "There has been an imbalance of energy for the past few years in both Palisphor and this reality. Your Father was tasked with discovering its source but became compromised. It appears he perished here in this reality." Seeing my look of confusion she hesitated then began again "I say appeared because that is all we believe it is;

for appearance sake."

I put my head in my hands "Elvis said something along the same lines."

"Elvis?"

"When did you see him?"

"What did he say?"

I was bombarded with questions from all directions.

"He showed up at BonHaven one morning a few weeks ago. We were all stunned of course, but he said he wanted to talk to me; and to Wallace evidently."

"But what exactly did he say? Try to remember exactly how he said it. This could be extremely important?" Mae said seriously.

"He spoke of Palisphor. He said there had been some disturbances there and he was sent to and I quote "snoop around some". He didn't say much else."

The women all sat back as one and sighed. I could tell I had disappointed them.

Leonora said "I still believe we should try to make contact through her." Her statement was directed to everyone. "It certainly can't hurt."

Mae made eye contact with each woman getting their silent agreement.

"Alright. Everyone please hold hands and close the circle."

"Wait, don't you have to do this at midnight with candles and salt and burning sage or something?" I asked wide eyed.

They all just laughed at me as if I were indeed that small child that desperately needed guidance; maybe I did.

As we all adjoined hands, I felt it. Power. Huge amounts of energy unlike anything I had ever felt before. This was followed by a high pitched vibration; like standing near a live power line. That's the only way I can describe it.

The next moment was accompanied by a blinding light in the room. A light that made the morning sun look like twilight. In that light I saw my Father. He was sitting in a cavernous room filled with filtered blue light and florescent looking things draped along the walls. It looked to me like he was writing something; maybe even writing in a journal. He appeared to be startled and looked up; straight into my soul; or so it felt. He smiled. Then I saw the face of a little girl with big dark eyes. She told me to Hurry; then the light dimmed and I was back in the bright sunlit room of Aunt Mae's.

I opened my eyes and looked at the women seated around me. They were all smiling at me like a student that had finally mastered a really difficult lesson.

"That settles it." Aunt Mae said. "Fraser is alive. Now the question is where."

I pushed away from the table and looked down at my cell phone. It was twelve fifteen and I had eight messages. Where the hell had the last three hours gone?!

I stood "I have to go. I have an appointment in less than an hour. What happened to the time? I just got here?"

"It's alright Al, what we just did is very disorienting for even an experienced Guide. For someone like yourself it must be terrifying; but you did well; very well. In fact I doubt we could have gotten through without you. I believe you were the reason Fraser let down his guard. I have been trying for two years now with no success." Now I was feeling guilty. Maybe there was a good reason Daddy was keeping everyone out. If that was even what this was all about. I'm not sure I believed it; any of it. Daddy was dead. Wasn't he?

38

Arriving back in Blakely was helpful. I felt more like myself by the time I arrived back at the station. Even though I was off today, one of the eight messages I had during my time at Mae's was from Captain Sampson requesting my presence back at the station pronto. Several of the other messages were from Bobby and Lyle with the same info; each message getting more frantic than the last. Evidently Sampson would not talk to anyone until we were all together. That could be really bad or maybe we caught a break in the case and finally have a strong lead. Other than the Antiques dealer who I still have not talked to again since I was stuck in who knows where.

I parked in the lot and got out of my car. I had to lean against the car for a minute to steady myself. It was like I had a few drinks then took too short of a nap; that didn't get enough sleep feeling. What the hell happened to me? Maybe I just need a soda and a Moon Pie. That's it. I'm heading straight for Lum's as soon as we are done here.

I finally got it together enough to walk into the station and headed for Sampson's office. I was cut off at the pass when I was joined by Lyle and Bobby.

Bobby stared at me hard "What happened to you? Are you coming down with something?"

Now Lyle looked at me "She looks fine to me" he said with a cute smile.

"That's because you haven't known her for as long as I have"

"Ya'll stop it right now. I'm fine. Maybe one day I will tell you what happened; when and if I ever understand it myself." I said confusing them both and walked past them to Sampson's door.

They both scrambled to catch me but I reached the door first. I reached out to knock but Bobby stuck his arm over my head and reached the door first. When I looked up at him he stuck out his tongue.

"In" Captain mumbled. "It's about time Babineaux. Where the hell you been 'cher? We been waitin all day."

"Sir" It's my day off. I was out of town. I came back as soon as I got the call." Sort of, I thought to myself

"I wanted to tell ya'll all together. We ID'd the body in the Bastian case. Name's Victor Torres; goes by Vic. He's only been in town for two years; works part time for Blo and Mo in the summer season. Not sure what he does the rest of the time. That's for you to find out. But your cousin's name came up in the bio, Al, something to do with Jimmy Don's company" he checked his paperwork for the name "Chaser's."

Good Lord!

We were obviously dismissed. He handed the file over to us on the way out and I tucked it under my arm.

We went back to our desks and I tossed the file on Bobby's desk.

"OK. I'm outta here. There's a cold RC cola and a Moon Pie with my name on it at Lums's. Then maybe we can meet up and swing by the Antique store. I don't want to come on too strong just yet. I still want to make sure we are not harassing an innocent old man." I said walking away.

"Umm, Al. You may want to wait a minute." Bobby said in a funny tone of voice.

When I turned to face him he had the file open on his desk. He picked up the photo of the victim and held it up so I could see.

"Holy Shit!"

"That about covers it." Bobby said scratching his head.

"Hey, isn't that the man in the sketch of the thief?" Lyle said helpfully.

"Holy Shit!" I said again. The photo of Vic Torres, the victim tied to Bastian in the murder case was a dead ringer for the sketch of the man who stole the jewels from BonHaven. Pun intended.

My Moon Pie was temporarily forgotten as I sat down at my desk. I wasn't sure I could keep getting shocks to my system like this and be OK.

"Alright, I guess I'm back on the clock."

"Where should we start?" Lyle asked me and Bobby.

""I guess we should go see Jimmy-Don, but honestly, I don't think I'm up for it yet." I said and slumped over my desk.

"What the hell did you do today?!" Bobby asked with concern.

"Not now" I said "Maybe after a few drinks tonight."

"How about this plan? Let's go by the antiques store first, swing by Lum's and get some sugar into you then hit Torres address and end up at Jimmy-Dons then you will be home. How's that sound?" Bobby sounded pleased with himself and his route planning.

"Exhausting" I answered with a sigh, but I said it as I was getting up and heading for the door.

We all decided to go in Bobby's squad car as he drove the SUV and it was more comfortable. I let the big apes sit in the front while I took the back. Then I would know now one was watching me too closely. Or so I thought until I caught Bobby checking the rear view mirror. I made eye contact and gave him my dirtiest look. It must have worked as he didn't do it again.

We pulled up to the antiques store in just a few minutes as the Police Station was on the other opposite end of Main street from DeCompanse Antiquities. We parked right in front so Mr. DeCompanse would see the squad car. But as soon as we got out of the car we knew it would not matter. There was a big closed sign on the door. I walked up to check the posted hours thinking maybe I got it wrong. He was supposed to be open at one today. Yep; it says he should be open at one; the time was now 1:45.

I walked over to where John was standing yesterday. In plain view on purple velvet display board was Alma Sue's brooch. My brooch! Now I was pissed. Everything I had experienced today hit me like a ton of bricks. I wanted blood. Someone was going to pay!

I had not moved in a few minutes and Bobby and Lyle were staring at me. OK, say something reassuring.

"I'm okay." That's all I got

Lyle just went and opened the SUV door for me. I climbed in and put on my seatbelt.

"Can't you get the air on for Christ's sake" I yelled and Bobby hustled in the car and turned on the ignition.

"We need to head back to the station. I want a warrant for that Antique store. Something is definitely up. The stolen merchandise in the front Damn window is enough for probable cause."

No one said a word as we headed back.

39

Within fifteen minutes we were turning off Highway 49 onto Randy Road. The warrant was being processed for Mr. De-Companse; both his store on Main street and his private residence on Jackson Street. The fact that he had one portion of the stolen goods on public display gave credence to the notion he had the valuable portion hidden away. Whether he was guilty of the theft or just fencing the items, he was in possession of stolen goods and that was good enough for Judge Connelley to issue the search warrant.

Our next destination was the residence of the victim. Victor Torres lived in the Randy Road Recreation Park; a large mobile home park on the east side of town. It also provided over two acres of spaces for temporary recreational vehicles and RV's just passing through off the Highway. There was a large park like area with a small river that ran between the two mobile parks for fishing and camping. All in all it was pretty nice; it was also a good place to blend in and not be noticed if someone was looking for that sort of thing. Of course we didn't know anything about our victim yet, but if he was the thief and was connected to DeCompanse in some way, then he might have chosen this place for exactly that reason.

We pulled off Randy Road and into the entrance to the Mobile Home side of the park. Two giant iron gates flanked either side of the entrance. It probably was very grand on opening day. The giant flamingos that adorned the gates were a great example of ironwork. Very delicate with layers of iron appearing as ruffling feathers of flamingos. My guess is they were once a bright pink, but had now faded to a rust colored rose on the iron. It was pretty depressing actually; a reminder of times past that had been forgotten by the world. Depressing.

As we pulled into his small driveway and parked under his carport, one word came to mind; nondescript. Space #55 was tidy without being showy. Everything was in its place. Shades were closed, but around here that's standard to keep the heat at bay. The hose was curled neatly around the facet. Sidewalk swept. No clues.

Bobby, Lyle and I looked at each other. We had all made the same sweep.

"Nothing" We said together and proceeded to walk up the small platform of stairs.

"Hey, there's an apple under there" Lyle said bending down to look under the trailers footing. "It looks fresh."

"Alright Inspector Clouseau, Thank You for the unbelievable observation that our victim likes fruit, prefers apples" I said pretending to talk into a handheld recorder. "This was the break we've been waiting for. I think this will blow the case wide open!"

He just looked at me. His meaning was undecipherable; I wasn't sure if I had pissed him off. That made me realize with a jolt, that I really didn't know him. I knew absolutely nothing about him other than he was hot, handled weirdness well and had a great sense of smell.

Lyle took two steps back down the stair platform and stood on the ground placing his hands on his hips. UH OH, he WAS pissed. He held out his arm pointing to a small willow tree in the front yard of the victim's trailer. "Go pick your switch!"

"Go pick you switch" is a phrase used when you get in trouble and are getting a spanking, usually from your parents. In my childhood I picked a LOT of switches, but usually from my Grandparents. I could usually talk my way out of everything with Momma and Daddy.

Lyle pointed again and said "I'm serious." Buy at this point the left corner of his mouth was turning up so I knew he was kidding; but for a minute there I was worried.

Bobby burst out laughing with me and Lyle following suit. Within thirty seconds we all had tears rolling down our faces.

Good Lord! I needed that. I was so tense and didn't even realize it. I think I was still floundering from my morning session in St. Elmo's. Reeling from what I didn't really know and wasn't yet ready to really think on it. Combine that with the shock at the station of finding out the murder victim in the case I'm currently working on and was found on my property, tied to Bastian no less, and he was the thief who was in my house was a little much. I don't think I could withstand much more today.

Bobby had pulled the key from the file and opened the door. Lyle bounded up the steps and slid past me to enter next. I pulled up the rear again. This was starting to get annoying. I was picking up on the feeling that both Bobby and Lyle were protecting me; and I did not like it one bit! Bobby never acted like that before. It must have something to do with what he is picking up on between Lyle and me. I was putting a stop to that right now. I opened my mouth to say something to the both of them as I stepped inside and was stunned into silence.

Stepping inside Vic Torres mobile home was like walking into a time warp circa 1975. The burnt orange carpet was once fabulous for sure. The brown tan and orange plaid sofa was once found in every recreation room across the country for several years; probably this exact model. The matching recliner was well worn and obviously the favorite place to sit in this room. The small kitchen was scrupulously clean with nothing out of place. It seems our Inspector Clouseau was correct in his deductions; our victim did indeed prefer apples as there was a wire basket of apples sitting prominently in the center of the small round dinette set that looked straight out of a period movie. It was the type collectors went nuts over at auction with the Naugahyde vinyl cushions and the metal trim. It looked a little sad with a solitary place setting waiting for someone who would never return. Jeeze what was with these weepy thoughts? Come on Al; Cop mode!

As we continued on to the rear of the trailer, we passed a small bathroom; again immaculately clean. The cramped hallway led to the bedroom in the back. A small full size bed was made with military precision. The coverlet was brown with cream flowers and looked new. It was cheaply made but clean. The pillows were new also. It seemed maybe out victim was a little bit of a clean freak; or he was a professional criminal and was used to keeping things clean and neat so as not to give anything up.

"There are absolutely no personal items around. Did you notice that?" Bobby asked. "Kind of weird considering he has lived here for two years. How could you not collect at least some junk in that amount of time?"

"I don't know" I said "but I would love to know his secret."

Lyle was looking around the bed. On the far side pressed close to the wall was a night stand with an old fashioned ringer type clock. Underneath on a shelf was a small basket and a framed photo of a young girl.

"Hey" Lyle said holding up the basket and the photo "I have something."

Lyle handed them to me across the bed. When I turned the photo over I stared at it for a while then sat down on the bed. Hard. It probably would have been defined more as a collapse from someone watching; like Lyle

The photo was of a beautiful little girl with big dark eyes; the same little girl that I saw this morning.

She told me to hurry.

"Bobby. You better get in here." Lyle yelled calmly

Bobby came running back to the back end of the trailer. Through the ringing in my ears it sounded like an elephant lumbering as fast as it could. Bobby was a pretty big man; sometimes I forgot.

"What's wrong?" He said slightly bending down to put his hands over his knees in a classic let me catch my breath posture. "Then he looked up and sees me sitting on the bed. The look on his face let me know if I didn't get up and shake this off, I was going to become a girl in his eyes. That was never gonna happen.

"This" I stood up and tossed the framed photo to him "is what's wrong."

"So, it's a picture of a little girl. Do you think it's his daughter?"

"I'm not sure, but I don't think so."

"No. It's not his daughter. It's his sister." Lyle said holding up a yellowed newspaper clipping. He had been looking through the small basket he found tucked away on the shelf under the nightstand and found several clippings. "Evidently she was kidnapped when she was eight years old and never seen again. Victor Torres is listed as her older brother, age seventeen."

"Wow." Bobby said running his hands through his hair "That could definitely mess someone up. Not that that is an excuse for becoming a criminal, but it does give him a better reason than most; especially if he didn't have a family to lean on. Statistically speaking most families don't remain intact. Within a year most families give up the struggle and blow apart. It's hard enough to deal with that kind of grief yourself, but if you're trying to help everyone else, the pressure is just too much for most folks."

Lyle cocked his head at Bobby. "Wow. I'm impressed. It's not just the stats thing. You really get what it is for a family goes through. How come? Someone you know?"

"No, just seen it happen too much." He grimaced then looked at Al. "But what else; something's up with you. Why did the picture rattle you so much?"

Bobby really knew me too well.

"I think it may be a long story. I still don't understand it all myself, but can we just hold it till later. Maybe after a Margherita or Martini or two or three I can explain it, or at least try."

"Deal. Let's finish up here; even though I don't think we'll find anything else, and then head over to Jimmy-Don's. Sampson said he would contact one of us when the warrant came through, so until that happens were just waiting anyway."

"So much for a day off" I said with a shrug "I had errands today too." I slapped my forehead. "Oh my God! I have to pick up the boutonniere for Lyci's date. Junior Prom is tonight; I have to have it there by 4:30!" I started to panic. Momma would kill me if it wasn't there for pictures. She has a very strict timetable for these things.

"Chill, it's only two fifteen. We'll go back to the station and split up. You can take your car and run by the florist, pick up the corsage thingy and drop it off at BonHaven. Bobby and I need to get our own cars anyways, 'cause we'll end up there too." Lyle looked pleased with his scheduling capabilities.

"It's called a boutonniere for boys Lyle." Bobby corrected knowledgably

"Sugar would be proud" I said sticking my tongue out at Bobby.

"And you better stop at Lum's too and get yourself that RC and Moon Pie. You're cranky." He stuck his tongue out back at me.

It did sound like a good idea so I didn't bother to respond. I wasn't that petty. Today.

"Then let's plan to meet at Jimmy Don's at four. That will give us all a little break." Bobby said as we all walked outside while he pulled the key back out of the file and locked the door to the mobile home. We all climbed back into the car and Lyle leaned over the front seat to hand me the basket with the old newspaper clippings. They felt so delicate and brittle. I glanced down to see her name; it was Victoria, how cute Vic and Vickie.

I was still holding the framed photo. I couldn't seem to get her voice out of my head.

"Hurry" she pleaded.

40

As we arrived back at the station and played musical cars, I felt a burst of energy. Maybe it was the fact of me knowing I would be at Lum's soon to get my sugar fix. But I think it was more than that. I felt a glimmer of hope that maybe Daddy wasn't dead. I still didn't believe it was possible, but my gut told me there was something going on. Figuring out what was my next move. I also felt hopeful I could help the little girl in the picture. I was investigating her brother's death. Now that I had a connection it didn't seem as strange as if it were just out of the blue; although, out of the blue IS pretty normal for me. I'm not sure why I even question anything.

My good mood faded a little when I arrived at the florist. There was a huge line at Some Enchanted Florist. Everyone else must have forgotten this errand and remembered at the same time also, just like me. The big man behind the counter recognized me and called my name.

"Hi'ya Al!" Are you here to get Lyci's order?" It was Karl, Sugars latest object of fervor.

He seemed like a great guy and honestly anyone who could get me out of this line and closer to Lum's was my new best friend.

"I am. I forgot all about it until about ten minutes ago. I can see everyone else did too."

"Naw, this is pretty normal; been like this all day, but great for business. Let me run to the back and I'll get her order."

"Thank you." I yelled out to his huge back.

While I stood there and received all the dirty looks from everyone that I took cuts in front of, I was surprised I didn't explode from the hateful thoughts.

Karl came right back through the swinging glass doors that separated the refrigerated work room from the front show room carrying a good sized sapphire blue box with a clear plastic top. He handed it to me carefully, almost reverently.

"What do you think? She asked for unusual." He asked cautiously. He actually seemed nervous for my reaction. Maybe because he knew whatever I thought would get to Sugar real fast.

"The box is beautiful" I answered before I even looked inside. "I'm sure the flowers will be great." Then I looked inside the box. The boutonniere was spectacular. It was some type of exotic orchid. It was a deep blue that bordered on purple with white stripes delicately running along each bloom. Vivid yellow spots dotted the inner folds of the petals. It was bright without being gaudy; but very subtle at the same time. I had never seen anything like it. It actually took my breath away.

"It's unbelievable. I've never seen anything like it." I looked up at him for a brief moment before looking at the flower again. "Where did you get this?"

"Oh, I have my sources. It's a secret." He said with a smile that lit up his entire face. I could see the attraction that drew Sugar in. "Jason's mom already came in and picked up Lyci's corsage or I would show you. It matches of course, but if you like this, you'll be blown away by hers. I took photos for my advertising flyers." He said with pride.

"If it looks anything like this one, you definitely should. Hell you should enter it a Florist competition. Wait do they have those? I asked.

"Actually they do, I just never felt confident enough to enter."

"Well, you definitely should! Especially with something like this" I said with a smile as I lifted the box.

"Thank you for the vote of confidence, and there's no charge for that" he said pushing away my debit card I had produced from my back pocket.

"No, really this is a work of art. You have to let me pay for it."

"Uh unh, No way. Sugar would kill me." He was serious.

"O.K., then you and Sugar come to brunch at BonHaven next weekend."

"Deal." He said shaking my hand.

"And thank you again. Lyci will love it, and more importantly, Momma will love it!" I said walking out the door. The crowd waiting in line had grown and people had to make a little path for me to get out. Most were trying to figure out why I was receiving special treatment. I felt like a rock star.

After a quick stop by Lum's to get sustenance, I felt like a new person. The drive back to BonHaven was a pleasant one. The humidity wasn't really that bad today, so I rolled all the windows down and reveled in the air blowing through the car. I took the back roads from town so I could drive by all the overgrown honeysuckle bushes growing wild along the country roads. I loved the way the air rushing in through the open windows were so laden with fragrance it would stay with my clothes after I got out of the car. My hair on the other hand was another story. I pulled into our drive and started the long path to the house. The Spanish Oaks lining the drive were draped with moss and swaying in the wind as I drove by. Ever since I was a little girl I imagined the trees were swaying in a welcome home dance for me. Jeeze, who knows; at BonHaven they might really be dancing.

I pulled around the circular drive dodging the other cars haphazardly parked. A few of Lyci's friends were here getting ready for Prom together.

I walked in through the front doors and placed the box from the florist on the entry table and was just admiring the pretty blue box when I looked up and caught a glance at my reflection in the huge mirror that hung over the table.

Good Lord! I should stop driving with the windows down. My ponytail was all disheveled with hair sticking up every which way. The rest was in huge snarls and tangles down to my waist. Crap! I have ten minutes to get to Jimmy-Dons. I ran up the stairs and headed to my room to try to repair the damage. I heard the screaming coming from Lyci's room, but tried to ignore it until I had dealt with my own issues.

I was able to get some semblance of order to my ponytail and was just fixing my mascara when Wallace popped in. I saw his face over my shoulder in the mirror. See, I didn't even flinch.

"Yes, may I help you?" I asked politely

"No I was just checking. I was in Lyci's room watching her do her hair with her friends." He knew I had just fixed my hair so the next comment was just to get a rise out of me, and I wasn't going to fall for it. "I was just wondering how Lyci turned out so beautiful when you both have the same genes. It is pretty improbable you know." and disappeared.

OK so, he got a rise out of me.

On my way back out I stopped in by Lyci's room and over the screaming and laughing got in a hello. I told them they all looked beautiful and to have fun but I was ignored; or at least I thought I was. Lyci caught my eye as I turned to leave and smiled and mouthed Thank You – love you. She's a good kid.

41

I got back in my car and rolled all the windows up and turned on the AC full blast. Even though I was only driving down the road to Jimmy-Don's, I wasn't showing up with the Medusa hair from earlier. I had changed into my uniform as this was an official visit. Plus Jimmy-Don responded well to intimidation; and I didn't get many chances to let my inner Towanda out, but since he was my cousin, I could and I wasn't letting the opportunity to give a hard time slip by. Childish maybe, but I was still gonna do it.

I pulled up to the Giles house and parked between Bobby and Lyles cars. Walking up to the front porch I realized I had not been there in years. I think it was a Christmas part or maybe New Years Eve; I honestly don't remember much about it. I must have been twelve or thirteen; and I remember really not wanting to be there! Our family left right after midnight, so it must have been New Years Eve.

I rang the doorbell and Aunt Bettina answered the door.

"Hello Alma Sue! How are you dear? Come in. I know this is official business so come on in, the boys are all in the rec room with Jimmy-Don and Bubba." She said as she ushered me downstairs. It's a good thing she did because I didn't recognize any of the floor plan. They must have remodeled since I was here last. Then again, I was thirteen; maybe I just didn't pay attention.

"Here we are." She said as she pointed me towards double doors open at the end of the hall. "If you'll excuse me, I was just getting to the good part of my book." She said smiling and took off back upstairs.

Bobby and Lyle were sitting on barstools at a nice setup in the corner with a huge wrap around bar. They were drinking sodas and watching Jimmy-Don and Bubba play some video game on a seventy inch screen projected on the wall. Jeeze, what were these guys, twelve.

They stood up when I walked in the room and said "We were waiting for you to get started."

"Yeah, and Bobby turn is next." Lyle tattled with a smile.

'Kiss ass" Bobby whispered

"Hey Jimmy-Don, can you put that on pause so we can ask you a few questions? It's important."

"Yeah, that's what Bobby Glen said. Can you wait a minute? I'm almost at level 84."

"That's what you said fifteen minutes ago." Bobby said a little petulantly. I think he was just mad he didn't get his turn before I showed up to end the boy's day out.

Lyle walked over and pulled the plug on the game.

"Hey that's police brutality" Bubba said.

"No Bubba. It's not. What this is Bubba, is a serious investigation involving your friend." Carlyle stood tall and put his hands on his service belt. "And you need to take it very seriously." Ooooh, me like. Lyle in control was awesome. Bobby and I made eye contact and he waggled his eyebrows.

Jimmy-Don and Bubba out their controllers on the table and sat up straight.

"Well what's this about?" Jimmy-Dona asked beginning to understand he might be in trouble.

"Do you have someone in your employ with Chasers named Victor Torres?" Lyle asked him flipping through his notebook.

"Yeah, Vic works for me sometimes as a videographer, why? What's he done?"

"We are not at liberty to say at this time. But we can tell you he was murdered. He was the victim found at the base of Bastian last week." Lyle informed him in an officious voice.

"Holy Mother of God!" Bubba yelled then burst our crying.

Jimmy-Don just stared at Bubba. "What are you cryin'for. We hardly even knew him."

"But what if it could have been us? Maybe they were after any Chaser's employee. You were just saying he didn't answer any of your calls. You were really mad at him." He sobbed

Jimmy-Don looked up real quick "Don't even think it; I wasn't made enough to kill him. I couldn't kill anyone!"

Jeeze; as if he had the brains to pull off something like this. I pulled the sketch of the robbery suspect out of my file and showed it to Jimmy-Don and Bubba. "Who does this look like to you?"

Both of them looked hard at the drawing.

"Well that's a dead ringer for Vic" Bubba said through his sobs.

"Yep." Jimmy-Don said. That's definitely Vic. But why does it say he is a robbery suspect? What did he rob?"

"BonHaven. Some valuable antique jewelry was stolen the day of the murder.

"Who'd be dumb enough to steal anything from BonHaven? That place is creepy! Do you know it's supposed to be one of the most haunted old plantations in the..." Bubba broke off as he realized I was standing right behind him. "Sorry, I didn't mean anything by it. He's the one who said it." Bubba said jerking his thumb at Jimmy-Don. So much for friendship.

"It's fine Bubba. Some people just like to gossip." I said narrowing my eyes at Jimmy-Don.

"Well maybe that's what Vic was doing talking to that funny little man with the bow tie. When I described him to my Momma later at supper, she said it sounded like just Dr. DeCompanse, the Antiques dealer downtown, right down to the bow tie and the funny two tones shoes." Bubba said excitedly. He was proud of himself for figuring out the mystery Mr. DeCompanse handed Vic in that envelope. He was probably just being helpful, right?"

"Bubba, think very carefully. When did you see this happen?" Lyle questioned "And where were you when you saw it happen?"

"Well, I was at the library downtown. Remember you sent me to look for that book JD? Alabama Ghost and Their Favorite Haunts?" He lifted his chin to Jimmy-Don.

"Yeah, and I remember you said you couldn't find it. It was already checked out or something." Jimmy-Don said still mad.

"Well it was." Bubba said pouting.

"So if you were in the library, how did you see Vic and Mr. DeCompanse?

"I was sitting at a table trying to figure out how to find the darn book and staring out the big window in front. You know the big glass one? That's when I noticed Vic sitting on a bench in front of the library like he was waiting on something. Then I saw Mr. DeCompanse trying to get his attention from across the street; he made a big show of putting an envelope in the crack of the brick wall in the alley then he left with that white envelope sticking out where he left it."

"What happened next Bubba?" I asked

Vic got up off the bench and walked across the street to the alleyway. He just walked right by that envelope then reached out and snagged it and put it in his back pocket. He never stopped walking or nuthin'."

"Smart." Bobby said locking gazes with me. I understood exactly what he meant. Since the two of them were never seen together there was nothing linking them; except Bubba saw the exchange. But without the envelope and whatever is inside the envelope, there is no proof to take into court. Everything else is speculation.

"Yes, very smart." Lyle agreed. He understood too.

Walking into the room carrying a letter Aunt Bettina said "Sorry to interrupt your meeting Jimmy-Don, but the mail just came and there is a letter here for you. It's from Ghost Hunters, Inc. Isn't that the company you sent your audition tape to? I know you've been waiting to hear back from them. I knew that was an understatement as David, our shared mailman, told me Jimmy-Don basically threw a tantrum every time he delivered the mail and didn't have a letter from Ghost Hunters for him. It was pretty funny to hear David complain about his route and how rude everyone was; how they were always complaining about their mail being delayed or getting lost. It seemed to me David did most of the complaining. But he did it with a lot of humor and he had a pretty severe eye tick so it always looked like he was winking at you between his jokes. So I basically thought it was free entertainment and I got all the local gossip without having to get involved.

We all waited patiently as Jimmy-Don read the letter. He reread it several times. You could read his face and body language getting worse with every reread. It was not good news.

"What does it say JD? Are we getting the gig?" Bubba asked with enthusiasm. Bless his little heart.

"No Bubba. We are not getting the gig. They said, and I quote" he looked at the letter again "the flicker on the tape indicates it has been edited or tampered with in some way and in no way meets our high standards in the quest for verification of the paranormal."

"That was my shot. And now it's gone. It's that damn tree's fault. He caused this somehow!"

"Now Jimmy, you know that's not true honey" His Momma tried to console him.

"I think we should leave you all to some time alone." Bobby said ushering me and Lyle out of the room. "We can see ourselves out Maam."

As we all hurried back up the stairs and out onto the front porch, we barely made it before we all exploded in laughter.

"Oh my God, I didn't think I was going to make it!" I said

"Me either." Lyle was bent over laughing.

As we tried to get control of ourselves, Bobby was checking his phone. He held up his finger indicating for us to hang on while he listened to his messages. Maybe Captain Sampson called about the warrant. It should be ready soon. Bobby listened to several messages before he put his phone back in his pocket.

"OK. You are not going to believe this."

"What? Did Sampson say we can serve the warrant?" Lyle asked

"No" Bobby replied "Actually the message from him was that the warrant wouldn't be ready until tomorrow."

"Bummer" I said. "Oh well DeCompanse isn't going anywhere. So what's the news?"

I had a message from Jenny Katherine. She spoke with her nephew the punk; he refused to talk to me as he said "I ain't helping no pig". So Jenny Katherine evidently read him the riot act and threatened to turn him in for his weed and he squealed like a stuck pig. No pun intended. Anyway, the kid said he recognized the carvings on Bastian. He had seen them in a painting Wiley used to have hanging where his big screen T.V. is now. Wiley used to talk about his piece of art all the time, but I never saw it. Evidently Jenny Katherine and Wiley fought about it a lot because of how much money Wiley spent on it. He considered it an investment but Jenny Katherine just thought it was trash and he was throwing their money away. Guess where he bought the painting?"

I raised my hand "I would like to choose antiques for one hundred please."

"And you young lady have just won final Jeopardy!"

"We need to get back to BonHaven and talk to Grady. He can confirm the voodoo symbols on Bastian and in the painting are the same." I said.

"No Momma, I will not calm down!" we heard being yelled form somewhere in the house. This was definitely our cue to leave.

42

We all pulled into the drive and skidded to a stop spraying crushed gravel everywhere. I was going to hear about the mess from Hollis tomorrow. We all ran inside and into the library where we had left everything about the case lying out. Wallace and John were playing chess in the corner like regular people. No one said anything. Lyle walked over and looked at their board and said it looked like a nice game then sat at the large table beside me.

Grady came running into the room. "What's up? I know something's up!"

"A lot" Bobby said. "It's looking more and more like our murder victim was also out thief and most likely working for the Antiques dealer Mr. DeCompanse. We think Mr. DeCompanse decided it was time to get rid of the hired help."

"But why the voodoo symbols on Bastian?" Grady asked

"Probably just to throw us off; make it look like a ritual killing by some kids maybe." Bobby shrugged. The problem is tying Vic and DeCompanse together. No judge is going to go after an upstanding citizen with no priors just because of circumstantial evidence."

"How about a signed confession?" Lyle asked

— 297 —

"Of course that would work, but what kind of idiot would do that?" Bobby laughed

"This kind" Lyle said holding up an envelope. He had been looking through the basket we found at Vic Torres mobile home. In it were several envelopes containing letters. All were on creamy thick stationary written in an old fashioned ink pen. Each letter detailed a specific job Vic was hired to perform for Mr. DeCompanse. Most of them were illegal. Some were only distasteful, but all were charges that would stick.

After a lot of high fiving, Bobby left to get that warrant expedited with the new evidence attached. I don't think any jury will have any trouble at all seeing the little bow tied man in a different light now. I am still curious how he could actually go through the act of murder the way he did, but that can be left up to the prosecutor.

Lyle walked up behind me "you never explained what happened to you today." He said in a concerned voice.

"Let's leave that for another time alright? Let's just enjoy our success for now." I said with a sigh. As the day had worn on, I just didn't have the energy to bring everything back to rehash and figure out.

"I will take you up on that. Don't think I will forget either." And he meant it.

Lyle could tell Al was still bothered by something and he was pretty sure it had to do with her father; but he couldn't say anything without opening that door wide open and that wasn't his decision to make. But watching Al stare blankly out the arched windows as Grady challenged

Wallace to the next game, Lyle came to a decision of his own.

"I think I'm gonna take off ya'll. It's been a long day and tomorrow will be even longer what with the arrest of a killer and all."

"See you later water man." Grady said making eye contact with Lyle. So he knew Lyle thought. Ha. Obviously he knows how to keep a secret. Grady went back to watching the chess game intently.

"Good bye young man" said John without looking up.

"Yes, Good bye." Wallace chimed in looking directly at him with a sneaky smile. He makes me nervous Lyle thought to himself.

He walked over to Al and touched her shoulder. She jumped like she had been shocked, but even when she looked up at him, he could tell her mind was a thousand miles away.

"I'm taking off. I'll see you tomorrow?"

"Yep. See you tomorrow. I'm off again, but I'll check in once the arrest warrant comes through so I will see you all at some point." She said with a weak smile.

"OK. Goodnight."

He walked out the rear door thought the veranda as the library was right there at the rear of the house. It was only five thirty. He had plenty of time. Once he made his decision, he wanted to leave as soon as possible.

43

Lyle arrived at Alassi in the early evening. He made great time leaving straight from BonHaven. He had to speak with Fraser. Walking into the antechamber of Fraser's room, he was still trying to decide what to say to Al's father.

"Hello Carlyle" Fraser said warmly coming towards Lyle. "What brings you back so soon? I just saw you last week. Is everything alright at BonHaven?" he asked at the tense look on Carlyle's face.

"I have a lot to tell you." Carlyle said as he sat opposite Fraser. They talked for a solid half hour with Fraser mostly just listening. In the end Fraser agreed he needed to see Al, if only to briefly explain. Then he would go back into hiding.

44

Al had a really great night sleep last night. Wallace left her alone. Thurman was relatively quiet. All in all it was a good night at BonHaven. Coming downstairs for breakfast my spidey senses started tingling. Oh Good Lord! Now what! But when I entered the dining room only Uncle Howard and Momma were at the table peacefully reading the newspaper.

"Good morning everyone" I said cheerfully

"Good morning darling" Momma said

"Good morning to you" Uncle Howard said from behind his paper.

"I'm assuming Lyci got in late from the Prom festivities." At Momma's nod over her cup of coffee I went on "Where's Aunt Merle?" I asked hesitantly. Her absence might be why my spidey senses were on high alert.

"She came down to get coffee quite awhile ago, but went back up to sleep a little longer. She said she didn't get much sleep last night."

Uh Oh. "Did she say why?" I asked hesitantly

"Now Al, why do you think it's always something bad? No, I don't think anything is wrong, but she did say she had a message for you."

Oh God. What did she bring me?

"Oh, I almost forgot." Momma said pulling a small wrapped gift from her pocket. "John said to give this to you." She said with a smile. "Go on, open it."

I pulled at the delicate pink satin ribbon wrapped around what looked like a cloth handkerchief. Inside was my brooch. Alma Sue's brooch. The brooch stolen from our house; the one that was supposed to be in the front display window of DeCompanse Antiquities.

"John said it was the least he could do; whatever that means." Momma said gently touching my arm.

Just then Merle came into the room stifling a big yawn. "I heard you had a message for me" I said clutching the brooch close to my heart.

"I do indeed." She said handing me a small piece of paper she pulled from her pocket. A small girl with big laughing dark eyes holding the hand of a young man who looked almost exactly like the sketch Lyci had me draw gave it to me.

The paper was a thick creamy white that looked as if it had been torn from a larger page. There were only two words on it with a child's smiley face made with two dots and a half circle

Thank You

45

Later that day after all the excitement of the antiques dealer's arrest had made the rounds of the towns gossips and the telephone had finally stopped ringing, I was sitting on my bed when I finally made a decision. I was going to call Lyle and ask to meet him for a drink later tonight. I would tell him everything that happened to me yesterday. Maybe he could help me make sense of what it all meant. I picked up the phone to call him, but it went to voicemail, so I left a message asking him to come by BonHaven around sun down.

Now I just had to decide what to wear.

Lyci came in and helped me pick out an outfit then went back to take a nap. She was still wiped out from Prom. I thought I looked pretty great and was just pinning Alma Sue's brooch, well, our brooch, to my blouse and was feeling pretty good about the upcoming evening when I ran into Wallace walking towards me in the hall. Oh Good Lord! I do not need this right now. I braced myself for his worst insult.

"Very Nice Al." was all he said.

I blew out the breath I had been holding and turned around to thank him, but he was gone.

I was still stunned when I walked out on the front veranda to wait for Lyle, assuming he would come when he got my message. The night

— 305 —

was promising to be sultry. I love this part of the day; the moment right before full dark falls like a velvet curtain

I was sitting in a wicker chair tucked into the side of the porch watching the sun go down and being mesmerized by the lightening bugs perform their nightly graceful modern dance routine when Lyle came up the road. I followed his progress into the circular drive as he parked in front. It looked like there was someone in the passenger seat and I was a little disappointed as I thought we would be alone. I started down the steps for a closer look forgetting to be on the lookout for Thurman. He wouldn't dare tonight. That is precisely the moment when I was hit by a large dirt clod from above and Lyle opened his car door turning on the interior car light illuminating his passenger. I think it took me a moment to process what I saw.

Two thoughts went through my mind. The first was that Thurman's aim was getting better which was a scary thought.

The second was a much scarier thought; Daddy is that really you?